The Judas Star

BOB WEAVING

THE JUDAS STAR
A ROY JOBE MYSTERY

2007

The Judas Star

ACKNOWLEDGEMENTS

Special thanks to: Dan, Lisa and Jake Francesconi, Kelly, Victoria, Josh and Sammers Miles, Kim and Pete Aguayo, Dana Demars, Eva and all her magnificent daughters, Liz and Ray Nowakowski, Derman and his family, Warren Yoshida, Michael Schinner, Connie and Candace Upman, Mark Gomez, Don Lucas, Dan Burton, Mark Ledwith, Barbara and Sam Marshall and their extended clan, Brenda Eckert, the Connecticut Weavings, Riyu Itakura, Ashwani Bindal, Ramin and Arman Arami, George Dean, James Russo and crew, Oscar and Samantha Olivas, Milt, Veda, Edwin and Sharon Armstrong and family, Jay Boyarski, Jean and Frank, Tad Williams, Dr. Choi, Werner Rogmans, Dang Lee, Frank Fiore and his gracious family, Justin, Eddie Lee, Brian Sasville, Bo, Bronco, the entire crew at AB and the crew at Skywest Golf Course, Hayward.

Dedicated To My Beautiful Baby Sister, Jacqueline Rose.

PROLOGUE

San Francisco
Sunday

On a day as glorious as this, I should've been golfing. I should've been staring down a sleek, dewy fairway, decked in plaid and holding a three wood made of titanium and betrayal. I should've been inhaling the scent of short grass and long cigars, and I should've been grappling with the irrational optimism that always precedes my first profanity.

Failing that, I should've been in bed with the Sunday paper and a willing mammal.

Instead, I was scouring the City for a man named Ira Lanski. Ira was a plastic surgeon of note who'd amassed a rapper's ransom by specializing in transumbilical breast augmentation and something called "SMAS-platysma facelift." He had a 4,000–square-foot office in the Transamerica Building, with four operating theaters and a waiting room filled with lattes and low self-esteem.

I was looking for Ira because I had a five-pound subpoena with his name on it distorting the profile of my very fashionable Dolce & Gabbana jacket. While normally an even-tempered, compassionate man, graced with patience and empathy, I resented the unsightly bulge it formed in my coat, and I resented the fact that I had to chase a Harvard-educated MD. around San Francisco on a Sunday made to waste.

The attorney who issued the summons however, is a good client and a better friend, so I took this job as a favor. Delivering paper isn't very profitable, but when a friend puts his hand out, you grab it without hesitation.

The reason my attorney friend reached out was because the two process servers who preceded me met with some resistance. This resistance took the form of two very large, very belligerent goons who broke the nose of the first process server and administered a near fatal wedgie to the second. That, in anyone's book, is some pretty serious resistance.

It was conveyed to me that Ira liked to hang around Mob types, trading work on wives, girlfriends and daughters for the privilege of hanging around guys a lot tougher than him. Hence the goons. I suspected Ira had become a little too enamored with *The Sopranos*.

The contents of a subpoena are never my business. I'm supposed to be a neutral, disinterested party, much like Switzerland. But I couldn't resist a peek. The subpoena disclosed that Ira had apparently gotten a couple of saline implants mixed up, resulting in a 36 double-D on the left and a 34 B on the right. The problem was further exacerbated by the fact that the patient in question had come to Ira for a rhinoplasty, which is a swanky word for nose job.

Finding Ira's home wasn't particularly difficult; I simply followed the scent of lucre. He lived in a multi-layered cake of a house in a posh neighborhood off 19th Avenue. It was a three-story Spanish Colonial with a big hedge out front and a roundabout leading to the front door. The house had a red tile roof and a number of quatrefoils, with stucco walls thick as hay bales. It was painted in the obligatory beige with dark brown trim and sat almost 50 feet from the street.

I pulled my car into the driveway and parked behind a yellow hardtop Porsche with one of those hideous whale-tails on its back. The vanity plate said *liftman*. A nondescript Chevy Suburban, black with windows to match, was positioned near the exit.

Taking into consideration the fact that Ira had two wiseguys hanging around, and possessing a keen instinct for conflict avoidance, I decided to forego the front door and squeezed myself through two bushes leading to the back yard. When I emerged, I was greeted by a wide expanse of lawn that flowed south for a while until it wrapped itself around a pool shaped like an internal organ. A short, portly bald man was laying on a chaise lounge at the far end of the pool, sipping something bubbly from a glass. He had somehow managed to stuff his important parts into a Speedo, which fit like a sausage casing. I knew instinctively that this particular image was going to haunt me for the rest of my life.

Between the sausage guy and the subpoena in my pocket, with their backs to me, stood two suit-wearing gorillas, about the size and shape of Frigidaires.

So much for conflict avoidance.

The guy in the Speedo, whom I assumed was Ira, squeaked and pointed.

"Hey!" said Ira.

"Hey, yourself," I quipped.

The two gorillas rotated slowly toward me. It was like watching a pair of aircraft carriers turning into the wind.

"You're trespassing," Gorilla One said.

"That I am."

Gorilla One lurched at me, reaching for a lapel. This was a mistake. I was already upset about the subpoena marring my jacket's contour, and the thought of his hand wrinkling my very expensive linen dragged me to the brink of insanity. I shifted to the right and intercepted his hand, grabbing his thumb. I performed a neat little twist and it popped out of joint. He pulled back, howling, and I pushed him to the ground.

That apparently upset Gorilla Two because he came at me with mayhem in mind. I believe he expected me to give ground, because he seemed very surprised when I leaned into his face with my fist. He collapsed like an ethics bill in the Senate.

I stepped over Number Two and fished the subpoena out of my pocket. When I was about 10 feet from Ira, I heard a familiar sound behind me. I turned to see Gorilla One on his knees, pointing a revolver at my chest, hammer cocked.

I sighed. "It's a fucking subpoena," I said. "You sure you wanna' elevate this?"

He stared at me; I stared at him. He lowered the gun.

I turned back and stood in front of Ira. He looked like a guy who'd just found a horse's head in his ziti.

I dropped the subpoena onto his Gherkin.

"Bada-bing," I said, cheerfully.

CHAPTER ONE
Monday

Today was a picture postcard, the kind that showed Coit Tower or Alcatraz sheathed in gold. It was 80 degrees and balmy, with a breeze light as a baby's laugh. The sky was an azure vault; the Bay, a glass table with boats.

I turned left on Broadway and passed Gough, then let the hood of my car tilt upwards toward Pacific Heights. This stretch of road was a corridor of elite homes, butted up against each other like stacked bullion.

The place I was looking for sat on a large, incongruous lot, a couple of blocks past Divisadero. It had been primped to PGA standards, with extravagant flowerbeds and a spotless, doublewide sidewalk. Apparently, standard sidewalks weren't allowed in Pacific Heights, because they're pedestrian. Like bad puns.

From here I had a 180-degree view of the Bay, taking in Angel Island, the Marina Green and the lesser homes below, inhabited by the wealthy-lite. Jags and BMWs populated the street, because the Bentleys got the garages.

I parked, had a smoke, then ambled over to 66962 Broadway.

The house I faced was Italianate, two stories and taupe. Ornamental Juniper trees ringed the perimeter, trimmed out to look like Zulu spears. I followed a tiled walk to the door, which was a wall of polished teak. It had black iron hinges and a black iron spy cage and black iron rivets the size of a monkey's fist. I rang the doorbell.

Eventually, an old guy in a butler getup opened the door. He wore a black suit with tails and a white shirt that had a collar stiff enough to launch a half-gainer. He was blue-eyed and bald, with a neatly trimmed swath of white hair horseshoeing his head. His face reminded me of an old tapestry, faded and rich, with the kind of matinee idol looks that would've made the young girls squeal…in 1960.

"May I help you?" he asked.

"I'm here to see Peter Aguayo."

"May I ask who's calling?"

"You may."

That annoyed him. It's a gift.

"Your name?" He bit it off, like I bite carrots.

"Roy Jobe."

"One moment."

I stared at teak.

Three minutes later the door reopened.

"Mr. Aguayo will see you now."

He turned and went into the house and I followed like an obedient schnauzer.

The foyer was cavernous, with a floor paved with marble the color of butter. The ceiling soared the full two stories, with a grand staircase centered about 40 feet from the door. A bunch of Ming vases were scattered around. Gladiolus fanned from their mouths.

Jeeves turned to his right and opened a set of doors. He stood stiffly to the side while I entered a room not quite large enough for two dirigibles.

The room swam all the way to the back of the house, its floor an ocean of gray. Pieces of furniture dotted the carpet, like islands in a dark sea. At the far end of the room, highlighted by floor-to-ceiling windows, was a desk. A man sat behind it.

"Mr. Jobe," he bellowed. "Please come in."

I weaved my way through furniture atolls, using his voice as a navigational aid.

A leg cramp later, I faced a large man with skin the same tone as fresh tobacco. He was wide as a down lineman and looked as strong, but was shorter than me by three inches. Arctic white hair and a perfect matching beard framed his face, and the contrast to his skin was startling. I was pretty sure his eyes were glittery and black, but I could've been wrong as I was temporarily blinded by his diamond cufflink, close in size to a ferret's head. I was confident, however, that he smelled faintly of orange groves.

Smiling, I shook his hand.

"Good to meet you, Peter," I said. "And please, call me Roy."

"My pleasure, Roy." He waved at one of the two chairs facing his desk. "Have a seat."

"Thanks."

Peter Aguayo was CEO and Grand Poobah of Advanced Marketing Associates, a multinational firm that specializes in mass-market trends and consumer behavior. Basically, they tell companies what consumers want, then they tell companies why they want it, then they give them a bill. Peter was also the author of *Modeling Consumer Behavior*, a *New York Times* bestseller.

I knew this because Gerald Bosworth, of Bosworth, Schinner and McCreedy, told me. The aforementioned Bosworth is an attorney and one of my best clients, meaning he pays on time. He recommended me to Peter Aguayo, and that's why I'm sitting in an airplane hangar, staring at a quarter-billion with legs.

Peter settled himself into his chair.

"My attorney speaks very highly of you," he said.

I shrugged. "I bought him a puppy once."

Peter smiled. It made him look like a Samoan Santa Claus.

"He also tells me you consider yourself somewhat of a wit."

"Modesty precludes me from commenting," I said, demurely.

He pursed his lips and raised a brow, which is a lot harder than it sounds.

"I'm assuming you signed the nondisclosure agreement?"

"I did."

"Good," he said. "Let's get down to business."

Peter impressed me as a "get-down-to-business" kind of guy, and I got the feeling he was a man whose good side you'd want to stay on.

"Tell me a little about yourself, Roy."

I spread my hands, palms up. "Not much to tell. I'm 40, an ex-Marine, and an ex-homicide inspector. I've never been married because I don't want to be an ex-husband. I made it all the way to the tenth grade and I think the designated hitter is a contrivance spawned by Satan."

I paused and tried to think of something that would impress him.

"I've had my P.I. license for five years," I said, "and I'm tall."

He cocked a brow.

"So you lack a formal education?"

I grimaced. "*Lack* is such a harsh word, Peter," I said, "like *flaccid*. I'd describe myself as a man with a deep well of utilizable life skills."

He laughed.

"I understand, Roy," he said, smiling. "I never made it to university either."

This was good. We were bonding.

He half closed his eyes while he bobbed his head, but remained silent. I had no idea what that meant. The silence stretched uncomfortably, and since I had that thing to do at the place with the guy, and because nature abhors a vacuum, I did something stupid.

I pointed to a book on his desk.

"What are you reading?"

He picked it up.

"*The Concept of Dread*," he said, frowning. "I've been trying for years to understand the finer points of philosophy." He looked at it, puzzled. "But I confess to only a layman's grasp."

He turned his attention back to me.

"Have you read Kierkegaard?"

My first reaction was to prevaricate, but I've found that my chances of employment are significantly reduced when I succumb to impulse.

"Who hasn't?" I prevaricated, impulsively.

He wasn't amused.

"Do you like what he's written?" he asked, testing.

"No," I answered, confidently.

He looked disappointed. "What don't you like?"

This was starting to feel like a pop quiz, which I was never good at, because I have the attention span of bacon. I was regretting my foray into small talk, one of my many weaknesses, so I fell back on my canned response.

"There's no car chase."

This time he *was* amused, just like the nuns at Our Lady of the Holy Sepulcher were, shortly before my expulsion.

He put the book down and let it go, which was a good thing. Existentialism is another one of my weak areas.

"Gerald tells me you're a man to be trusted," he said, "that you have a delicate hand."

"When it's called for."

His head bobbed some more.

"Do you carry a firearm?" he asked.

"It's Pacific Heights, doesn't everyone?"

He didn't smile, but I was pretty sure he thought it was funny. *I* certainly did.

Peter sat up a little straighter and adjusted his already-perfect tie. He looked like a man who'd come to a decision.

"Very well, then," he said. "I'd like to engage your services."

I nodded and said a silent prayer that this wasn't a divorce job. I don't do those.

"For what specifically?"

He shot his cuffs and cleared his throat.

"I believe my wife is going to kill me."

CHAPTER TWO

I gave him a look I usually reserve for televangelists, then I snorted. "You and every cop I know."

His face went dark. Two frown lines appeared above his nose. It was more than a little scary.

"I assure you, Roy," he said. "I'm very serious." He paused. "I believe my wife intends to murder me."

I sat up a little straighter. "All right," I said. "I'll bite. What brings you to that conclusion?"

Peter smiled grimly. "Behavior patterns, nonverbal display, phraseology," he said. "I'm an expert. My wife has engaged in behavior that I've interpreted as—" he waved his hand at the air—"hostile."

I gave him another look. "You'll excuse me if I have difficulty in making that assumptive leap."

"I didn't expect you to, Roy." He fussed with a lapel, and looked a little arrogant doing it, like a judge smoothing his robes. "As a matter of fact, I'd be surprised if you did."

I leaned back and reached for my cigarettes. I stopped, but not before Peter noticed.

"Smoker?" he asked.

"Only recreationally."

He smiled. I didn't like it; it bordered on smug. He noticed that, too.

"Forgive me," he said. "Force of habit. I make my living reading gestures and body movements. I meant no offense."

"None taken," I lied. "Let's get back to your wife. What kind of behavior makes a man think he's going to die?"

Peter sighed and rubbed his face.

"That's the problem, Roy. Reading people is not an exact science. If I explained to you the nuances of her behavior, you'd be able to put forth a convincing argument that they were completely innocuous."

He picked up a Mont Blanc pen and tapped it on the desk.

"It's just that I'm very good at what I do." He pointed the pen at me. "And I'm not being immodest. I make a damn good living selling my opinions to corporations."

That last statement was the first one, so far, that rang true.

He went back to the tapping, a little harder this time.

"But an incident two Saturdays ago convinced me to contact our mutual friend and ask for a recommendation for a private investigator."

"What incident?" I prompted.

Peter grimaced and stared at the pen he was playing percussion with. He stopped, guiltily.

"The Star of Siddhartha," he said quietly.

My eyes must've gone vacuous, because he started explaining.

"The Star of Siddhartha is a 38-carat alluvial diamond, shaped like a five-pointed star—"

"Alluvial?"

"It means it's a riverbed diamond, found in or around rivers, as opposed to mined."

I nodded wisely.

"Do you know anything about diamonds, Roy?"

"Not a thing." Which was another lie. I knew they were expensive and silly.

Peter waved dismissively.

"It doesn't matter. Suffice it to say that the Star was a gift to my wife when we married, five years ago."

"And the Star is missing," I deduced.

Peter smiled, this time with warmth.

"Very good, Roy," he said, somehow without condescension. "You, of course, are right. Two Saturdays ago we had a dinner party. Sandra, that's my wife, wore the Star to the affair."

"What happened?"

Peter suddenly looked like a man holding a lot of WorldCom stock.

"Sandra left the party early. She says she remembers placing the Star on the bedroom dresser." He leaned back and put a finger on his lower lip. "She went to the bathroom to shower, then retired for the night. The next morning she realized she hadn't returned the Star to the wall safe and went to fetch it. It was then she noticed it was gone." He shrugged. "That's the last time it was seen, or so she says."

"And you don't believe her."

Peter rubbed his face again, this time with both hands. "I'm just not sure, Roy. If I couple the Star's disappearance with her behavioral display, I come to a rather unpleasant conclusion."

"Since the diamond is hers," I ventured, "I can only assume she would steal it for the insurance money. Then she could break the Star into smaller stones and sell it piecemeal after things cooled down." I paused. "If indeed she was the one who nicked it."

Peter looked embarrassed.

"It's not technically hers," he said. "I bought it as an investment, and it's protected by our prenuptial agreement. It belongs to my estate, and my son is the beneficiary." He sighed.

"When I die, Sandra would only get an annual stipend." Peter raised a finger. "However, she, or whoever, ah, *nicked* it, could realize a substantial windfall on the black market. There are collectors aplenty who would gladly look the other way to get the Star."

"How substantial?"

"Eleven million dollars."

I whistled and he bobbed his head.

"What about your son?"

"He's four," he said. "My son gets everything when I pass. My attorney, Mr. Bosworth, is the executor. Even with a generous stipend, my wife's lifestyle will be substantially..." again with the waving, "...crimped."

"I see," said I. "What are the chances that someone else took it?"

Peter perked up.

"I'm glad you asked,"

He slid a piece of paper across the desk. There were four names on it. "This is a list of Sandra's friends who attended the party. I'd like you to investigate whether they had anything to do with the theft."

I picked it up and gave it a read. "How many guests were at the party?"

"Twenty all told."

"Tell me again why I'm not questioning the other 16."

The corners of his mouth turned down. He looked slightly indignant. "They are my clients and personal friends. I can vouch for each and every one of them."

"But you can't vouch for Sandra's friends?"

Peter fiddled with his pen, moved some papers around and avoided my eyes.

"My wife has her own set of friends," he said, carefully. "People I don't know all that well."

He was very uncomfortable now, and the pause that followed could've used a midwife.

"We…to some extent, have our separate lives."

I waited expectantly, but he didn't elaborate. Instead, he changed the subject.

"I'm sorry, Roy. I've been a terrible host. Would you care for something to drink?"

"I would care deeply," I said.

Peter looked past my shoulder. "Samuel, would you fix us a drink?"

Jeeves the butler, now known as Samuel, was standing no more than three feet behind me. The old boy was quiet as a leopard. I never heard him. It gave me the creeps.

"Certainly, Mr. Aguayo." He came into view and addressed me. "And what will you be having, Mr. Jobe?"

"Scotch, please."

"How do you take it?"

"In a bucket."

That got a smile from him. Maybe Sam wasn't so bad after all.

"Of course, Mr. Jobe. That should have been obvious."

Then again…

We waited while Samuel went to the wet bar. He came back with what looked like a bourbon and soda for Peter, and two fingers of amber for me.

"Thank you, Samuel," I said, striving for niceness.

He placed Peter's drink on a coaster and retreated silently, back to my wing position. I gave him the nickname *El Gato*.

Peter picked up his glass and looked at it with admiration. I could relate to a man who appreciated his liquor. He took a long swallow and smacked his lips.

"Where were we?" he asked.

I sipped and swallowed.

"You were trying to convince me that you're not delusional."

He looked surprised. Candor can do that.

"Uh, yes, of course," he said.

I killed half my drink. It was good Scotch, much better than the stuff I was used to.

"Let me get this straight," I said. "You have a hunch, based on your expert opinion, that your wife intends to do you harm. Your theory is further bolstered by the theft of the Star. You want me to find out if your hunch is right, or wrong, by refuting or confirming the innocence of her friends."

"In a nutshell, yes," he said. "And understand that no one outside this family knows the stone is missing. I cherish my privacy. I'll only file an insurance claim when all other avenues are exhausted."

He leaned toward me, and his form suddenly took on the appearance of a Panzer.

"That's absolutely imperative." Close to a growl.

"I understand." I didn't. I downed the rest of the Scotch. Peter looked impressed.

"What if she didn't do it?' I asked.

He shrugged. "Then I'd be relieved and would consider this entire exercise to be the paranoid fantasy of a silly old fool."

I sat back and tried to give the impression I was juggling a schedule. Warning klaxons were going off in my head, but my wallet was pretending to be hearing-impaired. Business had been slow for two months, and Peter represented a week or two of much-needed billing. He might be a bag of nuts, but he was a bag of nuts with a checkbook.

"This happened 10 days ago. What kept you?" I asked.

Peter cleared his throat and glanced quickly at Samuel. "I've made some discreet inquiries on my own," he said, "unfortunately, to no avail. The situation has escalated to the point where the resources at my disposal have been unproductive. I now need the assistance of a professional." He pointed the pen at me again. "And that professional is you."

Ten days is a long time. Whatever trail there was had turned colder than my credit line. But if it were easy, anybody could do it.

"All right," I said. "I'll take the job." I put my glass on his desk, without a coaster. Samuel picked it up and wiped under it with a handkerchief.

"But we'll need a ruse."

"Ruse?" Peter asked, puzzled.

"Yes. I need an excuse to question Sandra's friends," I said. "If the theft is to remain confidential, I can't very well ask them about the Star." I gave Samuel a quick glance, just to make sure he wasn't sneaking up on me. He looked amused. "And if any of them had anything to do with the theft, they'd sure as hell never agree to speak with a private investigator."

I paused to make sure he understood where I was going.

"If I have another reason to approach them, however," I continued, "—a ruse, a misdirection, one not associated with the Star—they might be willing to sit down with me just to throw me off the scent."

Peter let it rattle around in his head for a while.

"That seems logical."

"It is," I said. "I'll use blackmail as the dodge. It's juicy enough to get attention, and I can dance around the specifics. I'll say I'm investigating a blackmail attempt against your family, one that went bad, and see where it takes us."

I thought I saw his eye twitch when I said blackmail, but

it could've been the Scotch, or the fact that I had a cigarette in my pocket screaming my name.

He pondered my idea for a moment.

"I think that will work, Roy."

"Maybe. I'll also have to speak with your wife, sooner rather than later."

He pursed his lips again and pondered some more. "That's fine," he said cautiously. "Just as long as you keep the questions limited to the Star. She's not to know anything about my other…concerns."

"Discretion is my maiden name," I said.

He grunted and studied his desk calendar. Unlike me, he had things to do.

"I'll arrange a meeting for you with her for tomorrow morning," he said after a minute. "I'll be in L.A. on business; you'll be on your own."

"I'm used to it."

"Very good. Anything else?" he asked.

"Yes," I said. "I'd like to see the scene of the crime, and I charge two thousand a day, plus expenses."

Peter did a credible impression of spitting up a lung. "Two thousand a day?"

"Plus expenses," I confirmed.

"You can't be serious."

"As serious as a cauterized stump."

I didn't scratch my nose, shift my body or alter my expression. Peter had made me too aware of my body movements.

He looked over at Samuel, who shrugged.

"All right. I agree." He sighed. "When can you start?"

"Right now."

CHAPTER THREE

Peter and I said our goodbyes. I got his cell number and promised to keep him in the loop. El Gato, my new best friend, took me upstairs to the bedroom where the pilfering had taken place. It was to the left of the staircase and we accessed it through double doors.

The bedroom, like the rest of the house, was enormous. Sunlight streamed into the room from a large skylight and the two French doors that led out to a balcony. The carpet was an astonishing pink, with nap deep enough to hide a backhoe. A canopy bed was centered against the wall with diaphanous curtains matching the carpet, and the French Bisque dressers and vanity were of a light-colored wood with a pinkish hue. The walls held pricey-looking artwork spotlighted cleverly by little lamps.

"This the dresser?" I asked, pointing to the one closest to the bed.

"Yes," Samuel replied. "I believe Mrs. Aguayo placed the Star there."

The dresser was one of those low jobs, about thigh high, and had a phalanx of framed pictures of a beautiful little boy on top.

"Good-looking kid," I said.

Samuel remained mute.

I moved around the room, getting a feel for it. The bathroom was off to the side and was also pink, with a sunken tub you could snorkel in.

I went into a large walk-in closet and considered leaving breadcrumbs. Long rows of clothing packed both sides, and a shoe collection that would've made Imelda Marcos spit blood sat under the outfits.

Back in the bedroom I circled the bed and noticed a GI Joe and some miniature ordinance on the floor.

"Does Peter's son play in here?" I asked the effusive Samuel.

"Yes. On occasion."

I pointed to a door at the far end of the room.

"Where's that lead?"

"That's PJ's room," Samuel said, "The door's always open at night." He smiled. "PJ starts out in his own bed, but he eventually migrates to Mrs. Aquayo's."

"This happen every night?" I asked.

"Without fail."

I walked over and opened the door. PJ's room was about half the size of Sandra's, which made it twice the size of my living room. It was painted robin's egg blue to Sandra's pink, and had a bed shaped like a racing car. A small bed stand was next to it with a Mickey Mouse lamp. The carpet matched the walls and the walls had framed posters of pretty much every kid movie made since color. The bedroom furniture was painted a shade darker than the carpet and a large toy storage box, resembling a treasure chest, sat at the foot of the bed. The place was neat as a drill sergeant's blouse.

I waved at the room.

"Who picks up after PJ?"

"Aside from the vacuuming and dusting," Samuel sniffed, "no one. Little PJ is a very fastidious youth."

"What about the toys left in the other room?" I asked.

Samuel smiled.

"He's still a four-year-old," he said. "Perhaps you should make some allowances."

I grunted and went back into Sandra's room. I looked around at the walls.

"Where's the safe?"

Samuel pointed to a still life with a vase, flowers and some fruit in a gilt frame. I went over and felt the sides and found a latch. I flicked it up and the painting swung out on oiled hinges. Inside was a safe with a keypad. I swung the painting closed and stood back to admire it.

"Please tell me that's not an original Georges Seurat," I said.

Samuel's faced twitched in surprise. "Why, yes, it is. I recommended Mr. Aguayo buy it, oh, two years ago. Its value has increased 30 percent since then."

Braggart.

I gave him a long, cool look. "What do you think, Samuel. Did she do it?"

He frowned. "I believe ascertaining that would be your area of expertise," he said coldly.

I harrumphed and made a note to use *ascertain* in a sentence the first chance I got. "Okay, I've seen all I need to." I held up my hand. "Don't bother walking me out, Samuel; I know the way."

He ignored my offer and dogged my steps, probably to ensure I didn't pocket an ashtray. At the door he put a hand on my arm.

"Mr. Jobe, I overheard you say you were a Marine."

"Semper fi," I responded.

He paused.

From out of left field, he asked, "Have you seen any combat?"

I was technically outside the house, on the front step, so I pulled out a Gauloises and lit it, giving myself time to think. I drew smoke deep into my lungs and exhaled, away from my inquisitor. "When I was 18 I did a couple of years in Nicaragua and El Salvador, off the radar," I said, "doing some things."

"Bad?" he asked.

"Very."

He mulled something over before speaking.

"I was in Vietnam," Sam said. "I was 25. Tet Offensive, Hue City."

I was impressed.

"Bad?" I asked.

"Very."

He held my eyes.

"Samuel, you got something you need to say?"

For the first time since I'd met him, his face turned human. He looked down and shuffled his feet.

"The Aguayos are very important to me, Mr. Jobe," he said quietly. "They're the closest thing I have to family." He brushed something invisible off his jacket. "I need to know what kind of man is assisting them in their time of trouble. I want to make sure they're in capable hands."

I squinted and drew on my cigarette, and spoke through a curtain of smoke. "Okay, you've seen me," I said. "What do you think?"

He thought for a moment, brought his eyes back to mine and started closing the door. "I think you'll do."

Walking back to my car, I was surprised to find myself whistling.

CHAPTER FOUR
Tuesday

Someone smarter than me said that fog comes on little cats' feet, but today it arrived on the paws of an adult Bengal. It moved through the streets and buildings of Chinatown with feline grace, muffling voices and softening the clamor of a city rousing from sleep. It made you want to touch it, because you knew it'd be soft as a puppy's belly.

I got up, made some coffee and watched the fog roil outside my window. Normally, if I stuck my head out far enough, I'd be able to see the Dragon Gate at the beginning of Grant. Today it was a sheet of white.

I showered, shaved and washed out my coffee cup and French press. I put on a white shirt and draped a decent suit over it. I don't wear ties because they're slipknots, which is a polite word for noose. Keys, cell phone and wallet went into the suit's pockets; my watch went on my wrist, the Smith and Wesson went on my ankle.

I went down the two flights of stairs to the street and made an immediate right, then walked 10 steps and ducked into the American Café. Why it's called the American Café, in the heart of Chinatown, remains a mystery. Some detective.

Inside, the warmth and smells embraced me like a fat aunt. I plucked a menu from the stack and grabbed a table.

The American Café was painted in institutional green, and the paint was faded. It was long as two boxcars and just as narrow. The tables that single-filed down the left side were Formica-topped and chipped, with enough chrome edging to shame a Buick. The chairs matched the tables, most of the time, and both matched the walls. On the right, a long lunch counter ran all the way to the back and dead-ended at the kitchen. The place was half-full, evenly split between regulars and early-bird tourists, the latter dressed in shorts and loud shirts and huddled over their coffee for warmth.

I perused the menu, the English side, and waited for my waiter to bring the coffee. He was a new kid and was surprised when I ordered in Mandarin. I asked for a mushroom and Swiss cheese omelet, with hash browns and a side of bacon. He gave me a funny look and left. I unfolded the paper I'd scooped off my doorstep and read a little about death, corruption and misery. I balanced that with a story about a cat that had 20 kittens. Cute.

My breakfast came. It was two eggs over medium, fried rice and a side of Chinese sausage. The new kid was smiling, and left shaking his head.

Eddie Lee came out of the kitchen's double doors and made a beeline toward me. Eddie owned the American Café and the parking spot I rented, six blocks from my apartment. He also owned my apartment.

"How many times I gotta' tell you, Roy? Stop ordering in Chinese." He looked exasperated.

I defended myself. "Everyone in my neighborhood speaks Chinese, Eddie," I whined. "I gotta' practice."

He pulled up a chair and pointed a finger at me. "You want to learn Chinese," he said, "go to Berlitz."

I gave him a hangdog look. "Can't afford it," I said earnestly. "Slum lord's sucking the life outta' me."

He laughed and poked at my plate.

"Try that sausage."

I cut a piece and chewed it.

"Delicious."

He nodded smugly. I swallowed the mouthful and chased it with a sip of coffee.

"Just for laughs, Eddie, what'd I order?"

He made a face.

"Not sure, Roy. Something to do with road construction."

"Jesus," I said, "not even close." I shook my head. "I suck."

"Yes," he agreed. "You do."

We sat and chatted, like the old friends we were. I finished my breakfast and he finished his coffee.

"Who's the new kid?" I asked.

Eddie looked back toward the kitchen. "Fresh off the boat. From my ancestral village, name's Wei Lee."

"He working out for you?"

"Yeah, he's a good kid. Works hard, sends money home to his family." He sighed. "Same old story."

"You help a lot of these guys out, Eddie." I looked at him wryly. "If I didn't know better, I'd think you were a nice guy."

Eddie got up to go back to work. "Yeah, but you know better."

"Ain't that the truth. See ya', Eddie."

"Later, bro'."

I got up and left a fiver for the kid. The breakfast came with the apartment.

Outside it hadn't cleared a jot, and the air carried a bite, along with the fragrance of fruits and vegetables, fish and last night's garbage. It was a heady perfume and made me giddy with something close to joy.

A human tide snaked around the vegetable stalls and the just-opened tourist traps, bunching up around those who'd paused. Thinly-clad tourists were scanning the skies, searching in vain for the sun that had baked them just yesterday. But San Francisco weather, like all things in life, had reverted to form, nudging the thermometer to a miserly 62. It'd warm up later, but not enough for shorts.

I stood under the café's awning and lit my first cigarette of the day, ignoring the hostile looks from the clean-living. Half a block down I saw Wei Lee, my waiter, talking to an Asian man dressed in black. The guy in black was close to six feet tall, with shoulders about as wide. He wore black jeans with a tight black shirt, black cowboy boots with silver tips and sported sunglasses and a mullet. He looked like an asshole. He was talking loudly and gesturing, none of it friendly. He grabbed something out of Wei's hand, and I saw the flash of green that denoted money. He jammed it into his pocket, yelled some more, then slapped Wei across the face. I moved toward the hostile prick, but Wei stopped me with a guilty look and scurried back into the alley leading to the café's back door.

I watched the back of the Johnny Cash-wannabe until he disappeared around a corner. I crossed the street and walked the half-block to my office, also rented from Eddie. Three flights later I was in my two-room office. The first room was for waiting and was minuscule, with a low coffee table and some chrome-and-fabric chairs. Some magazines were on the table, because customer amenities are important and I have a kind heart.

The second room, though, is where the rubber meets the road, where the buck stops, where the nose hits the grindstone, where the clichés rain down in sheets thick as lead. It's also enormous, like my ego.

Large though it is, my office is a simple place, because I'm a simple man. It has a nice wooden desk, walnut I think, with two matching file cabinets. The carpet's reasonable, beige and stretches from wall to wall. An iMac sits to the side on a desk extension, next to a combination printer and fax and copier and scanner and something else I haven't figured out yet. A couple of chairs sit in front of the desk and a Herman Miller chair sits behind it. I've got a double window behind the desk that lets me watch the street when I'm bored, and I watch the street a lot.

I went through the mail, 90 percent of which was crap. Then I went through my email; 100 percent was crap.

I checked the time—9:30—and called Gerald Bosworth. His secretary put me through.

"Hiya', Roy."

"Hiya', Gerald."

After a couple of pleasantries, he asked me about Peter Aguayo.

"How'd it go yesterday?"

"All right, I guess," I answered. "I got the job, but he strikes me as a man who's hiding something."

He chuffed. "Yeah, he's evasive, and when you shake his hand, count your fingers."

"You know something I don't?" I asked.

"It'd take a year to list."

I chuckled.

"Just remember," he said. "You don't amass that kind of money without breaking eggs. He's smarter than you and me put together."

"Speak for yourself."

He laughed. "Just be careful, Roy. He's got some history."

"History, huh?"

"Yeah, he's ex-British intelligence, real slick and real clandestine, you know what I mean? There's a lot more there than meets the eye."

"That's exactly the impression I got."

"For once we agree."

I paused and scratched something mysterious off my desk. "All right, Gerald. Thanks for the heads-up, and thanks for the referral."

"No problem. This mean I get a discount on the next job?"

"No."

"Ha! Ungrateful wretch."

"I may be ungrateful," I said, "but I overcharge."

"That's an old, beat-up shtick," he admonished.

"But applicable."

"I'll attest to that," he said. "Keep me posted."

"Will do." I hung up.

I left my office and walked the six blocks to my car. The parking lot was slightly larger than a panty liner and held eight cars, one of which was mine. Eddie Lee and his family owned a lot of parking spaces in the City, and even more buildings, the extent of which I could only guess. He worked the café in the mornings, because he wanted to, but in the afternoons he managed his real estate empire from the office next to mine.

I carefully extricated my car and drove back up to the Aguayos' and parked in the same spot as yesterday. Samuel answered the door.

"Welcome back, Mr. Jobe." Distant and formal.

"Good to be back. Is Mrs. Aguayo in?"

"She's expecting you."

I followed him in, this time to the left, and entered a sunken living room deep enough to give me vertigo. The carpet was white Berber and the walls, leather sofa and chairs matched it. It was bright and cold and sterile, like an operating room. I feared for my gall bladder.

Samuel gestured toward a chair. "Make yourself comfortable. Mrs. Aguayo will be with you shortly."

He made an exit, then came back a minute later bearing a tray with coffee and its accoutrements. He put out two cups and two saucers and poured.

I heard a voice to my right.

"Thank you, Samuel, that will be all."

"Certainly." He left.

The voice was attached to a tall blonde gliding down the three steps leading into the pit. She wore a blue, gauzy creation that clung to all the right places and made everything below my chest ache. Her face was made of marble, flawless, like Grace Kelly in her prime. A wide, lush mouth flashed teeth perfect as snowflakes. Big, blue eyes, with lashes long enough to braid sat above the mouth, but they were cold as Hoffa's trail. They were the kind of eyes that could count the bills in your wallet from a passing car.

"Mr. Jobe." She offered her hand. I stood and took it.

"Mrs. Aguayo."

"Sandy. Please call me Sandy."

"Only if you call me Roy."

"Deal." She sat. We picked up our coffees and sipped gingerly, almost in tandem.

"As you know, Sandy," I started, "I've been hired to investigate the disappearance of your jewel."

"Yes, Samuel told me."

"Have you spoken to Peter about it?" I asked.

"No, he's in—"

"—L.A., on business," I completed.

She frowned.

"Do you do that often?" she asked.

"Do what?"

"Finish people's sentences."

"Only when I'm nervous," I replied.

"Then stop being nervous. It's annoying."

I nodded and gave her what I hoped was a sheepish look, which is hard for a guy with so much masculine confidence. "I have that effect on people," I said, hating myself for sounding like a mewling lamb. "It won't happen again."

"Very good."

I handed her the printout with the four names on it. "Peter tells me these are your friends," I said. "Can you give me some background on them?"

She looked the list over, frowned again and tossed it on the table. "Are these the only ones you're questioning?"

"They're the only ones I have permission to question, yes."

Her frown turned into a smirk. "Figures."

"How so?" I asked.

She crossed her arms over her breasts and pouted. "This is so typical of Peter. He immediately suspects *my* friends, but *his* friends are above it all." Bitterness crept into her voice. "He thinks just because they're part of his circle, they wouldn't stoop to palming a jewel."

She reached into her clutch and pulled out a pack of Camel lights and waved them at me. "Mind if I smoke?"

I pulled out my Gauloises. "Not if I can join you."

She smiled and I reached over to light her cigarette. She took a long, luxurious drag. "Peter hates that I smoke."

I smiled. "That's nothing. Perfect strangers hate that I smoke."

She smiled back.

We puffed contentedly for a minute, feeling like we were getting away with something.

"Sandy, how often do you wear the Star?" I asked.

She looked at me quizzically, like she was surprised that I'd asked something intelligent.

"Funny you should ask. That Saturday night was only the second time I've worn it. The first time was at our wedding. Then it went straight into a safe-deposit box at our bank." She nibbled on her finger. "Then out of the blue Peter wants me to wear it to this party. He said it would be all right to keep it in my wall safe until Monday. Then we'd return it to the bank." She shrugged casually. "I guess he wanted to impress his little buddies."

I tapped an ash off and looked at my cigarette.

"So you wore it at Peter's request?"

"Insistence is more like it," she said, a little sharply. "I could care less if his associates were impressed or not."

I cleared my throat. "It seems that you have a relatively low opinion of Peter's friends," I ventured.

She gave me a look with frost on it.

"They didn't get rich by being choir boys," she snapped, "and neither did Peter." She flicked her ashes into the chafing dish we were using as an ashtray. "They're like piranha among goldfish."

I let her stew for a minute.

"I get the impression that you didn't come from money," I said, cautiously.

She laughed. It was music.

"That was risky, Roy. Some people might take that as an insult."

"Some people might," I concurred.

She shifted her body toward me, which pulled her outfit tighter around the places I was trying hard not to ogle. She tilted her head toward the ceiling and exhaled smoke. "I'm what people call 'trailer trash,' Roy," she said, "raised dirt-poor, and I make no apologies. I've been around the block a couple of times." The spark in her eye could've lit a pipe. "The scenic route."

She crushed her cigarette out.

"I grew up in Elkins, Texas, outside of Amarillo," she said.

"You don't sound Texan."

"I dropped the drawl when I left that shithole." Her voice sounded like a knife scraping bone, and her eyes looked as if she was remembering something she'd rather not.

"We're neighbors," I said.

"What?"

"We're neighbors. I was born and raised in Lubbock."

She shrieked a laugh, startling me. It transformed her instantly into a rowdy cowgirl knocking back Lone Stars at a roadhouse. I liked it.

"God *damn,* Roy, why didn't you say so?"

"I didn't think it germane."

"Germane? Kiss my ass, germane," she chided. "Hell, boy, we're practically kin."

"I wouldn't go that far."

She pulled her feet up under her. "All right, Roy, ask away," she said, friendly now. "I won't bore you with my opinions of Peter's friends. It's the least I can do for a fellow Texan."

"I'm forever in your debt," I said, humbly.

She flicked a hand at me. "Go on, you. Stop talking like a carpetbagger. Ask your questions."

I smiled and did.

She pretty much confirmed Peter's version of the events of the evening in question. She left early, went upstairs and forgot to put the Star back into its safe. The next morning it was gone. She described herself as tipsy, but not drunk. Being who I am, I took it with a healthy dose of salt.

I steered the conversation back to the four names Peter had given me.

The first of the four we discussed was Jenny Monroe, a lipstick lesbian Sandy had known for a couple of years. She described Jenny as young, beautiful and rich—trust-fund rich—and a very dear friend, which seemed fraught with meaning when it oozed out of Sandy's mouth.

Then there was Brett Jarrod, a financial consultant, whatever that means, for a firm called Advent Securities in the City. He was young, ambitious and did a lot of coke. Next was Rachael Stark, a waitress at a pricy vegan place on Geary called the Millennium Restaurant. Sandy used words like *hard*, *manipulative* and *grasping* when she spoke of Rachael. I deduced she didn't like her.

The last one we talked about was Elvis Boone, and Sandy went cagey as a priest facing a felony charge. She doled each word out like it had a Krugerrand strapped to it, but I did get that he was tall, dark and handsome, and a consultant of some kind. I put him at the top of my list.

She reeled off the addresses and phone numbers for them all, which told me she'd been at their homes at one time or another. Elvis lived with the much-despised Rachael, which told me something else.

"Well, I think I've got all I need to get started, Sandy. I'll be interviewing your friends for the next couple of days," I said as we wrapped up.

"You're not going to grill them like suspects, I trust?"

"Absolutely not. I know they're your friends; I'll walk softly."

"You'll ask them if they're thieves. How soft can that be?"

"No." I shook my head. "Peter wants to keep this confidential. I can't bring the Star into the conversation."

"That makes your job a little difficult."

"Yes and no. Peter and I agreed that I'd use a ruse, for confidentiality."

"Ruse?"

I nodded. "Yes. I'll intimate that there's a clumsy blackmail attempt against your family, one without merit. That way I get my information without talking about the Star."

When I used the term blackmail, she looked like she'd stepped on a snail.

"Is that necessary?"

"Unless you have reservations."

She shook out another cigarette. I lit it. She took a nervous drag. "No, I guess that'll be fine," she said, "It's just that..."

I leaned in to prompt her.

"...never mind."

I stared, but this well was dry.

"All right, Sandy," I said, rising. "I'd better start earning my keep."

She held her hand up and looked over my shoulder.

"Just a moment."

I sat down and followed her eyes.

Samuel approached with the little boy in the pictures. The kid was cherubic, with black hair and olive skin. He had bright blue eyes, like his mother, but everything else came from Peter. He wore khaki shorts and a blue polo shirt with a

Ralph Lauren logo over the heart. Ankle socks and blue Nike Shox were on his feet.

"This is my son, PJ," Sandy said.

I nodded to him and he nodded back.

"Mrs. Aguayo," Samuel said. "I really must be going if I'm to keep my appointment."

"Of course, Samuel, I'm sorry. I've let the morning slip by."

Samuel excused himself and left.

"Roy, could you be a dear and watch PJ for a few minutes?" she asked. "While I get dressed?"

I was nonplussed.

"Uh, sure, I guess."

She laughed and pointed at me.

"You should see the look on your face, Roy." She smiled. "I take it you're a single man, no children?"

"Very, and yes."

She waved away any concerns I might've harbored.

"Don't worry," she said. "PJ doesn't bite."

"So you say."

"Don't be a big silly. He's four years old. He's potty-trained and has his rabies shots."

"What about distemper?"

"Stop being difficult."

"All right, I'll watch him."

"You're an angel."

She kissed PJ and left in a swirl of chiffon.

The kid stared at me and I stared back. We stayed that way for about five minutes. Apparently, that wasn't getting the reaction he wanted, so he took a deep, bored breath, walked up to me and kicked me in the shin. I kicked him back. Actually, it was more of a foot push, but the result was the same.

He went sprawling on his backside, arms flailing. His face started the pre-wail collapse, but he was a perceptive child. He sensed that crying wasn't going to affect a man who would knock a four-year-old on his ass. His face settled down and he smiled mischievously. We had an understanding.

After 20 minutes of ignoring each other, Sandy came back to claim the little darling. He gave me a look, but remained silent. He might be spoiled, but he wasn't a rat. I respected that.

Sandy had on a smart, cream-colored pantsuit with a string of pearls and matching earrings. Her bag matched the suit and her shoes matched her bag and the blouse she had on under the suit somehow matched the pearls. Even her nail color was dead on.

She noticed that I noticed and looked down at her outfit.

"The Devil's in the details," she said.

I nodded stupidly.

"Thanks for watching PJ for me, Roy."

"No problem."

"Did you boys have fun while I was away?" she asked.

"Yep, we talked about man stuff," I answered.

She looked at PJ like the universe revolved around him. It was nice to see.

"Oh, really? What kind of man stuff?" she asked him.

"I can't tell you, Mom."

She looked surprised. "Why not?"

"'Cause it's man stuff."

I smiled and winked at the kid. He smiled back. I liked his style.

Sandy rolled her eyes in mock disgust and gathered PJ to walk me out. On the way, PJ slipped his hand into mine and I held it as if it were a butterfly. At the door I said my goodbyes and followed the sidewalk to the street. I looked back and watched as Sandy started closing the door and caught PJ peeking out at me. He gave a shy, tentative wave.

For some reason, it broke my heart.

CHAPTER FIVE

I got in my car and pulled a U-turn so I could watch the double garage doors at the base of the hill that supported the Aguayos' home. I stuck an earpiece into my cell and speed-dialed Sammy Mayfair.

"Hey, Sammy. Roy."

"Darling! It's been months!"

I smiled. Sammy can do that to you.

"Yes, it has, and that's Mr. Darling to you."

"Someone sounds cranky. You need a nap?" Sammy asked.

"That and a drink. You got a minute?"

"Of course, Roy."

"Thanks. Track these names for me, will you?" I gave him the names and addresses of the gang of four. In the background, Sammy's keyboard clattered insanely. Sammy was a good guy to know. I met him when I was still with the SFPD.

"While you're at it, run Peter and Sandra Aguayo."

"Spell that last name for me, pumpkin."

"Mr. Pumpkin."

He sighed. *"Mr.* Pumpkin."

I spelled it out and heard more clicks.

"Bam! Done. When do you want it?"

"End of day okay?" I asked.

"As you wish," he said. "I am but a humble non-union worker bee."

"The humble part could use some work."

"Yeah, I'll make it my life's priority. You coming to my show?"

"When and where?"

"I'll be at Maxi's, two Saturdays from now," he said. "You gotta' come. I've got a new dress. Emerald, sequined and low-cut. I'm stunning."

"I thought you were working on the humble thing."

"Quit avoiding commitment, Roy. Can I count on you?"

"I'll be there."

"Wonderful! I'll rock your world."

"Not likely."

"Don't be a stick in the mud."

"Coming from a gay guy, that's a poor choice of words."

He laughed.

"And you wonder why nobody likes you. I'll email you this afternoon."

"Thanks, Sammy. I appreciate it."

"De nada."

I hung up.

Ten minutes and a cigarette later, the garage doors raised silently and disgorged a Stygian BMW 7 series sedan. It was sleek and shiny and muscular and had 20-inch silver rims.

The car purred up to Broadway and turned left toward Chinatown. I followed. It meandered in the general direction of Market Street and at the 200 block of Stockton slid into a four-story parking garage. I waited behind another car and trailed it in. On the second level I saw Sandy with PJ at her side, unloading bags from the trunk. I took a chance that she wouldn't turn around and cruised past them to the third floor. I parked and hurried down the stairs just in time to see her lugging PJ and three or four bags toward the Neiman Marcus store on Stockton.

I shadowed her to the Prada counter, deftly dodging two women trying to cover me in sample perfume. She deposited PJ into a chair and pulled a bunch of purses and some shoes out of the bags. The clerk fumbled around for a bit, then left. Fifteen minutes went by, which she killed by trying on some neat-looking ankle boots and a pair of Caterina Lucchi slingbacks. The clerk came back with a manager who looked like Fred Astaire and walked like Cyd Charisse, only better. He smiled at Sandy like she was a favorite aunt and started counting out a stack of bills a foot high. She wadded them up, thought about it, then peeled some off for the ankle boots. Good choice.

I waited for her to leave, then went to the men's fragrance counter. I bought some Issey Miyake cologne and deodorant, effectively wasting 10 minutes. That gave her plenty of time to exit the store.

Back at the Prada section, I fingered some handbags with price tags about two zeros past sane. I approached the clerk who had assisted Sandy. He was middle-aged and had on a good suit. He sported a stainless-steel TAG Heuer watch with a gold bezel and wore a diamond stud earring that made him look like he was trying too hard. He was perfectly coiffed, but his shoes, while gleaming, had a lot of wear on the heels.

"I was wondering if you could help me," I said.

"Certainly, sir. What can I do for you?"

"That woman." I motioned over my shoulder with my thumb. "She do that often?"

He tilted his body to look behind me. "You mean Mrs. Aguayo?"

"Yes. Mrs. Peter Aguayo. Drives a BMW, lives in Pacific Heights," I answered.

He got huffy on me. "I'm not at liberty to say." He sniffed. "I don't discuss my customers' habits with strangers."

I reached into my pocket.

"Do you discuss your customers' habits with presidents?"

An eyebrow shot up. "Depends on which president."

I took out a C-note, folded it and laid it on the counter.

"How about Ben?" I asked.

He picked it up. "Ben was never president." I reached for the bill, but he pulled it away. "But he'll do."

He looked around. We were alone. He leaned in and dropped his voice an octave or two. "Comes in two or three times a month. Been doing it for about six months. Buys big-ticket items with a credit card, then returns most of it for cash. We don't complain as long as she keeps some of the merchandise. I figure she leaves five grand with us a month and takes home around seven or eight grand in cash."

I whistled.

"She ever come in here with a guy?"

"No, only her kid."

He shrugged.

"Lot of women do it. Hubby puts them on a budget, but the accountant does the credit cards. Hubby never sees it. She gets spending cash and no one's the wiser." He winked. "She's probably doing the same over at Nordstrom's and Macy's. They usually do it prior to a divorce. You a divorce detective?"

"No," I said. "I don't do divorce jobs."

He smirked. "Whatever."

I shot him a dirty look and left.

CHAPTER SIX

It cost me 12 bucks to bail my car out of the garage, and as I paid, the terms *extortion* and *shakedown* kept trying to jump out of my mouth.

Next on my to-do list was Elvis and Rachael. Their place was at the intersection of Jackson and Drumm, a high-rent location about 15 blocks away. I circled their block a few times and espied an SUV pulling out of a spot. I slid into it like a NASCAR points leader, got out and walked around the corner.

Their apartment building was suitably snazzy, with brushed-aluminum balcony railings and an elegant white-blue-and-gray paint job that made it fit nicely against the city skyline. It had a great view of the Embarcadero, the piers and the bay beyond. The building was triangular, with graduated floors, like steps, which made it look like a docked luxury liner. The only things missing were boarding ramps, paper streamers and fat men in loud shirts.

At the entrance I buzzed 4228. A woman's voice came out of a tinny speaker.

"What?"

Abrupt and to the point.

I spoke into the mesh.

"My name is Roy Jobe. Sandy Aguayo gave me your address. I'm a private investigator. I have some questions I'd like to ask."

I waited for several moments. I was about to reiterate

when the door buzzed. I went through, took the elevator up to the fourth floor and knocked on 4228. A woman—a stunning woman—opened the door.

Rachael Stark was about 28, with a nice tan and raven hair. She had sharp, elfin features and a mouth that would be unfamiliar with the word *no*. Dark eyes shimmered below pencil-thin brows. A tight black top hugged her torso and the leather pants had been applied with a brush. She had the kind of body that could start a religion.

She spoiled it all, for me at least, with a bunch of rings in her lips and nose and a thingy in her eyebrow that looked like it could draw lightning. One ring in her ear held a fair-sized diamond in a dewdrop shape, set in blued steel, like my revolver. Under her makeup she had a black eye.

She jerked her head. "C'mon in. Sandy called and said you might be coming around."

I followed her into a large, bright apartment with all the furnishings a successful young couple was supposed to have. Everything looked Scandinavian, with sharp corners and slim lines. The colors were white, white and more white, with occasional splashes of salmon and something else. All the wood was blonde.

She motioned me to a chair and plopped herself into the couch.

"Thanks for seeing me," I said. "I know it's intrusive."

"Anything for the queen," she said sarcastically.

I ignored it and settled myself in the chair.

"The reason I'm here, Rachael, is because someone approached the Aguayos with a blackmail proposition."

Her face, like Sandy's, went tight at the mention of blackmail.

She got over it, quickly, and hooked an ashtray on the coffee table closer to herself with her foot. Her toenails were painted coral.

"What happened to your eye?" I asked.

She squinted.

"I head-butted a nosy guy."

I laughed out loud.

A pack of cigarettes materialized from somewhere in the cushions and she put one in her mouth. I leaned over and lit it.

"Thank you," she said, exhaling.

"You're welcome." I lit one of my own.

"Blackmail?" she asked.

"Yes." I confirmed, exhaling smoke. "It's a rather clumsy attempt, very amateurish."

Her eyes blazed. I'd somehow annoyed her. My gift again, but this time I wasn't even trying.

"So why come to me?" she asked.

"Actually, I was hoping to talk to you and Elvis together. Sandy said you three were friends. I thought you two might be able to clear some things up."

"Like what?"

"Is Elvis here?"

"No, he's working."

"Where?"

"You're pretty nosy," she said.

"You gonna' head-butt me?"

"Thinking about it."

I sighed and gave her a look of helpless innocence.

"Gimme' a break. It's how I make a living."

She blew smoke in my face.

"That's a pretty shitty way to make a living."

"Not really," I replied.

"Tell me one good thing about your work."

My eyes flicked to her legs.

"I occasionally get to meet beautiful women in tight leather pants."

She laughed. "Well, ain't you the charmer."

"Only when it's worth it."

She smiled and rolled her eyes.

"Jesus, you lay it on thick."

I grinned.

"My apologies; I pressed you there. It's the nature of my business."

I adjusted my lapels and showed her some more teeth.

"How about I ask a few questions and we get back on friendly footing?"

She gave me a sly, sidelong glance.

"All right, tall man, ask your questions."

I asked her about the sequence of events at the dinner party, telling her a blackmail note was slipped to Sandy early in the evening. She asked me what the note was about, and I told her I wasn't at liberty to discuss it. She didn't look very happy with my answer, but she didn't push.

The only thing she added that I didn't already know was that Sandy and her friends had taken turns going up to the bedroom to do lines of coke. A couple of Peter's friends had joined in. Brett Jarrod had supplied it. After Sandy had retired for the evening, the four stayed and drank champagne until 2:30 am. After that they went their separate ways.

"Did anyone go up to Sandy's room after she'd left the party?" I asked.

Rachael sighed.

"Maybe, maybe not. I wasn't keeping track. It was a *party*."

I nodded.

"Okay, point taken." I leaned back in the chair and asked casually, "Was there any unusual behavior that you might have noticed?"

"Like what?"

"Unpleasantness, self-immolation, maybe someone throwing a chair through a window?"

She put her finger to her lips and scrunched her face. It looked like it hurt.

"Actually, now that I think of it, Elvis and Jenny got into it in a corner. It looked like she was giving him an earful. I wasn't close enough to hear and never really gave it much thought."

"You didn't ask him about it?"

She smirked.

"Why bother? I figured he was trying to get into her pants. Thinks he can change her."

"Change her?"

"Jenny's a lesbian, or didn't Sandy tell you?"

"Sandy mentioned it."

Her lip curled and I saw a flash of teeth.

"Well, Elvis thinks he's God's gift to women. He thinks if Jenny went one night with him, she'd give up women forever." The statement had a deep vein of anger under the surface, but plain to anyone within a seven-iron.

"Is he?" I asked.

"Is he what?"

"Is he God's gift to women?"

She laughed. It came wrapped in spite.

"He wishes."

I let that marinate for a while and helped her stare out at the bay.

"How long have you been with Elvis?" I asked.

She blew a perfect smoke ring, and we both watched it rise toward the ceiling.

"I'm not *with* Elvis. He's my roommate."

"Then how long have you been roommates?"

"About six months."

"Do you sleep with him?"

Her eyebrows shot up, jiggling her scrap metal.

"That's a blunt question."

"I'm in a blunt business."

She looked at me the way I look at Porterhouse.

"I'm fucking Elvis for now," she said, "until something better comes along."

She blew another ring that encircled my head like a noose.

"Maybe something taller," she breathed.

It was tempting, but this was business, and she had too many holes in her face.

I pulled out a card.

"If you think of anything else, Rachael, I'd sure appreciate a call."

She didn't look all that disappointed. She took the card and walked me out, trailing Chanel No. 5.

"See you around, tall man," she said.

I shot her a smile that I hoped would ruin her for any other man.

She closed the door on my face.

CHAPTER SEVEN

Advent Securities, where Brett Jarrod worked, was at Sansome and Pine, too far to walk and too close not to think about it. I, however, had an expense account, so I drove the seven or eight blocks and parked in another larcenous garage.

The building that housed Advent was the kind I liked, old and dignified, with a lobby two stories high and a granite floor that had tasted about a million miles of shoe leather. The walls were brown granite that matched the floor and bulged here and there with Art Deco flourishes. In the center of the lobby was a kiosk with suite numbers, posted above the head of a tired old security guard. I found Advent on the board and went to the brass-faced elevators embedded in the walls.

I got out at the twentieth floor and followed the signs to suite 12. The door had *Advent* set in a gold plaque. I went in and sidled up to the counter.

A Rubenesque woman with a headset sat behind it, typing something important into her computer. I could see only her head and part of her shoulders. Behind her was a labyrinth of cubicles.

"Excuse me, I'm looking for Brett Jarrod," I said politely.

The woman stopped her typing and looked at me like a pawnbroker appraising a tin ring.

"You and me both, pal."

"Pardon?"

She shifted her body towards me.

"He's not here. Hasn't been here for a month. No call, no note, no nothing."

"I see."

"You a bill collector?" she asked.

"No, I just have some questions I'd like to ask him."

An impish smile tugged at her lips.

"You look like a bill collector. Tall and muscular, with mean eyes."

I feigned offense. "Tall and muscular, yes, but I take exception to mean eyes," I said indignantly.

Her smile blossomed, and it changed her whole demeanor. I estimated it at 2,000 watts.

"Don't get sore, big boy; it's just my way."

"I see."

"You already said that," she said.

This woman gave no quarter and took no prisoners. I liked her.

"So, he just disappeared?" I asked.

"Looks that way. Didn't show up for work. I called his house and left about 30 messages. Nada."

I mulled it over.

"Well, sorry to bother you," I said. "Perhaps I'll try him at home."

"No bother, handsome. Stop by any time."

I smiled and walked to the door.

"Hey," she yelled, "if you see him, tell him he's fired."

I nodded from the doorway and she blew me a big kiss.

Back in my car I reviewed what I knew about Brett Jarrod. Both Sandy and Rachael said he was a source of cocaine, and a user. As this was an expensive habit, I assumed he was either in a drug-induced, self-destructive spiral or he had another source of income that allowed him the luxury of walking away from his job. The best way to find out was to ask.

I drove out to the Sunset District, to the address Sandy had given me.

Brett Jarrod lived in a small stucco house on a side street off Judah. The home was white with a red tiled roof and needed a paint job, but not badly. It had a small, bushy lawn and gray flagstones that led up to the door. Planter boxes sat beneath the two front windows, and a couple of pink tulips had just flowered.

I knocked and waited.

A minute later a man answered the door. He appeared to be about 30, with a goatee that matched sharp brown eyes. Clad in only pajama bottoms, the beginnings of a potbelly crowded his navel. He wasn't particularly muscular, but he also wasn't terribly out of shape. A cigarette dangled from his lips.

"What can I do for you?" he asked, not unkindly.

"Sandy Aguayo gave me your name," I said.

"Oh, yeah, Sandy said you might stop by." He opened the door and motioned me in. "Come on in."

I followed him into the living room, wondering why Sandy had warned him and Rachael. Maybe she was just being helpful. I was used to that. Everyone wanted to help a nosy PI dig through the detritus of their personal lives, much the same way people were thrilled about helping the IRS with an audit.

The living room was comfortable, with overstuffed furniture in brown, green and burgundy. A rough-hewn coffee table supported an assortment of books and magazines. There were a couple of prints on the wall, good quality, of impressionist paintings. The carpet was relatively new and recently vacuumed, and a large entertainment center with a plasma screen dominated the room.

Brett's house was disheveled, but not offensively so. It didn't look like the lair of a serious cokehead.

He collapsed onto the sofa and I did the same with the chair.

"So what's this I hear about blackmail?" he asked.

"Where'd you hear that?"

"Rachael called, after Sandy. Said you'd been over there."

Our missile defense system should be so efficient.

"What else did she say?"

Brett went over my conversation with Rachael, parroting back almost the entire exchange. I kept nodding like I was interested. When he got to the part where Elvis argued with Jenny, I interrupted.

"So you saw the argument?"

"It was hard to miss. He was getting red in the face," he said. "I was actually getting concerned about her safety."

"Are you saying that Elvis threatened her physically?"

Brett grimaced.

"Elvis has been known to be liberal with his fists."

"What makes you say that?"

"Let's just say word gets around."

Brett didn't look like he was going to elaborate, so I moved on.

"Did you hear any details of the argument?"

"No; I was talking with one of Peter's friends, about investment opportunities. I'm a financial advisor."

Since he'd abandoned his job almost two weeks before the party, I wondered why he bothered. "I see," I said for the third time in an hour.

It seemed to me that Brett and Rachael were going out of their way to offer up information that might make Elvis look like a prick, or perhaps they were coordinating a story to take my attention away from them. Either way it smacked of subterfuge, and it had the opposite effect. Lies and guile speak volumes to me, and I was a man with a keen appreciation for both. I'd be looking at these two even more closely.

"Well, I think I have all I need. Thanks for spending time with me," I said as I got up.

"That's it?"

"Unless you have something to add."

"No, not really."

I smiled and walked to the door with Brett on my heels. I was about to exit when I turned and asked, "Do you have a girlfriend?"

He looked surprised. "No one steady. Why?"

"I thought I smelled perfume."

"Perfume?" Brett looked a little flustered.

"Yes, perfume." I waited a beat, then added nastily, "Chanel No. 5, to be exact."

"I don't smell anything," he stuttered.

I paused, then passed through the door.

"Probably just my imagination."

Brett nodded eagerly in agreement.

"Probably."

With a wave I left him and walked around the corner to my car. I got in and slammed the door. I don't like being played for a chump.

CHAPTER EIGHT

J enny Monroe lived out by Laurel Heights, on the corner of Clay and Locust. It was a nice neighborhood near the Presidio, within walking distance of Mountain Lake Park. I found her chic condo complex easily and parked about a block away.

It was getting close to two o'clock and my stomach was making the kind of noises a neglected stomach had a right to make, so I walked up half a block to a deli. I ordered a corned beef on pumpernickel with provolone and hot mustard and sprang for the "deli deal," which meant I got a bag of chips and some caffeinated sugar water for a buck more. I sat at one of the sidewalk tables and enjoyed the sandwich and the just-emerged sun, and pondered why the addition of potato chips and soda would elevate a sandwich into an entrée. I reached no conclusions.

After bussing my table, I washed my hands in the unisex bathroom and patted down some wayward hairs. Sated, I made my way to Jenny's condo.

The building was a five-story postmodern, with a few Romanesque accents that somehow worked. The front door was thick, oversized smoked glass with a stainless-steel frame and handle.

I buzzed Monroe and got no answer. Five minutes and five buzzes later I decided to try a shotgun approach and pushed a number of buttons at random. The tenth one rewarded me with the sound of the door being released and, never one to look a gift horse in the mouth, I slid into the lobby.

On the fifth floor I went to number 55 and knocked. No answer. I tried the knob and it turned, which was an obvious invitation that I of course, accepted.

"Hello? Jenny Monroe?"

I went down the wide hallway and was dumped into an enormous, well-lit living room. The design was contemporary Italian, graceful and luminous, with swooping lines and creamy, muted colors. The chairs were low slung and butter-colored with gold accents, and the sofa was shaped like a truncated S. Glass side-tables supported pink vases with cut flowers, while two floor lamps shaped like frosted tulips book-ended the couch. The coffee table was also glass and mirrored the furniture's curvature, and everything sat on a light mint carpet.

The limp body on the floor however, put a dent in the room's ambiance.

I moved around the coffee table and got a better look at whom I presumed to be the late Jenny Monroe. She was lying on her side and looked very much like she was asleep. Her outfit consisted of jeans and a pink Oxford shirt with two pockets. The visible ear had a diamond stud, and I assumed its twin decorated the other side.

I put on the latex gloves I always carry and felt for a pulse, but didn't find one. There was blood on the carpet behind where her other earring should be, so I carefully turned her head and brushed the hair away from the back of her neck. A neat little hole greeted me from the base of her skull.

"Don't move!"

I jerked in surprise, but otherwise obeyed.

"Let me see your hands!"

I put up my hands and rose slowly. I turned to see two police officers pointing Glock nine-millimeters at my chest. One was in his late twenties, big and wide with the shoulders of a bodybuilder. The other officer was Asian, about five-foot-six, and was very possibly the most beautiful woman who had ever held a gun on me.

"Move away from the sofa!"

This was getting tedious.

"It's more of a settee," I said reasonably, "and please lower your voice."

He thought about it.

"Shut the fuck up and do what I say."

"Better," I said, and moved.

Muscle Boy came up behind me and pulled my hands down and cuffed them, hard. He frisked me, badly, because he missed the .38 Police Special strapped to my ankle. It was sloppy police work that, frankly, pissed me off. His ineptness was putting himself and his partner in danger. I hate cops who don't take their work seriously.

He shoved me into the center of the room, none too gently, and admired his handiwork. The beautiful one holstered her gun.

Loudmouth came around the front and stuck his face into mine. His nametag said Officer Sean Stewby.

"Why'd you kill her, shitwad?" he asked.

"I didn't."

"Wrong answer," he said, and drove his fist into my stomach.

I buckled, but didn't go down. I remained bent over, trying to catch my breath, and noted that the other officer, Liz Ishida by her nametag, had the good grace to look embarrassed.

Stewby grabbed my hair and jerked me upright. "I'll ask you again; why'd you kill her?"

"I didn't."

"Wrong answer again," he said, as he delivered an open-handed slap to my face. It spun me almost completely around. Stewby was strong.

"That's enough," said Officer Ishida.

Stewby gave her a look that should have left an exit wound.

"What'd you say?" he asked as he advanced on her.

To her credit, she didn't back down.

"I said, 'That's enough.'"

Stewby's face was about a nose-length away from Ishida's, and he had a short nose. "Listen up, little girl," he growled. "When I want your *slant* on the situation, I'll ask for it."

Ishida didn't blink.

"What's going on here?"

We all turned toward the source of the voice. Petey Dempster, my partner when I was with the SFPD, walked into the room, followed closely by a compact Latin man I didn't know.

"Hey, Petey," I said.

"Hey, Roy." He walked around to the body. 'Who's the stiff?" he asked. Petey tends to talk like that.

"Jenny Monroe, I think," I answered.

He looked over at Officer Stewby. "Uncuff him," Petey said, pointing at me.

Stewby reluctantly uncuffed me.

"Go downstairs, you two, and call CSU. Wait for 'em," he directed.

As Officers Stewby and Ishida started to leave, I caught Ishida's eye and nodded a thank you. She nodded back.

"Hey, Stewby," I said.

He shot me an unpleasant look and I lifted my pant leg and wiggled my foot. He looked at my ankle holster, as did everyone else in the room, then turned magenta and stormed out of the apartment.

I turned my attention back to Petey. Petey Dempster was 53 years old and had mentored me as a rookie inspector. He was 5'10" and weighed close to 230 pounds, some of it muscle. His walrus mustache was almost all gray, with only a few streaks of black shooting through it. The thick shock of hair on top of his head was salt-and-pepper, and his hairline had held the same spot since birth. He had on a grey suit, Liz Claiborne by the look of the cut, with a white shirt and an electric-blue tie. His eyes matched his tie and were very sharp, like the brain behind them.

I tilted my chin toward the departing officers. "Is Stewby related to Deputy Chief Stewby?"

Petey looked over his shoulder. "You have to ask?"

I grunted.

"So what we got?" he asked.

I flicked my eyes over at the Latino man. "Aren't you going to introduce us?"

Petey rubbed his face. "Yeah, whatever. Roy Jobe, this is my partner, Octavio Sequoia."

Octavio was a short, neat man with olive skin and hair black as a publisher's heart. He had full, sensuous lips and a sharp nose, with eyes the color of chestnuts. The suit he sported was vanilla, and his shoes were made of some kind of exotic leather that matched his eyes. We shook hands warily.

"Roy and me used to be partners," Petey said.

"I feel for you, Roy," said Octavio.

"Better you than me, Octavio."

We smiled.

"All right, all right, enough with the pleasantries," Petey said irritably. "What are you doing here, Jobe?"

I summed up to Petey and Octavio my day so far, leaving out any mention of the Star. They listened quietly and gave an occasional nod to let me know they were awake. Petey didn't press me for names; he knew he wasn't going to get them. I just told him that there was a group of people I was looking at closely. I wrapped it up with my coming here, making no mention of Stewby's antics.

"So here I am," I concluded. "Now, what are *you* doing here?"

Petey was over at the body, poking at it with a pen. "Somebody called it in. Said we'd find a body here. Dispatch sent out Brain-Dead and the Asian girl. We weren't far behind."

"Man or woman?" I asked.

"Man," Petey said. "Didn't leave a name."

Octavio went over to the body and squatted. "You touch her?"

I held up the gloves I'd stripped off. "Only in a professional capacity."

Petey came over to me. "Any ideas?" he asked.

"Not yet," I said. "She's part of that group I told you about."

He looked at Jenny and shook his head. "So young. God damn heartbreaking."

"Tragic," I agreed.

"Any rough stuff in this case of yours?" he asked.

"Nah, just an everyday purloin."

He gave me the patented Dempster stare. "You'd tell me if there was anything here I needed to know, right." Which was more of a statement than a question.

I batted my eyes. "Yeah, Petey, I would."

Petey sighed and rubbed the back of his neck. "All right, Jobe, get out of here before CSU arrives."

He shook my proffered hand.

"Good seeing you again, Petey."

"You too, Roy." He held on to my hand. "Don't leave town," he said, more than half-serious.

"Perish the thought."

As I turned to leave, I asked, "You mind if I give you a call later?"

"Why?"

"To ascertain whether any information you garner has any bearing on my case."

Petey waved me off. Octavio sniggered. "Stop talking like an asshole," Petey said gruffly, "and no, you can't."

"Okay," I said. "I'll call you tonight."

He pointed to the door. "Get out."

I waved to Octavio and went downstairs.

Outside, Sean Stewby and Liz Ishida were busy not speaking to each other. Stewby gave me a nasty look, which I ignored. Liz said hello and I handed her my card. "Call me later," I wheedled.

She looked at the card, then slid it into her shirt pocket. She gave me a Mona Lisa smile and my knees were suddenly tapioca.

"Maybe," she purred.

CHAPTER NINE

Back in my office I checked my email to see if Sammy Mayfair had any early information for me, and was delighted, again, with his alacrity.

Based on the Social Security numbers Sammy had hacked from the subjects' places of employment, Brett Jarrod lived in Galveston, Texas, worked at a software company and was married with two children. He owned a three-bedroom house outside of town and had coached little league for the last five years. He was 5'8" tall, and 140 pounds with blue eyes and blond hair. In short, Brett Jarrod was not the man with whom I had just spoken.

Rachael Stark also was someone other than she claimed to be. Sammy's information stated that Rachael Ortega Stark, again of Galveston, Texas, was a floor manager at a Toys 'R' Us and was still employed there. She was married, 5'1", Hispanic, owned a condo in town with her husband and had one child from a previous marriage. This kind of information is commonly referred to as a "clue" in the detecting business. A big, fat, sit-on-your-chest-and-yell-at-you clue.

At least Jenny Monroe was Jenny Monroe. She had been a trust-fund baby, as Sandy had said, with a portfolio worth around $17 million. She'd attended UCLA and apparently had majored in bong hits. No aliases or police record of any consequence, other than possession of bong material.

I did find an interesting tie-in with Brett and Rachael,

though. Jenny's family was in oil—Texas oil—and they also hailed from Galveston. That's three names out of the same town, two of them phony and one of them dead. I knew it meant something, but I'd have to do some more digging to discern exactly what. Regardless, it was a solid thread to chase.

Elvis Boone turned out to be the jackpot. Boone had just gotten out of Huntsville Prison in Texas a scant seven months ago. He'd done six years for armed robbery and assault, and I immediately thought of Rachael's black eye. There was no probation tacked on, so he was free to go wherever his felonious little feet took him.

If you threw Sandy into the mix, all the people involved were from Texas or had stolen identities from Texas, and I believe in coincidence like I believe in wood sprites.

Sammy had provided me with a snapshot, as was his practice, and I could expect more information as it trickled in. His email said I'd get the Aguayo backgrounds tomorrow, if not sooner, along with any further details on the other four. I emailed him back, telling him to forget about delving deeper in Brett and Rachael's background.

I made my notes in one of the black composition notebooks that I keep in a file drawer and wrote "Aguayo" on the cover. I put it in my "active file" area, which means it went on top of my desk.

I had some time to kill before my next appointment and I needed something stupid to do while I mulled this over, so I lit a cigarette and went through my bills. As usual, Eddie Lee got his pound of flesh, but other than that my overhead was pretty low. I'd bought my Lexus SUV used from Eddie, for cash, and I wasn't part of the landed gentry, so I didn't have a mortgage to sweat. Phone, health insurance, cable and a couple of charge cards later and I was done.

I got my coat and locked up, then went next door to Eddie's office to see if he'd buy me a drink. No such luck. He'd escaped.

I went downstairs and walked to Clay and took a left. A block and a half up I ducked into the Red Pagoda, a local bucket of blood. It took a moment for my eyes to adjust to the murky interior, and as my vision cleared a wave of red and gold rushed to greet me. Red vinyl booths with gold trim took up the left half. On the right, a long bar, in the same hues, fronted a backlit display of liquor. The walls were red felt or velvet and had gold dragons and gold pagodas and assorted geegaws stuck on them. Eight people were in the bar, most of whom I knew, and who, like me, would be gone before the happy-hour crowd made the place respectable.

I sat at the bar on a stool close to the door and waited while Jumbo Choi brought over a Dewar's and rocks.

"Where you been, Dawg?" he asked. "Haven't seen you in a couple of months."

I looked up at the wall of muscle that made up Jumbo Choi. Jumbo and I went back about eight years. I'd met him as an SFPD homicide inspector. A jealous boyfriend had shot his sister and I'd worked 72 hours straight to bring the shooter in. His sister had survived and the boyfriend was cooling his heels in San Quentin. We'd been friends ever since.

"Business been slow," I answered. "I've been hanging out at McCoy's, hitting the speed bag."

He wiped the counter. "Got a fight coming up?" he asked facetiously.

I chuffed a laugh. "They don't have a seniors' tour in boxing, Jumbo. It's a young man's sport."

"You could hold your own," he said, charitably.

"For the first 30 seconds," I corrected.

He grinned at me with large white teeth. I sipped my Scotch and looked around to make sure we were out of anyone else's earshot.

"You know an Asian guy, dresses in black, wears cowboy boots with silver tips?"

Jumbo nodded. "Got a mullet; looks like an asshole."

I smiled. "Yeah, that's him."

He put his elbows on the bar and glanced over his shoulder before speaking. "He's a new guy, one of Khan's. Came down from Seattle. Takes bets and loans some money. He tried working this room a few weeks back. I had to toss his ass out...excuse me."

Jumbo went over to the soda station and splashed some ginger ale and Seagram's Seven into a glass, then slid it down the bar to a waiting patron. He walked back to me with his arms spread.

"Would you believe he threatened me?" Jumbo looked incredulous. "Can you imagine? He threatened The Jumbo."

I shook my head. "Fuckin' suicidal, that guy," I said.

"Goddamn skippy," he said.

I took another sip.

"He got a name?" I asked.

"Yeah, I checked around. Name's Randall Tang."

I grunted.

"What's he to you?" he asked.

I shrugged. "A kid I know is on his bad side. I'm going to take care of it."

"Need some help?" Jumbo asked.

"Why?"

Jumbo sighed and poured another shot into my glass.

"He's with *Khan*," he said, exasperated.

I sloshed the liquid around a little and thought about it.

"Thanks, Jumbo, I appreciate the offer." I drained the Scotch. It made everything in my chest cavity feel special. "If I need a hand, I'll come get you."

Jumbo glared. "You better."

I put a twenty on the bar, said goodbye to Jumbo and waved back to a couple of guys sitting in a booth.

Outside, Chinatown had ratcheted up a notch. Citizens done with work were hurrying home and the omnipresent tourists were trying hard not to get between them and dinner.

I walked back down to Grant and went a couple of blocks to Jackson, and then to Beckett. On Beckett I turned left into a gloomy, perpetually wet alleyway with overhanging fire escapes that did a great job of squelching any hope of sunlight. About halfway down I found a battered sheet-metal door that would have looked out of place anywhere except in a Bucharest slum. I gave it a rap.

Nothing happened for a few minutes, until a voice behind the door told me to go away.

"I'm here to see Khan," I said to chipped paint.

"No Khan here. Go away."

This charade went on for about 10 minutes, then I lost patience.

I went back up to Jackson to a tiny hardware store and cruised the narrow aisles. I found what I needed hanging on the back wall. It cost me $27, plus tax, and shelling out the money put me in a vile mood. The guy behind the counter insisted on wrapping it in butcher paper, and after a minute I saw his point. Back in the alley I tore the wrapping off my shiny new axe and swung for the fences.

The first swing sliced through the sheet metal and thunked into wood. The second sent splinters shooting out in all directions. It was kind of neat. The third never happened because some guy started screaming for me to stop.

The door swung open and a man stood there, glaring. He was big and pissed off and red in the face. I think he was Korean because he was screaming at me in something other than Mandarin, but I couldn't be sure, as my command of Mandarin is suspect at best.

He moved toward me with bad intent and I pointed to the axe. He stopped.

"What the *fuck* are you *doing?*" he asked, discourteously.

"Are you Korean?" I asked.

"What?"

"Are you Korean?"

He spluttered, "Yeah. So?"

"Nothin'," I said. "I'm here to see Khan."

CHAPTER TEN

Khan wasn't any happier to see me than the door was. The Korean guy had taken me back to Khan's office after getting permission via intercom. I'd followed him through a winding maze of claustrophobic corridors with exposed pipes and bare light bulbs. We went though a door somewhere in the bowels of the building and entered Khan's nerve center.

Jimmy Khan was a tall, handsome Asian man who should've been a movie star. Slim, with jet-black hair graying at the temples, Jimmy could play an international diplomat or an arms merchant. He was dressed in a black suit with a white shirt and a gold tie, and sat behind some kind of glass-topped, exotic metal-alloy desk that looked too cool to be in a basement. His office was in stark contrast to the corridors I'd navigated, with thick gray carpet and black leather everything.

"Wipe your feet," he said, pointing to a mat in front of me.

I did as instructed and sat in a chair in front of his desk. The Korean guy stayed at the entrance. I took out a card and put it on the glass top. He ignored it.

"That door you wrecked was expensive," he said irritably.

I snorted. "When Coolidge was president."

He smiled. "You're a funny man." The smile disappeared. "What do you want?"

I pulled out my Gauloises and offered them. He took one almost daintily, with manicured fingers. We lit and smoked.

"There's a guy working for you who's making problems for a friend of mine," I said. "I want him to go away."

Khan exhaled smoke toward the ceiling. "What kind of problems?"

"Probably loan-shark problems," I said. "I'm not sure."

He gave me a look. "Why come to me?"

"Respect," I said. "Normally I'd just break the guy in half, but the word is he works for you."

He swiveled in his chair a little and tapped off an ash. "Who?"

"Randall Tang."

He laughed, and so did the Korean guy behind me.

"Your friend must be small potatoes to owe Tang money," he said. "What are we looking at, two, maybe $300?"

"I'm guessing that."

He was still smiling. "So you wrecked my door to ask for a $300 favor?"

"Yep. Just a little favor."

"In exchange for what?"

"In exchange for not breaking Tang in half."

Khan stared at me for a minute. He opened a drawer and took out a Beretta nine-millimeter, chrome with a lot of custom filigree. He put it on the desk between us. "I know you, Roy Jobe," he said in a low growl. "You don't carry a badge anymore, which means you don't have the protection you used to."

I ignored the gun. "It's a two-way street pal," I said. "I also don't have a badge holding me back."

Khan's face went dark, and he frowned so hard his eyebrows clashed.

"Are you threatening me?" he asked, quietly.

"No," I said, just as quietly. "I'm just looking for a shitty little $300 favor."

Khan thought about it, then motioned the Korean over, but not before reminding him to wipe his feet.

"What's your friend's name?" he asked.

"Wei Lee. Works for Eddie Lee at the American Café."

His eyebrows went up. "I know Eddie," he said. "We went to Balboa High together."

"He owns it now," I said.

Khan laughed. "You're not far from wrong, Roy Jobe."

I grinned. "Tell me about it."

Khan whispered to the big Korean for a minute, then shooed him out. Giving me a level look, he said, "All right, Roy Jobe, I've done you a shitty little favor." He paused. "Now you owe me a shitty little favor."

"We'll see," I said.

He told me what it was, and after some thought, I agreed.

CHAPTER ELEVEN

Back in my apartment I checked my messages and found three. One was from Eddie, telling me to meet him for dinner at Il Fornaio around seven. The second was from Petey Dempster, ordering me to call him at home. The last was from Liz Ishida, asking me to call her back.

I prioritized. I called Liz and got her voice mail. I left a message with an invitation to lunch the following day. I called Eddie and told him I'd meet him at the restaurant, as long as he was buying, then I phoned Petey and he answered on the third ring.

"What's up, Petey?"

"Jenny Monroe," he said.

"You got something?"

"Nope. I want something."

"What?"

"We went through Monroe's iPhone," he said. "She's got a lot of numbers stored. I wanna' know which numbers I should be looking at."

I hesitated. Client confidentiality was a delicate subject between Petey and me. I needed to keep my mouth shut if I was going to make a living in this town. He needed to solve a murder, and he was a friend. I prioritized again.

"This never comes back to me, right?" I asked.

Petey sighed. "All you're doing is saving me time, Jobe. I've already got the numbers; I just need a nod in the right direction." He paused. "And I'm getting a lot of heat from upstairs."

"What kind of heat?"

"There's only one kind of heat. Monroe's dad is flying in tomorrow. He knows people."

"Let me guess," I said. "The mayor?"

"The governor."

"Oh."

"Yeah."

I lit a cigarette. "All right, Petey. Here's what I can give ya'."

I gave him the names I'd been chasing, and informed him that Brett and Rachael were not who they purported to be. He made a humming sound when he heard that, which was his way of expressing joy. I asked him to check into their real identities, suggesting that their last places of employment might be a good place to start, and listened as he asked if I thought he was an idiot and couldn't have figured that out himself. He also rambled on about the fact that he had taught me everything I knew, and had I received a massive head wound that had made me forget that? I didn't dignify that with a response. I told him about Elvis' record and suggested he be put at the top of the list, and got the "Do you think I'm stupid?" lecture again. I asked him not to contact the Aguayos until I talked to them. He agreed, as long as I talked to them first thing in the morning.

"All right, Petey, your turn."

"Nothing you don't already know," he said. "Monroe was shot, execution style. Twenty-two caliber to the back of the head. It was someone she knew, no signs of forced entry, no struggle."

"When did it happen?"

"Within a couple of hours of when we showed up. As usual, we're waiting for prints and toxicology."

"Anybody see anything?" I asked.

"Octavio is still canvassing. People are getting home from work about now, and he's hanging around to get some interviews, but so far, nothing."

"A classic whodunit," I said.

"Yeah." he agreed. "Listen, thanks for helping. I gotta' go. Sylvia's putting dinner on."

"God forbid you should miss a meal," I said with a grin.

"Bite me. I'll talk to you tomorrow."

"Okay, Petey." I started to hang up.

"Hey, Roy?"

"What?"

Petey's voice went almost to a whisper. "Stewby's sparring at the Third Street Gym on Thursday night."

"What's that to me?" I asked.

"Don't insult me, Jobe. His handprint was all over your face, and I know how that prick operates."

I pondered a minute.

"Thursday night, huh?"

"Yep."

"Okay. Thanks, Petey."

"See ya', Roy."

I hung and looked at my watch. I had just enough time to meet Eddie at Il Fornaio. On the way, I noticed people were giving me a wide berth. That was smart. Pity anyone who gets between me and a free meal.

CHAPTER TWELVE
Wednesday

The next morning dawned bright and clear, a perfect day for detecting. Sunlight poured into my humble little apartment and for a moment I imagined I was on a Tuscan estate, waiting for the maid to bring warm croissants with butter curls and strong, sweet coffee in a soup tureen. A car horn blared from somewhere outside my window and I was back in Chinatown.

I'd called the Aguayos last night after talking with Petey and arranged a meeting for 8 am, which meant I wasn't having breakfast with Eddie. It also meant I wasn't going to get in a workout, but I'd been working out for two months straight and I figured a break wouldn't kill me.

I took a long, hot shower and scraped a razor over my face. I put on some dark blue slacks and pulled on a long-sleeved, light blue shirt with a button-down collar. The collar had one of those tiny buttons on the back and I struggled for a couple of minutes with my elbows in the air before I battened it down. It would have been easier to button it before putting the shirt on, but that would've entailed thinking ahead. I put a tan Hugo Boss sports coat over everything and slipped my feet into brown Doc Martens with thick rubber soles. They were the same hue as my ankle holster, because color coordination is the well-dressed detective's best friend.

Some coffee, sans croissants, butter curls or maid, a quick cigarette and I was ready to face the world.

At the Aguayos, Samuel answered the door on the first ring.

"Good morning, Samuel."

"Good morning, Mr. Jobe. Please follow me."

He didn't have on the butler outfit today. Instead he was dressed in khaki pants and a peach polo shirt with a light gray jacket and a pair of crepe-soled leather shoes. Looked pretty sporty for an old guy.

I followed Samuel though the living room, another sitting-type room and a room with tiled floors and lots of plants and windows. We eventually made it to the kitchen, where Samuel left me.

The Aguayos' kitchen was as big as my apartment, without the walls, and looked like it could feed a brigade. On the business side, there was an eight-burner Wolf gas range, with a double oven and stainless steel smoke hood. A glass-faced refrigerator the size of a tool shed was next to it. You could see everything inside, which I guess is a good thing. There was a walk-in freezer further down, and the sinks were deep enough to wash a pony.

Seven or eight stools surrounded the red-tiled breakfast island, and Sandy sat at one, keeping coffee and bagels company.

"Want some coffee?" she asked.

"Desperately."

She poured a cup for me and I grabbed a stool.

The smell of honest soap and clean, damp hair wafted toward me, mingled with the scent of freshly scrubbed skin. Sandy wore no makeup, which made her radiant. She had on a fluffy white terrycloth robe that made you want to crawl inside it and wink out of existence.

"What's so important that you'd get me up at this ungodly hour?" she asked grumpily.

"I'm afraid I have some bad news for you."

Sandy hooded her eyes and looked at me warily. "How bad?"

"Jenny Monroe was murdered yesterday," I said bluntly.

Sandy set her cup down with a clatter. It was a harsh sound that sucked the warmth out of the room.

"Murdered?" It came out as a squeak.

"Yes." I explained how I found Jenny and went over with Sandy what Petey had run past me.

Sandy's eyes had welled at first, and then tears started making trails down her cheeks. Her face folded into itself and her mouth formed an inverted 'U'. I reached over with my handkerchief and she plucked it from my fingers.

She continued to cry silently, so I busied myself with spooning sugar and cream into my coffee. I poured her another cup and gathered the bagels and cream cheese and placed them on the counter behind her. I got a towel from the sink and wiped down the area in front of us and took my seat.

"Sandy?" I prodded gently. "I hate to press you, but time is of the essence. Is there any reason you can think of that someone would kill her?"

She blew her nose delicately. "I just need a minute."

I sipped my coffee. It was Kona coffee and normally would be delicious, but right now it tasted like warm pond water.

Sandy sat up straighter and inhaled. "I can't think of anyone who would want to do this to her. She was a joy to be with. She never hurt a fly." Sandy's vulnerability had vanished, replaced with the mask she had on when we first met. It seemed like some defense mechanism had kicked in, one that she'd honed to a sharp edge.

"I understand that Jenny had a disagreement with Elvis at the party. Do you think that had anything to with her murder?" I asked.

Her mask twitched in surprise, but only for a moment. "Elvis and Jenny were always arguing about one thing or another. I hardly think it grounds for murder," she snapped.

I tried another approach. "Do you have any idea where Elvis is? He's the only one I haven't been able to connect with."

"Try his house," she said curtly.

"I did," I said, just as curt.

"Then there's not much I can do for you. Maybe we should hire someone who's better at his job."

I ignored the slap; you get used to them in my business. People sometimes used anger as a way to distract themselves from pain, aiming it at whoever was handy. I've been used as a doormat before, by people with much bigger boots. Hell, I've been stepped on more times than a $10 eight-ball. I moved the conversation to another subject.

"I've done a background check on Brett Jarrod and Rachael Stark," I said. "They're both false identities."

Sandy frowned. "What do you mean?"

I gave her the information Sammy Mayfair had sent me, leaving out the fact that the stolen identities were from Texas.

She looked baffled. "I don't understand. Why would they do that?"

"I don't know yet, Sandy. How long have you known them?"

Her face creased in confusion. "Only about six or seven months. Elvis introduced them to me."

"So they were Elvis' friends?"

She shrugged. "I suppose so."

"How close did you guys get?" I asked.

She grimaced. "We just partied together—it wasn't like we were bosom buddies. I liked Elvis' friends...most of them."

"Not Rachael, though?" I asked quietly.

"Even a detective of your limited skills could see that I didn't care much for Rachael," she said irritably.

Another slap in the face. I was beginning to feel like the drunken brother-in-law at Thanksgiving dinner. It was probably a good idea for me to leave before I started slapping back.

"All right, Sandy, sorry for your loss. If you think of anything that would help, please give me a call."

She put her hand on my arm.

"I'm sorry, Roy; I'm being an ass," she said. "Jenny was very close to me." Her face started to collapse again, but she held it together. "This is difficult."

I patted her hand. "It's okay. It's a bad situation all around."

She looked up at me like I had some answers. Her eyes were swollen and her nose was red. "Do you think her murder had anything to so with the Star?" she asked.

"I don't know, Sandy," I said, "but I'm going to find out."

She grabbed my hand with surprising strength. "You do that, Roy. You find out who killed Jenny." Her teeth were clenched and her face was hard as sobriety.

"I will, Sandy."

She squeezed my hand harder.

"You promise?"

I thought about it.

"Yes. I promise," I answered.

She let go. "Thank you, Roy," she said quietly.

I got up to leave. "Is Peter back from L.A.?"

She shook her head. "No, he went to New York from there. He's not sure when he'll be back."

I grunted acknowledgement.

"Sandy, what's Samuel's last name?"

She looked surprised. "Becker. Why?"

"Just curious," I said. "Another thing—the police may come by with some routine questions. Thought I'd give you a heads-up."

She nodded and remained mute.

"All right, Sandy, take care."

She gave me a weak smile and I turned to go. At the door I looked back at her. She sat at the counter and stared at her hands. She looked like the loneliest person in the world.

CHAPTER THIRTEEN

I parked my car and humped the six blocks to my office. Glancing up, I saw runnels of blue sky peeking from between the buildings' outlines. It was like looking up from the bottom of an inverted river, flowing forever. With a little imagination, you could pretend you were a fish, swimming through concrete canyons, looking for a cozy spot to raise your fingerlings.

Or not.

By the time I got to my building, I was a detective again, sans fins, working for scale. I went upstairs and I immediately felt the little hairs on my arms stand up. My door was slightly ajar, which is not the way I had left it. In a quick, practiced motion I bent my knee and transferred my .38 from my ankle holster to my hand. I nudged open the door to the waiting room and was greeted by emptiness. It was quiet as an empty office should be, with only the muffled sounds of the street filtering up. I moved to my inner sanctum, noting the unlocked door and slid in, gun first.

Too late, I heard a stealthy footfall behind me and felt a sharp pain in the general vicinity of my ear. I went down and out.

***

Coming to is never a pleasant experience. First you feel disoriented, then you feel pain, and then you feel stupid. My assailant hadn't been in my office when I'd arrived—he'd been in the hall, around the corner, and entered behind me. I was lying on my side, and from this angle I could see that the nap of my rug was darker along the trail from the hallway to my inner office. The carpet in the corners was brighter and fluffier, and I made a note to have the cleaning crew come in and shampoo, which I wouldn't have done had I not been assaulted. Everything has a silver lining, you just gotta' look for it.

I did a quick survey of my body and was relieved to find that only my head had taken damage. I've had worse. There was a nice lump behind my ear, about half the size of a golf ball, but it wasn't bleeding. I propped myself up on an elbow, then a knee and waited for the nausea to pass. I got to my feet and swayed for a second, and then everything was okay.

My gun was on the floor and I snapped it back into its holster. I looked at my watch and noted I'd been out for about 15 minutes.

At my desk I saw that my Aguayo notebook was gone. My iMac was on and someone had gone through the files I'd gotten from Sammy Mayfair. Some new files were also on the screen that had just come in. Whoever had broken in now knew everything I did, which wasn't all that much. I checked around the desk and file cabinets, but nothing else seemed to be out of place.

I plopped into my chair and opened the top drawer of my desk and pulled out a bottle of Dewar's. I grabbed one of the glasses I keep next to the bottle and sloshed in a healthy dollop. The Scotch chased three aspirin down my throat, and I felt better immediately; it's amazing how fast aspirin works.

The iMac beckoned. Sammy Mayfair had sent me a treasure trove of information. I went through it carefully.

Things were starting to fall into place, but inevitably, when that happens, everything twists into knots, like a bag of asps.

With that in mind, I called Sammy, and let the phone ring 20 times. He was a night person, and tenacity, coupled with a complete lack of conscience, was the key in getting him roused from bed.

I heard him fumble the phone. "Whaa...?"

"Sammy, Roy here. Sorry about the hour."

"What time is it?" he mumbled.

"Time to get to work. I need some help."

"You're gonna' need a paramedic when I get my hands on you," he growled.

I was crushed.

"What happened to Sammy Sunshine?" I asked. "Man of joy and friend to all?"

"He's sleeping. I'm his evil twin."

I laughed. It hurt my head.

"Take this down and I'll leave you alone," I said.

"Yeah, let me get a pen." I heard some bumbling around and the sound of a shin striking an immovable object. He came back on and spoke through gritted teeth.

"All right, I'm armed. What you got?"

"Samuel Becker, about 60 to 70 years old, Vietnam vet. He works for the Aguayos."

I waited for him to write it down.

"Also, the Star of Siddhartha. It's a 38-carat alluvial diamond. I need background and history on both. You want me to spell *Siddhartha*?"

"No."

"Do you know what *alluvial* means?"

"Yes."

I muttered something unpleasant.

"That all?" he asked.

"Yep. Go back to sleep."

"Duh." He hung up.

Grumpy bastard.

I put down the phone and checked my weapon. All rounds present and accounted for. I left it on the desk.

I lit a cigarette and let things simmer for a while, and the longer I let them simmer, the more pissed off I got. The knot on my head wasn't helping either.

I poured another shot into my glass.

"A little early for that, isn't it?"

Octavio Sequoia was standing in the doorway. He had on a peach suit that looked like it had been made from the spinnings of honey-fed silkworms and woven by virgin Thai nuns, or something to that effect. His ecru shirt was the perfect ecru for the suit, and the creases in his pants were sharp enough for minor surgery. The only thing I disagreed with was the show handkerchief fluffing out of his jacket pocket; it seemed a trifle rakish.

"Nice suit," I said.

Octavio rocked back on his heels with his hands in his pockets and looked down at the front of his outfit. "What?" he asked demurely. "This old thing?"

I laughed. It made my head hurt again. "Grab a seat."

He sat in one of my office chairs and crossed his legs carefully.

I waved the Dewar's at him with raised eyebrows and he nodded. I got a glass and poured him one. He sipped and took in my disheveled appearance, the gun on my desk and the bottle of Scotch.

He made a show of looking at his watch. "I'm not interrupting anything, am I?"

I grunted. "Only my drinking."

He nodded noncommittally.

"What brings you here, Octavio?"

He reached into the inside pocket of his jacket and extracted some printouts. "Petey says you might have some background information on certain parties related to Jenny Monroe."

"Like who?" I asked.

"Like Sandra Aguayo."

"What do you want to know?"

"Everything."

I leaned back and appraised Octavio. "Not much to tell," I said. "I was hired to find something that went missing from their home. I was starting to make my rounds and found Jenny Monroe dead. She's part of that group we talked about earlier. I was collating my meager information when you decided to grace me with your presence."

"What kind of meager information are you collating?" he asked.

"That's confidential."

He squinted at me, then looked down at his printouts. "Sandra Aguayo, known as Sandra Voorhees prior to her marriage to Peter Aguayo." He looked at me over the printout. "Her birth name, however, was Sandra Boone." He paused. "Elvis' sister." He waited for a reaction, but didn't get one. "She had a little trouble in Galveston, Texas."

"You've been busy," I said.

"All-night busy, Roy." He raised his glass and knocked it back. He waggled for a refill. I obliged.

"It seems Sandra's previous husband met with an untimely death," he said, "out in the scrub brush of Texas. Hunting accident."

That information and the fact that Sandy was Elvis' sister were in Sammy's email, but I feigned ignorance. I'm good at that.

"A big brouhaha, a big investigation and a big fight over the last will and testament," he continued. "Elvis and Sandra were suspected of arranging the death. The family filed suit, the D.A. filed suit and nobody came away happy."

"Yeah?"

"Criminal charges were dropped, and the estate conceded half a million to Sandra to get her out of their lives. She took it and disappeared."

I took another sip. "What about Elvis?"

"The law watched him for a while," he said casually. "Elvis was stupid. Spent money like a shore-leave sailor, with no visible means of support. Gambled away plenty, then got in trouble with some local loan sharks." He fussed with his handkerchief. "Tried to make good on his debts by sticking up a jewelry shop. You know where that got him." He finished his drink and gave me the look a cat gives a mouse. "But that's not the clincher."

"There's a clincher?"

"There's always a clincher." He looked down at the printouts. "It seems that the Galveston incident wasn't the first time Sandra Boone had marital misfortunes."

I sat up a little straighter. That was information that I didn't have.

"Three years before Galveston, at 15," he said, "Sandra lost a husband in a boating accident."

He paused, and I motioned for him to elaborate.

"Do tell," I said.

"It seems that husband number one fell off a boat in the Gulf of Mexico. They never found the body. The guy owned a car dealership. Sandra came away with about a hundred thousand."

"Where was Elvis?" I asked, enraptured.

"Around," he said. "Around."

I shifted in my seat, looking for a comfortable position. I couldn't find one. "So you figure with Elvis out of jail, they're back to start this scam again, only for much bigger stakes."

Octavio stretched his jaw and cracked a knuckle. "Your client, Peter Aguayo, is worth—" he referenced the printout again, "—two hundred and sixty million dollars."

He glanced up at me. "And Peter is ex-British Intelligence, MI5. He's got to know all about this."

"Yeah, I know," I said wearily. "To paraphrase Winston Churchill, 'It's a mystery within an enigma wrapped in a tortilla.'"

"Con queso," he added.

"Con queso," I agreed.

"Where does Jenny Monroe fit in?" I asked.

"I don't know, Roy. I was hoping you'd tell me."

I sighed and massaged my neck. "I was out at Sandy's this morning. She seemed pretty broken up about Jenny. I don't know what that means. I think they were lovers, but that's just a gut instinct."

Octavio hummed. "That could mean a lot of things."

"Yeah."

He gave me a hard, level look. "So it's 'Sandy' now, huh?"

"I'm on a first-name basis with all my clients," I replied.

"Friendly fella', ain't you?"

"Friendly enough."

His hard look segued into suspicion.

"Maybe too friendly?" he asked.

"Not in the service industry. No such thing."

I sipped a little more from my glass.

"A man in your line of work, Octavio, can use all the friends he can get." Another sip, a small one. "And I'm a good guy to have on your side."

Octavio locked eyes with me for a minute. He broke contact and adjusted the crease in his pants and flicked something microscopic off the top of his shoe. "So Petey tells me," he said.

I twisted my neck to de-kink it and rubbed my new lump. It hurt like hell.

We were quiet for a while.

"Petey tell you about Brett and Rachael's aliases?" I asked.

"Yeah."

"You find anything out?"

"Nothing yet. How about you?"

"Nothing," I answered, tiredly.

"When you find something," he said, "you'll let me know?"

"Like I said, Octavio, I'm a good guy to have on your side."

He sucked his teeth, gave me another look, then got up and brushed at his clothes.

"All right. I'll be seeing you, Roy." He gave me a genuine smile. "Thanks for the drink."

"Any time."

At the door he paused.

"You ought to keep a dog in here, Roy, maybe some motion detectors. That second head you're growing looks like it hurts."

He was out the door before I could retort.

Just what the world needs. Another smartass.

CHAPTER FOURTEEN

I put my office liquor away and rinsed out the glasses in the bathroom. Octavio's visit had distracted me from pondering the who and why of my latest head wound and what it meant to my investigation. Now that I was alone, I tried to form a mental list of people who would want my information badly enough to dent my head. But no names magically appeared. No avenues lit up with neon. No flashes of brilliance or sparks of ideas or anything remotely combustible illuminated the darkness. I'd have to ponder some more later. Better to deal with what was in front of me.

I read a little more about Peter and Sandy, making notes in a new notebook, and then put the computer to sleep. My gun went back in its holster and I locked up carefully and shuffled down the hall to Eddie's office.

Eddie's floor plan is the mirror image of mine, with a long storage/utility room separating us. He wouldn't have heard my altercation this morning, but I wanted to check if he'd seen anyone. I also wanted to bounce some ideas off that melon he called a head.

Eddie's waiting room differed from mine only in the fact that his magazines were less than five months old and hadn't been pilfered from the dentist's office. And his carpet was cleaner, which was a discrepancy I intended to rectify. He was usually here after the café's breakfast rush, so I knocked on his door and entered his elegant little lair.

Eddie sat behind an elaborate, multi-level desk with three flat-panel displays at differing angles and heights and a bevy of printing and broadband and real estate empire-essential tech doodads linked to each other with too many wires to count. The floors were hardwood, expensive and gleamed like a freshly waxed Duesenberg. The two chairs that fronted his desk were squat and covered with brown leather, and paintings of bucolic French landscapes pegged the walls.

Eddie spun away from one of the computer displays when I entered.

"You look like hell," he noted.

"Thank you." I dumped myself into one of his chairs.

Eddie sniffed. "And you've been drinking."

"I have an excuse."

"It better be good."

I told him about my head's rendezvous with something hard, and chastising turned into concern.

"Jeez, Roy, you okay?"

"Yeah, I'll live. You didn't happen to see anyone skulking around, did you?"

He rubbed his forehead. "Naw. I got here early. Been working on a deal for a small building."

"How small?"

"Three stories, 20 offices."

"Nice."

"Could be."

He waited.

"So, I got this case," I said, nonchalantly.

Eddie smiled. He loved this. He leaned back in his chair and folded his hands over his belly. I know he lived vicariously through my little adventures, but we both chose to pretend otherwise.

I remained silent and let him sweat, because I'm small and mean. His smile faltered.

"Stop being an asshole," he snarled.

I laughed. "All right, here's what I got."

I gave him my case outline, up to walking in his office. Eddie listened raptly, nodding at the appropriate times and taking sharp breaths on at least two occasions.

He stared at me, impressed.

"You're on the job two days and you've already got a dead body."

I looked at my fingernails.

"It's a gift."

Eddie shook his head.

"I've never seen a dead body."

"Lucky you," I said.

Eddie nodded and pursed his lips. "All right. Here's my take. Peter Aguayo is playing you. That crap about behavior patterns, nonverbal display, phraseology—that's all bullshit."

"Yep."

"He's ex-British intelligence, which means he probably knows all about Sandy's two previous husbands. Probably knew it before he married her."

"Probably," I agreed.

"But the man's in love with this gal, and marries her anyway, has a child with her," he said. "The two dead husbands are always in the back of his mind though, spoiling an otherwise wonderful experience, like a curly red hair on his quiche."

"I wouldn't have put it quite like that," I said, "but I agree with your assessment."

Eddie waved a hand. "Whatever. He and Sandy cruise along in relative bliss for about five years, then six months ago Elvis shows up on his doorstep with—what's their names?"

"Brett and Rachael."

"Right. Brett and Rachael. Anyway, shortly after Elvis and friends show up, Sandy starts draining money out of her credit cards at an alarming rate...according to your snitch at Neiman Marcus."

I rolled my eyes at 'snitch.' He ignored it.

"So now Peter is getting nervous," he continued. "Sandy's long lost brother, with whom she might have conspired to kill her last two husbands, is back in town. Cash is being diverted from credit cards to God knows where, and I'll assume that Sandy hasn't come clean to Peter about Elvis and her past. Nothing happens for six months, because Sandy and Elvis know that if they knock off Peter, Sandy only gets an annual stipend, and apparently that's not enough to make all the parties involved happy."

Eddie sipped his coffee, then pointed his mug at the pot.

"Coffee's fresh if you want."

"Thanks." I got up and poured a cup and brought the pot over to top Eddie's off. I replaced it, then sat and sipped.

I squinted my eyes.

"You want me to tell you why Peter waited six months before hiring a private detective to investigate Elvis and friends?" I asked.

Eddie's face went taut and he placed both hands on his desk.

"No. Give me a minute."

I gave him a minute, then another.

His eyes were darting here and there like a cornered rat's. I looked at my watch. "Meter's running."

He gave me a dirty look, then scowled and slapped the desk.

"Damn it!"

He started rubbing the entire surface area of his face and neck. "All right," he exhaled. "I don't know. Tell me."

I grinned and started my lecture.

"Peter figures he's not in too much danger as long as Sandy and Elvis can't get at the big money. Sandy's credit cards are keeping them in ducats, for now, but there's a quarter billion dollars on the table and they're all drooling over it. Sandy's stipend is not enough reason to risk a homicide rap, so they're circling Peter like vultures, trying to find some exposed flesh. Peter doesn't investigate them, overtly, because he doesn't want to spook the horses."

"What's that mean?"

My smile was cynical as a Bangkok hooker's.

"It's important for Peter to play a shell game because he doesn't want to scare everyone off. He wants them to stick around. He's depending on their greed to keep them in the game. The last thing he wants is for them to scatter in the wind, only to regroup later and take another run at him. He's tired of looking over his shoulder like a rabbit, because it's not in his nature. He doesn't relish the role of being the hunted, so the Star's disappearance is perfect because it gives him an excuse to call in a shamus."

Eddie was getting it. He usually does.

"So he tells you that he thinks his wife is going to kill him," he said excitedly, "and turns you loose on her gang. The gang thinks you're investigating the Star, which they expect, and they're all willing to chat with you. That's why Sandy called around and let everyone know you'd be visiting."

"I believe so," I said.

I waved magnanimously at him.

"Now go on with your soliloquy."

Eddie leaned forward and gestured excitedly with his hands.

"Okay. A big dinner party comes along and Peter wants Sandy to show off his wealth by wearing the Star. Sandy is delighted. She sees this as her big opportunity to add 11 million dollars to the pot, so she fakes a headache or whatever and goes upstairs. Elvis or Brett or Rachael or all three follow with a couple of Peter's friends, just to muddy the waters, and they do a little coke while Sandy slips the jewel to one of her cohorts."

Eddie gulped some more coffee. His mind was at three alarms by now, blazing with excitement, and his enthusiasm was contagious.

"The next morning she's all Little Miss Innocent." Eddie's voice went into a high falsetto and he started waving his hands in the air in a parody of panic. "'Somebody's absconded with the Star,' she says. 'Somebody snuck into my room and stole an 11-million-dollar jewel that I absentmindedly left on my dresser.'"

I giggled.

Genuine admiration lit his face.

"The balls it must have took," he said.

"Shameless," I agreed.

"Anyway," he continued, "Peter now knows his days are numbered. Sandy's got the Star and has 11 million reasons to knock him off. She figures she can't sell it while Peter's alive, because he'd find out about it and drop the hammer on her. It sounds to me like he's dialed in to some kind of underground collectors' network and would know if a jewel of that magnitude were up for sale. Sandy knows this and knows she can't unload the gem until Peter is out of the picture. So, *bam*!" Eddie dusted his hands with a quick, slapping motion, then held them up. "Peter's fate is sealed."

I sipped some more coffee. I'd made it sweet, and it helped put some distance between me and the Dewar's.

"You're on target so far, Eddie. Keep going."

Eddie shifted in his seat and pushed a finger at me.

"But the Star is also an opportunity for Peter. It gives him an excuse to call a guy like you in to investigate the theft, which serves as a front for the real investigation."

"I just told you that."

Eddie was waving the finger now.

"I know; I'm just thinking out loud; stop interrupting," he said.

He took a deep breath. "So Peter now has carte blanche to have a pro snoop into the lives of Sandy and her friends without, as you said, 'spooking the horses.' You get to ask a lot of questions and poke around and do what you do. They're okay with that because they expect at least a little heat from the theft, and Peter's happy because he can finally start being the hunter."

Eddie drained his coffee. His eyes went a little wider. I was getting concerned about his heart rate.

"Now it's a foot race," he said. "Sandy and Elvis need to put Peter away before you expose the whole sordid mess. They're gambling that you won't find out about the plot, because you're not smart enough. You certainly don't look smart, but they're aware that there's an outside chance you might solve the riddle."

"Ouch."

Eddie laughed.

"Where's Peter?" he asked.

"Out of town," I said, "and he's going to stay out of town. He's not stupid. I've left six messages on the cell number he gave me. No return calls. He's going to stay incommunicado and out of harm's way until I've come up with something concrete."

Eddie nodded sagely, then shook his head.

"I don't know, Roy. It seems too complicated. Why not just rub Elvis out?" Eddie's mouth stretched itself into a grin. "Peter's ex-British intelligence. Doesn't he have a license to kill?"

I grinned back.

"Maybe. And maybe Elvis is innocent. And if he kills Elvis, what about Brett and Rachael? And Sandy? We have to at least entertain the fact that Peter loves Sandy, and knocking off her brother, and the uncle of his son, might put a little strain on the relationship. Peter won't take any action until he's absolutely sure that Elvis and Sandy are out to murder him. Ultimately, while I don't think he's too shy about bending the rules, he's not morally bankrupt, and he's got a lot to lose by moving too soon."

I shook my head.

"Nah, he's patient and methodical. He won't take any action until there's proof."

Eddie sighed. "You're right. You'd have to be a patient man to wait around for six months with the Sword of Damocles over your head. Impressive."

He tapped his fingers in an impatient gesture. I looked at them. He snorted and stopped drumming.

"I still think it's too complicated," he said.

"I'll make it even more complicated for you," I said.

Eddie was gleeful. He looked like a puppy eyeing a biscuit.

I held up two fingers. "So far, I see two scenarios." I tapped my forefinger. "In scenario one, as we've discussed, Sandy takes the jewel and starts plotting Peter's murder." I folded my forefinger, leaving only my middle finger up. "In scenario two, Peter purposely brings the Star out, only to fake the theft in order to get the ball rolling."

Eddie nodded appreciatively.

"I bring him enough proof that there's a murder plot afoot," I said, "and Sandy will get pulled over for a broken tail light or an unpaid parking ticket and the Star, much to her surprise, will be found in her purse, next to a big fat baggie of coke or China White."

Eddie's eyebrows burst to his hairline.

"Then Peter gets her thrown into the hoosegow with Elvis and whoever else is involved, " I said, "and he gets uncontested custody of little PJ."

"Ahh," Eddie said. "I forgot about PJ."

"Yeah," I said, nodding. "PJ's the key here. Peter has one son, his only progeny. If it gets messy, and without some slam-dunk evidence it most certainly will, PJ is stuck in the middle of a nasty knock-down drag-'em-out. The best I could probably do is bring Peter some fairly convincing circumstantial evidence, but it won't hold up in court. If Peter doesn't set Sandy up, she could use PJ to leverage some sort of deal with him, and the way California law is structured, she would probably get custody of PJ. But if Sandy is found with the missing jewel and some drugs, and if Elvis rolls over on her, she's either in jail, or if Peter is feeling generous, in South America with an agreement never to contact her son."

"You think Elvis will roll over?" he asked.

"Without a doubt," I said. "With his record, he'd be looking at some serious jail time."

I shook my head.

"I'll bet Krugerrands to Krispy Kremes that Elvis will do whatever it takes to save his own skin."

I held up a finger again.

"It's possible that the only reason Peter brought the jewel out was to stir things up. It's only been out of the safe deposit box two times in five years. The Star could be the bait at the end of a very sharp hook. If Sandy takes it, then murder is in the air. If she doesn't, it might mean something or it might not, but she's still not off the hook because of the credit cards and the fact she didn't introduce Elvis as her brother. That's going to be hard for her to explain either way. But if Peter's the one who nicked the Star, then he's holding it in reserve to frame either Sandy or maybe Elvis, based on what I can bring him."

"So you think there's a possibility of a preemptive strike by Peter," Eddie said, musing. "He could frame either one of them with the jewel, and force the framee to rat the other one out on the murder plot."

"Yep."

Eddie nodded again. There was a lot of that going around.

"That's good," he said, then held up a finger. "But when you mentioned PJ, another scenario popped into my head."

"I'm listening," I said.

The biscuit was now in Eddie's court.

Eddie leaned back in his chair and looked smug.

"Sandy has a child with this man." He hooded his eyes. "That changes everything. You don't have kids, so you wouldn't understand."

"That's about the most condescending thing you've ever said to me," I said.

Eddie thought a little.

"No, I've said worse."

"Nice."

He sighed. "You want to hear this or not?"

I flicked my hand at him. "Go on."

"Okay. There's a very real possibility that she's truly in love with Peter. But even if she isn't, if Peter's a good father, she's not going to casually deprive her son of his daddy." More head shaking. "Uh-uh. That would devastate PJ. Good mothers won't do that." He paused and became even smugger, if that were possible. "Elvis might be forcing Sandy to play out this scam…she might actually be paying Elvis *not* to kill Peter."

His finger went up again, and I wondered idly how loud he would scream if I bit it off. "Sandy could be an unwilling accomplice."

"So you're saying that Sandy might be stealing money, and possibly the Star, to protect Peter and PJ?" I asked, intrigued.

"It's worth considering," he answered. "She might have been trying to buy Elvis off with the credit-card thing. Then the Star shows up and she sees this as a chance to get Elvis out of her life. Maybe instead of being 11 million reasons to knock Peter off, the Star is 11 million reasons for Elvis to leave him alone."

It was a good point that I hadn't considered. That annoyed me. But what was more irritating was that it came wrapped in about 20 layers of smugness.

"I would have deduced that, given time," I said, lamely.

"Of course you would've."

"What about Jenny Monroe?" I asked, trying to trip the little weasel up.

Eddie sighed again. "No clue. But I still think everything we discussed here is too complicated. There's got to be a simpler explanation."

"There usually is, Eddie, but you know the drill. We've sat here a thousand times going over possible scenarios with other cases. We let our fevered little minds wander into every cubbyhole and we extrapolate every little scrap of information. That's why it's called 'speculation.'"

"And it's fun," he said.

I grunted, got up and smoothed my rumpled clothes. "Thanks for bouncing things around with me, Eddie. That's good input."

"My pleasure, Roy. Sorry about your head."

"Comes with the job," I said, like the tough guy I was. "Good luck with buying your building."

He gave me a grin that would've looked more at home on a wolverine.

"Luck's got nothing to do with it."

CHAPTER FIFTEEN

I went back to my apartment and changed my shirt and splashed my face with cold water. I got some ice and pressed it against my lump, but I abandoned the strategy because it gave me one of those headaches you get when eating ice cream too fast.

Eddie had opened up a new avenue for me to consider—I just wasn't sure if it had legs. He was right about my lack of insight into the mother-child dynamic, but I wasn't completely clueless. I understood the concept of that bond, but I also understood the concept of murder, the latter much better than Eddie. I'm sure motherhood changes a person, but so does murder, especially for the dead guy. Murders are like oysters; the first one's hard to swallow, but subsequent murders get easier and easer to digest, and then you start to like them. Regardless, it was all speculation. Factors of which I had no knowledge were out there impacting the case, and all these convoluted, twisted theories could end up amounting to a hill of beans.

And speaking of oysters, Liz Ishida had called the previous night to confirm our lunch date. Our conversation was relatively short; she was running out the door to catch a movie with a friend, but the give and take had been direct and genuine. I was interested in her and she was interested in me. I respected that. She warned me that she was a blunt person who got right to the point and I warned her that I was a sly, evasive person with base intentions.

Even though I had a lump on my head and a murder, a missing jewel and the machinations of a multimillionaire on my mind, I wasn't going to miss this date. Prioritization.

I went to my closet and took a box off the top shelf and rummaged for a while. I took out an item, checked to make sure it was charged and slipped it into my pocket.

Outside, the sky was still clear, and the temperature was rising to about 75 degrees. A lilting breeze carried the salty hint of ocean.

I made the jaunt back to my car without incident. Across the street from my lot, I noted a gold Lexus, one of those coupes with a hardtop that slid into the trunk. It had a ticket fluttering on its windshield.

I drove out to the Embarcadero and went right toward Harrison. Taking a slight detour, I went by Elvis and Rachael's place and quickly spotted the SFPD stakeout: two bored guys in an unmarked car that stood out like a wart on a beauty queen. I thought briefly of bringing them a Starbucks lowfat white mocha with whipped cream and chocolate sprinkles and maybe some powdered cinnamon, but like I said, I'm small and mean.

Rounding the corner I was surprised to see the gold Lexus behind me, playing peek-a-boo with a couple of Fords and a Mercedes. I cruised past the Gordon Biersch restaurant where I was to meet Liz and slid into a parking space about a block up. The Lexus sped up and passed me, but not before I saw a man with dark hair and sunglasses pointedly looking the other way. The Lexus was brand-new, with those cardboard license plates that touted the dealership from which it sprang. There were no numbers to trace. I watched it zip away and turn a corner.

I walked the block to Gordon Biersch and spotted Liz through the window, sitting in the waiting area. I paused for a moment to admire her.

Today was her day off, so there was no cop uniform and Kevlar vest getting in the way. She was dressed simply, with a long-sleeved, collarless black silk top that strained tastefully where it ought to. She wore blue jeans, fashionably faded, and held what looked to be a black leather blazer folded in her lap. The diamond studs in her ears twinkled like sunlight on water, and her long hair was done up in one of those baffling braids that only women knew how to weave.

I walked in and was surprised to find myself a little nervous. Liz got up, smiled and came toward me. Her smile disappeared. "You've been drinking."

"I have an excuse."

"It'd better be good."

The place reeked of déjà vu.

"Someone knocked me on the head this morning," I said, "and combed my files while I slept it off." I took her hand and put it on the knot behind me ear. She instantly went mother hen.

"Oh, you poor thing. Are you all right?"

She cupped my face with her hands and looked deep into my eyes, her brow wrinkled with concern. A little makeup was dusted on her perfect skin, and a close look at her lips proved them to be a danger to men with bad hearts. It felt marvelous, and I made a note to get knocked out more often.

"I'm fine. Comes with the job."

Her concern turned into a smirk.

"Tough guy, huh?" She pulled a punch to my stomach.

I smiled. This time it didn't hurt.

"Yeah, something like that," I said. "Let's eat."

Gordon Biersch was a microbrewery that wasn't micro anymore. They had about 15 restaurants, mostly on the West

Coast, and put on a good spread. Their beer wasn't bad either. The San Francisco place had high ceilings with walls painted beige, and elegant glasswork that brightened it up and made the restaurant seem even bigger than it actually was. It had a long bar that curved the way bars should, and the bar had stools with backs on them for those who needed it. It was loud and cheery and crowded, and I was at the older end of the patron spectrum.

Liz and I followed the hostess to our table and went through the menu. We agreed on the spicy ahi spring rolls with sriracha aioli and soy sauce as an appetizer. She ordered the blackened mahi mahi on a bun with Cajun remoulade and garlic fries, but only after extracting a promise that I'd take a share of the fries. I got the goat cheese ravioli with sautéed mushrooms, pine nuts and fresh rosemary in a brown butter sauce. We added a couple of frosty pilsners.

I felt my good artery spasm.

"Okay," she said after we ordered. "First, let's hear how you got conked on the head, and then tell me why you're not married."

I smiled, again, then gave her an overview of my escapade that morning.

"You have any idea who might've done this?" she asked.

"A couple, but it's too early to tell."

She hummed. "Okay, now let's get to the important question. How come a good-looking guy like you is still a free agent?"

I shrugged. "I was a cop, which says a lot. I don't believe in divorce, and that seems to be the way most relationships end up when you're in this line of work."

She gave me a level look. "What do you mean when you say you don't believe in divorce?"

It was a pushy, personal question that would make a lot of men run for the hills. I, however, had a weak spot for pushy, personal women.

I looked back at her and tried not to sound too serious.

"When I make a promise, I keep it."

She smiled. "That's good, Roy; you're scoring points."

I'm not quite sure how she did it, but her words didn't come out as a condescending pat on the head. It seemed to be an honest assessment, so I decided to voice an honest aspiration.

I looked over toward the kitchen and mumbled, "I hope to score a lot more than points."

She let out a deep, throaty laugh. "Oh, you are such a *rake.*"

I laughed with her. I was having fun. "Most of the time," I said. "Tell me about yourself."

Liz gave me the lunch-date lowdown on her life history. She was a 30-year-old rookie cop and was born and raised in Belmont, a city about 20 miles south of San Francisco. Her father was a carpenter, retired now and still living down south. Mom was a homemaker, and Liz had two sisters and one brother. She graduated from San Francisco State with a degree in criminal justice, did some graduate work and spent about four years in a variety of stupid jobs before joining the force.

She asked about my family, and I gave her the answer that I'd been doling out for the last 25 years. Even I was starting to believe it. Parents died when I was 15. Car wreck. Lived with a cousin until I joined the Marines. It was a short, manufactured history, steeped in tragedy. No one pursued it, for fear of dredging up bad memories. If they only knew.

Our food came and she dug in like a trouper. I liked that. She took off the top half of her mahi sandwich and cut off pieces that were equal parts fish, lettuce, tomato and bread.

Very neat, very efficient. I proved I was a man of my word by taking a handful of garlic fries and dropping them on my plate. The fries were crisp and oily, and had diced garlic stuck to their surface. To die for.

"How's it working out with Stewby?" I asked between raviolis.

Her face darkened. "Really bad," she said grimly. "Bad enough to think about quitting and going to law school."

"Better to be a hit man," I said. "It's a more honest profession."

She put down her fork and sighed. "Yeah, I know. It's just that he's everything a cop shouldn't be. I sometimes feel overwhelmed by what he and his little cronies do."

"Cronies?" I asked.

"Yeah. He's part of this group that sees things a certain way. They're all connected, either by family or association." She took a sip of beer. "There's a few higher-ups who consistently look the other way. Birds of a feather."

I swallowed some beer. "That's why I quit the force," I said.

She smiled a deliciously wicked smile. "I heard you were fired."

"Or fired." I grinned. "Whichever."

Her smile faltered a little, then she exhaled and looked gloomy. "There's a lot of good cops out there, Roy," she mused, "more good than bad. But I'm stuck on Planet Stewby." She nibbled her lip, making me wish I could too. "I really don't want to quit."

"Maybe I can help."

She tensed. "I don't need a white knight," she said coldly.

"That's obvious," I said quickly, "but a helping hand doesn't mean you can't handle it yourself."

She looked at me, eyebrow cocked.

"You got something in mind?"

I reached into my pocket and laid the item I took out of my closet on the table. It was about the size of an iPod Nano.

She poked at it with her fork. "What's that?"

"It's a voice-activated recorder," I said. "Top of the line. Real sensitive. It only kicks in when someone's speaking and has about eight hours' worth of memory. Completely digital."

She picked it up and turned it around with slim fingers.

"Pretty slick. You get this at PrivateDetective.com or something?"

"Actually, it was Gumshoe.org."

She laughed. I liked making her laugh.

"What am I supposed to do with this?" she asked.

I winked. "Use your imagination."

CHAPTER SIXTEEN

After lunch, before we said our goodbyes, I asked Liz out to Sammy Mayfair's show. She accepted. She gave me a peck on the lips that held the promise of better things to come.

I was in an exceptionally good mood when I got in my car, even considering the fact that I had spent part of the morning unconscious.

I pulled out and drove to Geary, keeping a close eye on the rearview mirror. My intentions were to get back up to Brett Jarrod's house, but I was going to take the scenic route. It wasn't until I passed Nineteenth Avenue that I spotted the Lexus, about six cars back.

I took Geary all the way out to the Coast Highway, past the Cliff House and Seal Rocks. I went down the Coast Highway a bit and pulled over and parked in one of the plentiful parking slots that overlook Ocean Beach. The highway was wide open here, with only a smattering of traffic.

I got out of my car and watched the Lexus come down the hill toward me, and leaned against my SUV with arms crossed. The little coupe passed and slowed down, then pulled a U-turn and came back. It U-turned again and passed me and parked about 20 spaces down the line.

There was a pleasant breeze coming off the water, smelling of salt and seaweed and far-off places. I could hear the seals barking from the rocks, and the crashing waves had an almost hypnotic effect on my shoulders. They loosened up, but tightened again when the coupe's driver-side door opened.

A tall man with black hair and sunglasses ambled casually toward me. He wore a hideous yellow suit with brown piping that covered a white shirt. The shirt was unbuttoned down to his ankles. A thick gold chain nestled in his chest hairs, both of them, and an E-shaped medallion dangled from the chain. From his ear hung a dewdrop-shaped diamond, set in blued steel. It had looked good on Rachael, but on him it was ludicrous. Next time I saw her, I'd scold her for letting this chowderhead borrow her jewelry. The shoes were tan slip-ons, and every finger, including thumbs, had a ring. His knuckles were bruised and skinned, like he'd been in a fight. *Probably in a bar, over a coke whore*, I thought uncharitably.

"Elvis Boone, I presume," I said when he was five feet away.

"How'd you know?" he asked, sincerely.

I looked at the E on his chest. "Lucky guess."

He didn't know what to do with that, so he left it alone. "I bet you're wondering why I followed you," he said.

"It's been keeping me up at night."

He didn't know what to do with that either, but he didn't like it.

He stepped a little closer. He was near my size, which is a good size to be. He had about 20 pounds on me, but they didn't account for much. He took off his ridiculous Gargoyles and showed me the same bright blue eyes as Sandy's. His face was the kind of handsome that lulled a certain type of man into thinking he could coast through life on it, but there was plenty of unhealthy bloating that came with bad living.

"I didn't kill her," he said abruptly.

"Who?"

"You know goddamn well who. Jenny Monroe."

"That's not what the police think," I said.

"Fuck the police. They couldn't find stink on shit."

A regular Faulkner, this guy.

"I'll be sure to let them know."

He gave me an ugly look. It didn't take much effort.

"You think I killed her?"

"It looks that way."

"Well, I didn't."

I shrugged and smiled. "Then that settles it," I said, brightly. "I'm convinced."

I could tell he wasn't liking anything I had to say.

"You some kind of wise guy?" he asked.

"What gave it away?"

He moved too close to me and spread his legs and bounced on the balls of his feet. "You don't want me on your back, pal," he said menacingly.

I pushed him, hard, with both hands to his chest. He stumbled back and stood there, breathing fire and clenching his fists.

"You come anywhere near my back," I said in a low voice, "and you'll think an Escalade fell on you."

We stared at each other for a few moments like two angry minks. Eventually he relaxed and let a grin stab his face.

"I didn't come here for trouble, pal," he said. "I've already got enough of that. I'm just trying to clear my name."

I relaxed a little too. I needed to hear what he had to say.

"All right, truce," I said. "And don't call me 'pal.'"

He nodded and walked to the cement wall separating the sidewalk from the sand. I joined him. We stared out at the Pacific, watching the sun glint off the ocean. Seagulls hung in the air, looking for lunch, while a couple of joggers and an old guy with a dog roamed the edge of the beach.

"My sister's something else, isn't she?"

"Yes, she is."

"Sits up there in her mansion, not a care in the world." His lip curled a little. "Done all right for herself."

I looked over at the Lexus. "You don't seem to be doing so bad yourself."

He followed my glance. "Yeah, we'll see," he said cryptically.

There was too much fresh air out here and too few answers, so I pulled out my cigarettes and offered them. He took one. I lit it; we smoked.

"So, you're out of Hunstville Prison, with no place to go," I started. "You make it back here and connect with Sandy. You and she decide it's a good time to start up your little deceased-husband scam again, but can't figure out how to get to all that money."

He looked surprised, but only for a moment. He didn't strike me as a particularly intelligent man, but he had plenty of gutter smarts.

"I ain't saying yes or no, but go on," he said carefully.

"You both figure out that she can get plenty of working capital from credit cards, but that's just chump change compared to what's on the table. You wait around, looking for an opportunity, and then the Star makes itself available."

He looked genuinely confused. "What Star?"

Me and my big fucking mouth.

"Never mind; I misspoke. Got it confused with another case," I said lamely.

He didn't believe me, but he let it go. I gave myself a massive mental kick.

I cleared my throat. "Anyway, you two are milking Peter, but sooner or later he's going to get wise to Sandy's history. He's probably already getting wise to the credit card thing, so that cash river is about to dry up. So you two decide that the stipend Sandy gets in case of Peter's death is as good as it's going to get, and you make plans for Peter to have an accident." I paused to let him comment, but he kept staring out at Hawaii.

"Somehow Jenny Monroe figures it out and reads you the riot act at the party. At that point, she becomes a liability, so you go to her house and shoot her in the head."

He puffed on his cigarette a moment, then gave me a Clint Eastwood squint. "Like I said, I ain't saying yes or no, but I *am* saying I didn't kill Jenny."

"I was over at your house," I said sharply, "talking with Rachael at the time Jenny was killed. You weren't there. I went over to Brett Jarrod's house shortly after; you weren't there either." I paused. "So where were you when Jenny was killed?"

He gave me a Cheshire grin.

"I was with Sandy."

CHAPTER SEVENTEEN

I let a couple of cars buzz past us, then I looked at him skeptically.

"You were with Sandy," I stated.

"That's what I said."

"Doing what?"

He gave me the look a Joe Pesci character gives to a guy who's late on his vig.

"I ain't saying."

I exhaled frustration and changed the subject.

"How long were you in my office this morning?"

Confusion again. It seemed to be his natural state.

"I wasn't at your office. I waited by your car—figured you'd have to come back for it sometime." He grimaced. "Got a fuckin' ticket."

"You weren't in my office?" I asked.

"I just told you that."

Now *I* was confused. Maybe it was airborne.

"Listen," he said, "I didn't kill Jenny. that's the only reason I'm talking with you. I got shit to do. I don't need an all-points out on me." He coaxed smoke from his cigarette and exhaled. "Not now. I'm an ex-con. I know how it works. Cops pull me in and they punch out and go home. Case solved." He dropped the cigarette onto the pavement and crushed it out with a neat twist of his ankle. "But I ain't your guy. You and the cops are wasting your time chasing me for the murder, and the guy that did it is still out there. Wise up and get the fuck off my back."

I was sure he was a good liar, but it didn't feel like he was lying now. The only time he could have been with Sandy would have been before I'd spoken with her yesterday. That was about the same time Jenny had been murdered, but his alibi wasn't ironclad. He still could have done it, but my gut was saying no. I'd have to ask Sandy about it.

"All right," I said. "I'll see what I can do. Where can I get in touch with you?"

He laughed. "Funny."

I took a card out of my wallet and handed it to him. "Keep in touch with me. If what you're saying is true, I'm a good man to know."

He put the card in his jacket pocket. "Okay. I'll be in touch."

He gave me a salute and went back to his car. I watched him drive out of sight.

Elvis had made me feel oily and dirty. Something was unclean about him, something he tried to hide, but couldn't. He was like a gangrenous wound doused with perfume.

Feeling a little nauseous, I jumped in my car and drove over to Brett Jarrod's house. Everything was pretty much the same, except the lawn had been mowed and the *Chronicle* hadn't been picked up off the doorstep. I knocked and waited, then knocked again. I tried the door. It was unlocked.

It was twilight inside, as the drapes were closed and no lamps were on. I went into the living room and poked around a bit, but found nothing approximating an 11-million-dollar diamond. I checked the small bathroom. Men's toiletries, none too neat, were spread out on the sink and the small shelves over the sink. A brush, a comb, tweezers, a small pair of scissors, a toothbrush and a tube of Colgate in a plastic cup rounded out the first shelf. The second shelf held a number of prescription bottles. Xanax, Valium and three bottles of Vicodin, all from different pharmacies and all from different doctors. Brett liked his drugs and knew how to get them.

I stole a couple of Vicodin and slipped them into my pocket. My head was going to need some help later, and I didn't think Brett would miss them.

I went to one of the two bedrooms and was greeted with boxes, a reclining bike, strewn clothes and some dumbbells on the floor. The next bedroom was the one in which he slept. It was surprisingly well-furnished, with a queen-sized sleigh bed made of light-colored wood, with slats on the head and footboard. It was centered under the room's double window, with a bed table and matching lamp on either side. The bedspread was a down comforter, with a patterned white coverlet, soaked in blood. The blood came from the body of Rachael Stark, sprawled on top like a broken doll. She was lying on her back, arms spread out at different angles. Her face looked like the floor of a busy butcher shop. The only reason I recognized her was because of the face rings, some of which were still attached. The location of her distinctive diamond earring wasn't much of a mystery; it was dangling from Elvis' ear. His trophy.

I carefully approached the body and felt for a pulse, even though I knew I wouldn't find one. I was right. I checked my shoes to see if I'd stepped in blood, which I hadn't. I went back into the bathroom and replaced the Vicodin I'd pilfered and wiped the bottle with my shirttail. I took out my latex gloves, snapped them on and opened the glass shower door. It was moist inside, like someone had showered recently. I moved some of the shampoo and conditioner bottles that were in the corners of the tub and spied pink at the edges of the puddled water. I looked closely at the water droplets that had dried on the door and walls, toward the bottom, and noticed some pink half-moons.

I'd seriously underestimated Elvis. He wasn't confused or ignorant, he was working me like the chump I was. He'd beaten Rachael Stark to death sometime this morning, then showered, changed his bloody clothes and stuffed them into a garbage bag. He then knocked me out at my office or, if someone else was the assailant, just hung around my car, waiting. He'd followed me to Gordon Biersch and waited while I had lunch. The thought that he'd seen Liz, and was capable of destroying a woman's face, drove a spike of anger through my already-aching head.

He had followed me out to the ocean, where we had our little chat. His bruised knuckles weren't from some barroom brawl, as I'd thought; they were from beating a woman to death.

I decided then and there that I would bury Mr. Elvis Boone.

CHAPTER EIGHTEEN

By the time I got to my car, my head was a mass of pain. I had spittle on the corner of my mouth, but I was too furious to wipe it off.

Jenny Monroe had been a corpse—a "stiff," as Petey had put it. I'd never met her and she wasn't etched in my mind as a living, breathing human being. That's how you handled death in the homicide business: you distanced yourself, you made jokes, you viewed the dead as bags of skin, as inert pieces of flesh with no emotional attachment. That's how you survived. Detached.

Rachael, though, was a woman I'd met, a woman I'd traded quips with, a woman with whom I'd shared a laugh. She was a living, breathing human being, and seeing her that way in my mind brought the vision of her broken face all the more close. There could be no detachment here, nothing to hide behind, no way to view her as another "stiff." Rachael was real, and so was my rage

I called Petey.

"Pete Dempster here."

"Petey, Roy."

He could feel my anger rip through the phone.

"What's the matter, Roy?"

"Plenty. There's a body at—" I gave him Brett's address. "It's Rachael Stark."

He let out a loud sigh.

"Jesus. What happened?"

I told him about my meeting with Elvis Boone, leaving out very little. I explained how I found Rachael, and my anger went up a notch, if that was possible, in the telling.

"He's a dead man, Petey. It's a done deal."

"Slow down, Roy—I know how you get."

"He's dead."

"Listen, wait for me there. Don't do anything stupid, all right?"

"He's dead, Petey, the man is dead."

"Okay, okay, but we've got to find him first. Just wait there for me."

I calmed a little. Petey's rock-steady voice helped.

"All right. I'll wait."

We hung up. I sat for a moment, reflecting on Rachael's face, pre-Elvis. Then I smashed my fist into the windshield. Thin cracks spider webbed on the glass and my hand immediately started to swell.

I didn't feel any better.

CHAPTER NINETEEN

Brett Jarrod's house, or whoever the fuck he was, had turned into a San Francisco City employee parking lot.

Three patrol cars, a coroner's van, a CSU van and two unmarked Fords were on or near the front lawn. The street was blocked off and uniformed police officers milled around with their hands on their gun belts, trying to look busy.

Petey, Octavio and I were inside. The CSU crew was in the bedroom and bathroom, poking around and taking pictures. The three of us stood in the living room, pacing like expectant fathers.

Octavio hadn't slept since the night before last, but he looked fresh as warm bread. I'd calmed down considerably since my phone call to Petey, but the rage was still there, right where I always keep it, next to revenge.

"So Elvis stood there talking with you like nothing happened?" Petey asked.

"Cool as silk sheets." I shook my head. "He was pleading innocence on the Jenny Monroe killing, then gave me his alibi and told me to get off his back."

We were quiet for a moment.

"Did he know you were coming out here?" Octavio asked.

"Couldn't have," I answered. "I made the decision after you and I spoke in my office. No way he'd have known."

"So maybe Rachael was supposed to be found by Brett Jarrod. Maybe it's a message," Octavio deduced. "Or maybe Brett Jarrod is buried in the back yard."

"Very much a possibility," I said.

"Elvis the guy that knocked you around this morning?" Octavio asked.

"I don't think so," I answered. "Someone else out there doesn't like me."

"Take a number," Petey grunted, then laughed. I gave him a nasty look, which he ignored.

"He's a dangerous one," Octavio muttered. "Beating a woman to death is like making a ham sandwich to him, same difference."

I nodded. "That's why I don't like him for the Jenny Monroe murder," I said. "Calculated execution versus murderous rage."

Petey sucked his teeth. "Not good enough, Roy. He's probably a psychopath. You don't know what he can or can't do."

"Could be," I said. "But if you saw the guy, you'd know that he's not a 22-caliber mook."

"Maybe he used a small caliber 'cause it's quiet," Petey lectured.

"Nah," I said. "If Elvis wanted something quiet, he'd just snap her neck."

Petey scratched his face and watched the CSU crew through the open doorway.

"Maybe yes, maybe no," he said, "or, as usual, maybe you're making everything more complicated than it really is."

I shook my head. "Uh-uh. He didn't do Monroe." I gestured toward the bedroom. "That's more his style."

"Yeah, we'll see," Petey said, then changed the subject. "We found out Sandra Aguayo owns a gold Lexus, so we figure that's what Elvis was driving. He's an experienced con, so he's dumped it by now. We're looking for the Lexus and Rachael's car."

"What'd Rachael drive?" I asked.

"Black BMW, the small one. New," Petey said.

"If Brett's not in the back yard, where is he?" Octavio asked rhetorically. All three of us were calling "Brett" and "Rachael" by their stolen names, simply because we knew of nothing else to call them.

"Don't know," I answered. "I'm going back to his last place of employment to see if I can shake something loose, and then I'm swinging by the Millennium Restaurant."

I gauged Octavio's face.

"Wanna' come?" I asked.

Petey nodded to Octavio.

"Go ahead. Then swing by Rachael's place and turn it upside down. Let Roy give you a hand."

Octavio gave me a look, a measuring one. I couldn't tell to what conclusion he came.

"All right, Petey." He arched an eyebrow. "What about you?"

"I'm here for the duration. Then I'm going to brace Sandra Aguayo, hard. She's gonna' feel like she's inside a cement mixer."

"You got my new cell number, Petey?" I asked.

"Yeah. I got one of your cheap cards somewhere in my wallet," he said, "which doesn't mean I'm gonna' call. If I find something here, I'll call Octavio. He'll decide whether to let you in on it or not."

That was politic of Petey, and good policy. He knew I wouldn't resent it and it would ease any tension Octavio might have felt for having me foisted off on him.

I had a lot of thoughts swirling around in my head, very few of them good. If Sandy Aguayo had anything to do with Rachael's death, I was going to make it my life's work to see that she hanged for it. She was already a two-time widow, and her supposed lover, Jenny Monroe, was lying on her back somewhere in the morgue. People around Sandy Aguayo seemed to have a knack for getting dead.

Octavio and I went outside.

"You all right with this?" I asked.

He thought a moment.

"Petey trusts you. I trust Petey. I'll live."

I smiled, for the first time in an hour.

"Let's take my car. You can have a uniform take care of yours."

He nodded and spoke to a young officer, then walked the half block with me to my Lexus.

"So where do you buy it?" Octavio asked as we shut the car doors.

"Buy what?"

"That garlic cologne."

I laughed. It was thin, but it was a laugh.

"Gordon Biersch garlic fries at lunch."

He grunted.

"What happened to your windshield?" he asked, pointing.

"Anger management," I said.

CHAPTER TWENTY

The drive to Advent Securities took Octavio and me about 15 minutes. The same gal was behind the counter, and she gave us both a smile bright as a signal flare.

"Well," she said, "if it isn't tall and handsome and short and handsome."

I smiled, and so did Octavio.

"This is Octavio Sequoia," I said, gesturing. "He's a homicide inspector. We were wondering if you could tell us a little about Brett Jarrod."

She looked surprised, concerned and interested at the same time, then took off her earpiece and walked around the counter. As she came around the partition, I realized my previous description of her as Rubenesque was flawed. The correct word was *voluptuous*. She had on a long-sleeved linen blouse, cream-colored, tucked into black gabardine slacks. A shiny black belt was wrapped around her surprisingly small waist, and it did a good job of accentuating her generously proportioned chest and hips. Her shoulder-length black hair was pulled back in a ponytail, which gave a clear line of sight to a round, pleasing face. Big brown eyes and full lips, painted red, were framed by smooth, porcelain skin. Her nose was perfectly formed and her ears were cute as a kitten's. I figured her to be under 35, but I could have been off; it's happened before. She was a little shorter than Octavio, but her two-inch heels brought her eyes even with his.

"I have to apologize," I said. "The last time I was here I neglected to get your name."

"Ruby," she said, holding out her hand. "Ruby Kanzis."

"Like the state?" I asked.

A tiny smile twitched the corner of her mouth.

"Kansas is flat and dry," she said. "I'm anything but."

We didn't react to her statement. I mean, what do you say to that? I just loved this gal.

She spelled it out for us. "K-a-n-z-i-s. Kanzis."

Octavio and I nodded like two country bumpkins.

Eventually I shook her hand, as did Octavio, except Octavio held on to it a split second longer than I did. She didn't seem to mind, and neither did he.

"Somebody get killed?" she asked.

Octavio took the lead. "Yes." he said, nodding. "An associate of Brett's was murdered. We want to question Brett, but we can't seem to find him. We were hoping you could assist us."

"Who got killed?" she asked.

"We can't discuss the details of the case, uh, Ruby," he said.

"That makes sense. What can I do for you?" She said it without taking her eyes from Octavio.

Octavio was the first to look away. He shuffled his feet a little before continuing.

"We know where Brett lives, but we're trying to find out if he has somewhere else to stay. Has he ever mentioned a friend's house, or a business associate's where he might go?"

Ruby thought for a moment, then shook her head. "No. Brett pretty much kept to himself. He was an underachiever here, although he was smart enough. I never really figured him out."

"Did he make any friends here at all, any girlfriends?" Octavio asked.

"No, not really. He hit on me a couple of times, but hell," she spread out her arms, "can you blame him?"

I laughed out loud and Octavio went 10 shades of red. It went well with his suit. I liked Octavio, so I bailed him out.

"How about phone calls?" I asked. "Is there anyone who called him regularly?"

She sighed. "We make over a thousand calls a day." She gestured behind her. "I've got 20 brokers making cold calls to drum up business. It'd take you 20 years to track the outgoing calls, and the incoming calls are almost as high. If my brokers make or take personal calls, it's on their own cell phones."

"'Your' brokers?" I asked.

"Yep." Ruby waved toward the cubicles. "This sweat shop's all mine."

I could see that Octavio was impressed, as was I.

"Do you have an employee file on him? And if so, could we take a look at it?" Octavio asked. "There might be something in there that could help."

"Sure. Hang on," she replied.

Ruby spun on her heel, leaving a trail of pure femininity in her wake. Being men, we watched her round, muscular backside until she turned a corner.

I looked at Octavio.

"Don't say a word," he growled.

"Like what?" I asked, innocently. "Like, I think she just turned you into a quivering mass of Latin pudding? Like that?"

"Yeah, like that," he said. "And Latin pudding is called *flan*."

"Okay," I said.

Ruby returned with a thin file and a black scheduling book.

"This is all I've got on him. I can tell you now that you won't find anything. It's as thin as his last commission check." She handed the file to Octavio. "But I might have something else that would help."

We waited while she went through the scheduler.

"A couple of months ago, while he was still in my good graces, he called in sick." She rifled through the book and stopped at a page. "He asked me to forward his client calls to this number." She leaned in to Octavio to show him. I thought he was going to melt into a puddle.

"Let me write that down," he said, fumbling for his notepad.

I gave him my pen. "Yeah, Octavio, write that down."

I should've burst into flames, the look he gave me. This was fun, and I could do with a little fun after the morning I'd had.

He wrote the number down and tucked the file under his arm. He kept my pen, out of spite.

"All right, Ruby," he said, "you've been very helpful." He shook her hand. "We'll be in touch."

As we turned toward the door, I stopped.

"Ruby, I'm taking a date to a show that a buddy of mine is putting on Saturday after next. Octavio and a few friends are coming along. Would you care to join us?" I asked.

Ruby smiled and wrote something down on a business card. She walked over and handed it to Octavio. "Love to," she said.

He smiled and put the card in his pocket.

When we got to the door she called out, "Octavio?"

"Yes?"

"Nice suit."

CHAPTER TWENTY ONE

As we walked back to my car, Octavio seemed to have a bit of a spring in his step.

"I'm not sure if I should kiss you or kill you," he muttered.

"Is there a third option?" I asked.

"I can kill you slowly."

"I'll get back to you."

We got in my car and made our way up Geary to the Millennium Restaurant. While I drove, Octavio made a call to have the phone number Ruby had given us matched up with a name and an address.

The Millennium was ensconced in the Savoy Hotel, a small hotel that would've looked at home in Paris. The building itself was a cross between the Queen Anne and Second Empire style, with bay windows curving gently out from its face. The restaurant took up the ground floor, with a façade made of dark, polished mahogany and big windows that offered views of the street.

Inside, there was more mahogany, with a checkerboard tile floor in beige, white and brown, and tables with lots of linen. Small mirrors, framed in wood, ringed the room at waist level.

It was too late for lunch and too early for dinner, so the place was empty, much like a Bobby Brown concert.

A young man in a black suit approached us. "May I help you gentlemen?" he asked.

Octavio flashed his badge. "We need information on Rachael Stark."

The guy's face went white. "Is something wrong?" he yelped. "Has something happened to Rachael? Is she okay?" The questions tripped over themselves like kids rushing out for recess.

"I'm afraid there's been some trouble," Octavio said. "Do you work with her?"

Concern turned to panic. "What happened?" he asked loudly. "Is Rachael all right?"

"Settle down." Octavio raised his hands, trying to calm him.

He started to splutter.

"What's your name, fella'?" I asked.

"Uh, Joey, Joey Kimble."

Joey was a good-looking kid, no more than 25. He was almost as tall as me, but built like a long-distance runner. He looked a little like a young Pierce Brosnan, but with a weaker chin.

"Rachael Stark was murdered this morning," Octavio said bluntly.

Joey looked like he'd swallowed a hamster. He fumbled for the back of a chair and collapsed into it. We joined him in our own chairs as he struggled for control. His eyes darted over the table, desperately looking for I don't know what. His mouth was hard at work, mouthing mute words. A few minutes went by.

Eventually, his jaw unclenched and his breathing became somewhat normal.

"What happened?" he asked.

"I can't go into details with you, Joey," Octavio said calmly. "Suffice it to say we think Rachael died as a result of foul play." Octavio watched Joey carefully. "We need as much information as we can get, fast, in order to bring whoever did this to justice." He paused. "Can you help us?"

Joey sat up a little straighter. "Yes, of course I'll help."

"Good," Octavio said. "When was the last time you saw her?"

"Sunday night. The dinner shift. She didn't show up last night and we tried to reach her at her apartment, but no one answered."

"Has she ever missed work without calling?"

Joey shook his head. "No. Rachael was very responsible, always on time. That's why I, uh, we were so concerned."

"Do you have any idea who would want to do Rachael harm?" Octavio asked.

Joey frowned. "Yes," he said quietly. "Yes, I do."

"Who?"

Anger flashed in his eyes. "Her ex-roommate. Guy named Elvis."

"Ex-roommate?"

"Yes. They were still living together, but it was over." Joey looked down at his hands. "She was going to move in with me."

That explained a few things.

"When's the last time you saw Elvis and Rachael together?" I asked.

"Sunday night. Rachael was done with her shift and I walked her out to her car, as usual," he said. "Elvis was there waiting for us. They started screaming at each other, then Elvis punched her in the face." He paused, and I could see impotent fury twisting his features. "I tried to stop him, but he knocked me down. Rachael pulled him off me and said it was going to be all right, that she would handle it."

He looked down at his hands again, then tears pattered the table.

"But everything isn't all right, is it?" he sobbed. "Rachael's dead. He killed her, didn't he?"

Octavio reached over and put his hand on Joey's shoulder. "Yes, Joey, we believe he did."

We waited while Joey's weeping subsided.

"Joey," I asked quietly, "does Rachael have a locker here, or someplace where employees keep their personal belongings when they're working?"

He took a linen napkin off the table and wiped his eyes.

"Yes. We've got a bank of lockers in the back. I suppose you'd like to see them?"

"We'll get to them after a few more questions," Octavio said. "Are you up for it?"

Joey nodded.

"Okay, Joey," Octavio said. "Have you heard of a man named Brett Jarrod?"

"Yes. He comes here often with a few of Rachael's friends."

"What other friends?"

"There's Jenny Monroe, Sandy Aguayo and, uh, Elvis Boone. They come here as a group a lot."

Octavio and I exchanged glances.

"Have you ever overheard their conversations?" asked Octavio.

Joey grimaced. "No. I'm the maitre d'. I'm usually at the front."

"Did you and Rachael ever discuss these guys?" I asked.

Joey shook his head. "Never. We talked about Elvis a little, just in the context of her leaving him, but she was adamant about not discussing her relationship with the group."

"Didn't that strike you as odd?" I asked.

"Of course." He paused, and I could see pain ripple across his face.

"But I was in love with her. If she didn't want to talk about them, then we didn't talk about them."

I nodded, for lack of anything better to do.

"Can we take a look at her locker now?" Octavio asked.

"Yes," he said. "Follow me."

Joey got up and we trailed him through the kitchen and up a small flight of stairs. It deposited us in a small room with worn carpet and five or six folding chairs. A mirror was near the door for last-minute checks before going out to battle, and a folding table held a couple of tin ashtrays. On the left side was a bank of steel lockers, battered and chipped, just like the ones in junior high. About 20 half-sized lockers, one row on top of another, stood with locks on half of them.

"This is her locker." Joey pointed to a top locker farthest from the door.

Nothing was remarkable about the locker except for the very stout, very expensive brass padlock that guarded its contents. The other locks were all mostly courtesy locks, more appearance than function. Rachael's lock, however, was built for security.

"You're not seeing this," I said as I pulled out my lock pick kit. It was a good lock, but 90 seconds later it was open.

We pulled out the contents and placed them on the folding table. Inside was a small black nylon bag with a variety of cosmetics, two hairbrushes and a tin of breath mints. A couple of rolled t-shirts and an extra pair of comfortable jeans were in a plastic bag. A men's shaving kit contained a woman's wallet with credit cards, a checkbook, some coupons for hair care products and a driver's license from Texas with the name Rachael Parker on it. The credit cards and checkbook also had Rachael Parker on them. I found two other sets of drivers' licenses and credit cards, one for Rachael Simpson and one for Rachael Rogers.

The only other things in the locker were a cheap calculator, an assortment of pens and a zippered mesh bag with what looked to be about $50,000 in it.

"Hello, Kitty," I said.

"Jeez," Joey said.

"Fuck me," Octavio said.

I shook the bills out on the table. "Let's start counting."

"Joey," Octavio said, "we need you to witness this, okay?"

Joey nodded and we started counting.

My initial estimate of $50,000 was slightly off. The bag contained $47,260.

CHAPTER TWENTY TWO

We left the Millennium Restaurant with Rachael's things stuffed in a plastic bag Joey had rustled up for us. It made a sad little lump on the floor of my car.

"I still haven't heard how these murders tie into whatever your client has you looking for," Octavio said.

I grimaced. "I know, Octavio," I said, "but that has to stay confidential. When we find the murderers, we'll find what my client hired me to get." I paused. "I hope."

Octavio grunted. "That's only going to be good enough for a little while longer."

I blew out a breath. "I know."

On our way to Rachael and Elvis' apartment, Octavio called Petey to let him know what we'd found. Petey had also found something interesting at Brett's place: a scrapbook. It held newspaper clippings and photos of Sandy and Peter's wedding, society photos of Peter and Sandy at charity balls, some articles, a shot of Peter glad-handing the mayor and a *Sunset Magazine* article with photos of the Aguayos' home.

I asked Octavio for the phone.

"Petey, when you talk to Sandy, find out where she went after Galveston, and if you can, see if you can find out how and where she met Peter."

"What makes you think I wasn't gonna' do that already?" he asked.

"You're getting old, Petey. Old men forget things."

After another lecture on how he taught me everything I know, and how lucky I was that he was letting me tag along with a real detective, he hung up.

I handed the phone back to Octavio.

"You enjoy rattling Petey's cage, don't you?" he asked.

"What's not to like?"

He chuckled.

We drove over to Jackson and Drumm and I pulled parallel to the unmarked police car watching for Elvis. Octavio got out and chatted with the two cops, bringing them up to speed. He let them know we'd be in there for about an hour, and left his cell number in case Elvis made an appearance, but they told him not to hold his breath.

Upstairs, the place was a post-hurricane FEMA site. In one closet, empty clothes hangers clutched the closet pole in a tangled mass, mocking us. Elvis had been here, and he had taken his fashion-disaster wardrobe with him...in a hurry.

Rachael's stuff was still here, scattered around in clumps, like discards on a Goodwill loading dock. Books were strewn around, and all the paintings had been torn out of their frames.

"Looks like Elvis beat us to it," Octavio said. "When do you think he got here?"

"Could have been any time," I said, eyeing the destruction. "Probably saw the stakeout and slipped in the back entrance."

"Yeah," he said. "Easy enough to do. I bet I know what he was looking for."

"A bag with 50 grand in it." I said.

He smirked. "Really?" I think he was being sarcastic.

"Let's get to work," he said.

We went through the leftovers, and as I handled Rachael's things, I felt a suffocating sense of loss. Everything I touched seemed to radiate sadness, from my hands to my shoulders and into my chest. I never knew much about Rachael, never knew if she was a good person, never knew how many would mourn her death or if she was kind to stray cats, but I knew she hadn't deserved being beaten to death. Nobody does.

A book caught my eye. It was titled *Diamonds: An Illustrated History*. I picked it up and leafed through it, fanning the pages, hoping something would fall out. It was a coffee table book, about 12 inches by 16, and was filled with world diamond history and beautiful full-plate shots of stones worth the GDP of small European countries. Nothing was folded inside, or if there had been, Elvis would probably have it.

But Rachael had struck me as a smart woman, so I took off the glossy protective cover to see if anything was taped inside. Nothing. I opened the book, tilted the edge toward me and looked into the gap of the spine, and felt a little shiver run up mine. Something white was rolled up inside. I wet my finger and worried it for a moment, then pulled out three sheets of paper.

It happens sometimes. A USDA, prime-cut, bona fide clue drops in your lap, and all you can do is squeal like a little girl and hyperventilate and run around in circles waving your hands in the air and drop to the floor and make snow angels. But I wasn't alone, so I didn't.

There was a Xerox of an article, rough, like it had been copied a few times, but readable. It was from the *London Times* and was dated August 10, 1975. There was also a more recent newsprint photo, black and white and magnified, of a diamond on the neck of Sandy Aguayo. The *London Times* article was about the Star of Bombay, a 38-carat alluvial diamond that had disappeared from a British diplomatic pouch. It was part of an ensemble of diamonds and Indian artifacts that were on loan to the British Museum and had vanished into thin air. A little history was written on the gem and a lot of stuttering backpedaling by the "British authorities" on how they were exploring every avenue in order to locate the blah, blah, blah.

I looked at the photo of the diamond on Sandy's neck. The stone was encircled by precious metal that only did a halfway decent job of disguising the five little points that your eye formed by following the line of the diamond. It was a subtle enhancement that masked its true shape, but if you were looking for it, you'd find it. I had the distinct feeling that my client confidentiality was about to fly out the window.

I handed the sheets to Octavio.

"Look at this."

Octavio read the article, then pointed to the photo. "This Sandra?"

"Yep."

"This what you're supposed to find?"

"Yep."

"The Star of Bombay." He said it almost wistfully, like he was in love.

"Actually," I said, "I was supposed to find the Star of Siddhartha, but I'm going to make a leap here and assume they're one and the same."

He looked at the article again. "Oh, dear." He gave me a wicked smile. "Time to 'fess up."

"Yep," I said, then spent the next 15 minutes violating my confidentiality agreement.

CHAPTER TWENTY THREE

We finished tossing Rachael's place, but found nothing worth mentioning. Octavio asked me to drop him off at the Hall so he could write a report, then he'd go home and get some sleep. He promised to fax over a copy of what we'd found and connect with me some time tomorrow.

I parked my car in the lot and trudged the long, slow walk back to my office. Inside, I checked my email and got nothing, but my voicemail had a few messages: one from Liz Ishida, one from Jumbo Choi and one from a man who said he could get me a great deal on a mortgage.

I called Liz and got her machine, so I left a pleasant, extraordinarily witty message. I called Jumbo Choi, who picked up after the fourth ring.

"Hey Jumbo," I said.

"Hey Roy, glad you called. Khan wants to meet you over here at 7:30, which is"—he paused, and in my mind I saw him squint at the wall clock—"in 10 minutes."

"What about?"

"Don't know."

"All right, see you in a few."

We hung up.

I locked up and checked in with Eddie, who wasn't there. At the Red Pagoda I let my eyes adjust, and spotted Jimmy Khan and the Korean guy at the bar. I sat next to Khan.

"You wanted to see me?" I asked.

Khan didn't look too happy and the big Korean looked even less so. "We got a problem," he said.

I waited.

Jimmy took a swallow of his gin and tonic, and I gratefully knocked back half the Dewar's that Jumbo had put in front of me.

"Randall Tang," he said with disgust. "Rupert here—" he thumbed at the Korean "—went and had a chat with him after you and I met. Randall told him to fuck off."

Rupert, the Korean, broke in. "Can you imagine? He told *me* to fuck off."

I looked over at Jumbo, who merely shook his head.

"First things first," I said. "Your name is Rupert?"

Rupert looked hostile. "Yeah. Rupert Park. You got a problem with that?"

I smiled. "No."

"All right you guys, focus," Khan said irritably. "Tang's left the reservation," he continued. "He's gone over to the Joy Boys."

Rupert, Jumbo and I snorted in unison.

"Fuckin' Joy Boys," Jumbo said. "Cowboy meth runners."

"Yeah," Khan said. "Been a thorn in my side for two years. They're like herpes with hats." He sipped again. "But that's not your problem."

"No, it isn't," I confirmed.

"What is your problem, and mine, is that Tang put Wei Lee in the hospital." Khan finished his drink and motioned for another. I did the same.

"How bad?" I asked.

"Broken jaw, broken arm," Rupert said grimly.

I waited for Jumbo to come back with the drinks, then I took a long pull.

"All right. What else you got to tell me?"

Khan made a face that was half grimace, half scowl and half regret. "I can't go after Tang without touching off a war with the Joy Boys," he said, "which normally wouldn't bother me." He sipped his drink. "But right now, I've got some things in the works. Let's just say it's a delicate time." He wiped some condensation off his glass. "But I can't let Tang slide." He looked over at Rupert, who nodded. "Some low-level hump leaving my organization without permission makes me look bad. I can't have that."

I waited, but he didn't elaborate, which I didn't expect him to.

"I'm not hired muscle," I said.

"I know that, Roy—don't insult me. But if you go after Tang, you go after the Joy Boys, and that's a war whether I'm involved or not."

"So?"

Khan sighed. "Chinatown getting shot up is never a good thing, and right now, regardless of the participants, it's a real bad thing for me."

"What's that to me?" I asked.

Khan's jaw clenched. "I can't let Tang disrespect me like that—you know how it works. He needs to be spanked."

"Oh, he'll get spanked all right," I said.

"I know that," Khan said quietly, "but it needs to be handled diplomatically. It needs to be handled my way." He paused. "I would consider this a favor."

I let a minute disappear.

"All right," I said.

Khan nodded.

"Go see the Joy Boys," he said. "Tell them it's personal."

"It is," I mumbled.

He ignored me. "I've already let it be known that whatever you do is okay with me. If they've got half a brain between them they'll back away from Tang. Take Rupert with you, as a representative. That'll let them know there'll be repercussions if they move on you."

I looked over at Rupert. He was big and mean, and he had a name that gave you the impression his parents hated him. A good guy to have watching your back.

"And if they don't let me administer justice?" I asked.

Khan gave me a look that could've frozen Guam.

"Then I'll cut their hearts out."

CHAPTER TWENTY FOUR

I got back to my apartment and noticed my head hurt. A lot. I was beginning to regret putting the painkillers back in Brett's bottle. I settled for some Advil.

My apartment was musty and it felt like I hadn't been there in a month, or maybe it just smelled that way. Regardless, I opened a window and let Chinatown in. The din from the street swept into my place, along with the scent of the Pacific and fried onions. It was oddly comforting, kind of like a life-force thing I shared with the anonymous faces passing below, or something deep like that.

It was 8:30 and I was tired. In the last two days I'd found two bodies, been knocked unconscious, got few answers, raised more questions and received some bad news about a hardworking Chinese guy trying to nibble off a small piece of the American pie. I'd been slapped around by my client's wife, slapped around by a punk cop, duped by a murderer in a bad suit and given up my entire case to the police, which would probably come back at me in the form of a lawsuit six feet deep.

On the other hand, I had lunch with Liz Ishida.

Feeling better, I put on some Bob Marley and ordered up a jerk-pork salad and asked my delivery guy to pick up a six-pack of Red Stripe beer, in keeping with the Jamaican theme.

While I waited, I lit a cigarette and worked on my boat.

Calling it a boat, though, borders on insult. *Boat* besmirched the name of Admiral Horatio Lord Nelson and the Royal naval architect, Sir Thomas Slade, and I can only blame my exhaustion for the blasphemy. My *ship* is a fully-functional scale model of the *H.M.S. Agamemnon*, a 64-gun Ardent class ship-of-the-line. Launched in 1781, she was one of the most famous, and beautiful warships of the Royal Navy. Lord Nelson considered her his favorite, and who could blame him? He commanded her between 1793 and 1796 and lost his right eye on the *Agamemnon* during the siege of Calvi, which must have hurt. She'd seen action in the Saints, Copenhagen, Trafalgar, and eventually went down in Maldonado Bay, off the coast of Uruguay.

Too much information for most people, but absolutely necessary for those of us who had social lives best described as "marginal."

She was one of my passions, that and the sweet science and golf, and of course, the pleasure of being an under-appreciated, occasionally-assaulted, always self-amusing private detective.

I was working on the *Agamemnon* because I belonged to the "Plank Walkers Society," a group of nerds, lawyers, surgeons, stevedores, as well as various and sundry malcontents, with a passion for period-model ships. On one Sunday every summer, we have a regatta on Spreckels Lake in Golden Gate Park. The regatta is a frivolous ode to men with too much time on their hands and not enough places to waste it. For the regatta, and only for the regatta, our vessels are fitted with small electric motors so they can glide on the glassy surface in majestic formations, very much like synchronized swimming, without the beautiful women and tanned legs.

The regatta's been in existence for five years now, and we've been written up in the *Chronicle* a couple of times. Last year the mayor came, and this year he'll probably show up again, as the crowds get bigger and bigger.

The Regatta was two Sundays away, and I needed to put some finishing touches on my little nautical beauty. Between bites of salad and swigs of beer, I worked on her rigging and oiled her mahogany and made sure whatever brass there was gleamed like the buttons on a Prussian general.

There was going to be a little friction within the Society this year as a serious breach of etiquette had occurred at the last regatta. A two-year member named Stan Keith had shown up with his new boat, a twin of my *H.M.S. Agamemnon.* There was an unwritten law that no two members would showcase the same vessel, and yet Stan had flouted this tacit agreement and brought forth his doppelganger. I'd made some modifications to my ship to avenge this slight. Mr. Stan Keith was in for a nasty little surprise come the regatta.

Working on the *H.M.S. Agamemnon* is the closest I get to meditation, and as I rubbed and glued and fussed with her, the vision of Rachael Stark's broken face retreated a bit.

The phone rang. It was Eddie.

"You hear about Wei?" he asked.

"Yeah."

"What's going on?"

I repeated both my conversations with Khan, blaming myself for Wei's misfortune. Eddie told me not to, but it sat in my stomach like a clump of nails. I outlined what I was going to do and he listened without comment.

"You need any help?" he asked.

"No, Eddie, thanks. But maybe you can tell me why Khan's so keen on keeping things peaceful."

"Khan's got three liquor licenses up for renewal, and a building permit pending for a condo conversion. Everybody knows he owns Chinatown, and as long as things are quiet the City doesn't bother him. But if it turns into the OK Corral..."

"Got it," I said. "You gonna' be around tomorrow?"

"Same Bat-Time, same Bat-Channel."

"All right, I'll see you."

"See ya', Roy." He paused. "And stop kicking yourself in the ass for what happened to Wei—you were trying to do the right thing."

"Thanks, Eddie." I hung up, considered it, then kicked myself in the ass some more.

CHAPTER TWENTY FIVE
Thursday

The next morning I felt the Scotch and the beers and the welt on my head. More Advil went down the hatch, mixed with some strong French roast.

I took my time in the shower, letting the water blast my forehead for a few minutes. It seemed to loosen the skin and the muscles holding my brains in and I could feel the pain and tension sluice down my body and pool with the water at my feet.

By the time I toweled off, I felt like the price of a two-bedroom, two-bath San Francisco condo.

I dressed in a pair of loose-fitting jeans and a yellow oxford shirt with buttons made from nuts. A sand-colored Liz Claiborne lightweight suede jacket, which the saleswoman insisted was "fawn," rounded out the ensemble. Fawn, my ass. I know sand when I see it.

I went down to the café. The place had the regular mix of customers, except for the two hard cases sitting at the far end of the counter. They were taking a stab at being inconspicuous, but one guy had long, oily hair pulled back in a wispy ponytail and was sporting an extravagant fu manchu. Hard to miss. His partner had a shaved head and a goatee, and both had more tattoos than a Thai pirate. They were dressed in t-shirts, one black and one that used to be, and jeans. They both had the obligatory black engineer boots and I could see part of either

Loser or *Louvre* tattooed on the shaved guy's massive bicep. I put my money on *Loser*.

The rest of them were massive too. Big, bulging slabs of muscle, honed by hours of prison-yard weightlifting, stretched the tolerance of XXL t-shirts.

They'd given me a quick appraising glance when I walked in, then immediately tried to hide the fact by concentrating on their coffees.

I wasn't fooled. I'm a detective. It says so on my card.

Eddie came over and sat.

I pointed my chin at the big boys. "How long they been here?"

Eddie had his back to them, but he knew enough not to look around. "Two hours," he said. "Drinking all my coffee." He shook his head.

"I'm thinking of instituting a policy of limited refills."

I muffled a laugh. "Cheap bastard."

Eddie did his Chinese guy doing Marlon Brando doing Don Corleone. "It's not personal, Sonny." He scratched below his jaw. "It's business."

I laughed out loud this time. Eddie was good. "Don't make me laugh, Eddie; it hurts my head."

He sniggered. "Like you said, tough guy, comes with the job."

"That I did. What am I having for breakfast?"

"What difference does it make?" He smirked. "It's always good."

"True," I responded.

Breakfast came and proved Eddie right. A cheese-and-mushroom-and-spinach omelet with fresh tomato slices on top. Diced red potatoes, with the skin on, mixed with green peppers and onions. A medium-sized bowl of sliced melon, apple and banana, with a handful of seedless grapes tossed in. An English muffin with melted butter filling the craters. Orange marmalade in a jar.

I ate and he watched. We talked a little about Wei's situation. Eddie made me feel a little better by telling me Wei was covered by his insurance and was doing as well as could be expected. We didn't talk about what I was going to do about it. He knew, I knew, and that was that.

"What about these bruisers?" Eddie thumbed over his shoulder.

I spoke around a mouthful of omelet.

"Gonna' employ an old detective trick."

"And that would be?" he asked.

"Play it by ear."

He snorted. "What shit."

I shrugged. "You asked."

More snorting.

I solicited a favor from him, finished my coffee and everything on my plate and waddled to my office. I went in, leaving the door unlocked.

The phone was ringing. I picked it up.

"They left two minutes after you did," Eddie said.

"Thanks," I said, and hung up.

I hurried out of the office and slid into the utility room, leaving the door open a crack. Five minutes later the two steroid poster-kids came into view. One had brass knuckles on. They paused at my door, then quickly and quietly went in. I hustled out of my hidey-hole, gun in hand and slammed open my office door.

"Surprise!" I said.

They were.

My assailants-in-waiting were on either side of my inner office door, preparing to storm the place. It crossed my mind that this was the strategy my attacker had used on me yesterday. So much for originality.

I motioned with my gun. "Reach for the skies," I said. "Grab some air." A dramatic pause. "Or I'll push a pill in you."

They showed me their armpits. The guy with the ponytail looked at me askance.

"You're trying too hard," he said.

"Trying too hard?"

"To sound like a shamus."

Fucking critics.

"Into the office." We filed in. Both had big, black, greasy wallets sticking out of their back pockets attached to chains. "Sit down, and keep your hands—"

"—where you can see them dance," said Baldy, rolling his eyes. I believe he was making fun of me.

"Are you making fun of me?" I asked.

"That wouldn't be jake," he muttered.

I gave him a look, then sat behind my desk. I placed my revolver on top of it.

"Okay," I said. "I've called this meeting to ascertain why you two mugs are here and, as an ancillary objective, to determine the identity of the gee who fingered me as the pigeon."

Baldy looked over at Ponytail. "You're right," he said, with mild disdain. "He's trying too hard."

"You just made fun of me," I said, indignantly.

"Did not."

"Did to."

"Did not."

This was going badly.

I slapped the desk. "Enough! What are you doing here?"

Baldy took off his brass knuckles and flopped them on my desk.

He had me there.

I tried to salvage some pride. "It was a rhetorical question," I stated.

This time, they both rolled their eyes.

"You're doing it again," I said, sharply.

"Am not," they said in unison.

This was going very badly.

I picked up my revolver and fired a round into the wall above their heads. They ducked, then looked at me like I was crazy. I felt a little better.

"Go easy with the roscoe," Baldy said, straight-faced.

He was *definitely* making fun of me. I chose to ignore it. "Who sent you?"

They looked at each other.

Baldy sighed. "Fuckin' Elvis."

Now we were getting somewhere. "Spill," I said.

They looked disgusted. "We would," Ponytail said, "if you'd stop trying to sound like Phillip Marlow."

"Or Sam Spade," grumbled Baldy.

"It's fucking annoying," Ponytail added.

I slumped. "All right," I said, chagrined. They both looked relieved.

"Elvis called and asked us to rough you up," Baldy said, resigned. "Said you were asking a lot of questions and he wanted it to stop. We told him to point you out. He got us a rental car so we could follow him around. He *fingered* you at the beach."

"Why did you need Elvis to point me out?" I asked. "Whatever happened to address and description?"

"That wouldn't have been professional," he said.

Ponytail shook his head. "Very unprofessional."

I took a minute to absorb this information.

"You guys know Elvis from Huntsville?" I asked.

"Yeah," Ponytail said. "We had the pleasure."

"So he flew you out to work me over?"

They looked at each other guiltily. "We took the bus," said Baldy.

"You took the *bus*, from *Texas?*"

They fidgeted a little.

I leaned forward, frowning. "What's he paying you?"

They exchanged another look. "Five hundred each," said Ponytail, quietly. "Plus bus fare."

"Five hundred?" I shouted.

Baldy shrugged and spread his hands. "It's a bad economy."

"Reflects the recent downturn," Ponytail said.

"Off shoring," Baldy added. "It's nothing short of the complete evisceration of the American workforce."

"Evisceration," Ponytail agreed, nodding.

Jesus wept. "So all I'm worth is five hundred, plus bus fare," I stated.

Baldy shrugged again. "It's what the market will bear. The 'trickle down' theory of the Reagan administration has thus far failed to reach the bottom rung of the economic ladder."

"Reagan?" I yelled. "That was *decades* ago."

Baldy held up his hands, palms out. "Which proves my point," he said smugly.

I rubbed my face and tried to figure out where I'd lost control of the situation. "How long you guys been in the leg-breaking business?" I asked.

Ponytail looked down at his Timex. "About," he did some head math, "three hours."

CHAPTER TWENTY SIX

I gave them the dirtiest look in my repertoire.
"Wonderful."
They looked sheepish.

"You got a cigarette?" Baldy asked. "My nerves are shot."

I shook out a cigarette, flipped the pack to him and nudged at an ashtray. We all lit up and smoked.

"We wouldn't have gone through with it, you know," Baldy said. "I don't think we're cut out for this kind of work."

Ponytail tapped an ash. "Too stressful."

"How do you think I feel?" I asked.

"Yeah," Ponytail said. "Sorry about that."

"All right," I said, exhaling. "Fill me in."

Their names were Larry and Sean. Larry had the ponytail. Sean didn't. They'd met Elvis in Huntsville Prison, where they spent two years for Internet fraud—identity theft, to be exact. They'd been out for about eight months and then had the misfortune of joining a small company that went belly-up three months ago. Money was tight, and then Elvis called.

"We figured it was time to get out of Texas anyway," Sean said. "Come to Silicon Valley and do some programming."

"You're software programmers?" I asked, surprised.

"Yeah," Larry said. "Self-taught."

Sean nodded confirmation.

Who woulda' thunk? I pulled on my cigarette. "Tell me about Elvis."

"Elvis was a big talker," Larry said. "Always yakking about how he was going to score big in San Francisco. We didn't think too much about it, but then he calls us up."

"What did he propose?" I asked.

"He said you were throwing a wrench in the works," Sean said. "Said money was tight right now, but if we did this job there'd be plenty of work for us out here."

"And you believed him?"

He smirked. "Of course not. Elvis is a bonehead. We just wanted to get out of town and start fresh."

"By busting me up?" I fingered the brass knuckles. "With these?"

Larry waved dismissively. "Nah. That's a prop. We figured we'd put the fear of God in you. Warn you off, as it were."

"The best-laid plans of mice and men," I said.

"Something like that," Larry said.

"If you're software programmers, why'd Elvis pick you for a muscle job?" I gestured toward their torsos. "Aside from your appearances."

They squirmed a little.

"In prison," Sean said, "it's best to give the impression you're something other than a white-collar criminal." He paused. "Avoids a lot of conflict."

"Makes life a little easier," added Larry.

"So what impression did you give?" I asked.

"Larry here," Sean said, waving toward his partner, "murdered five people at a party." He smiled. "With a hatchet."

Larry waved back at him. "Sean bludgeoned his whole family to death," he said, "with a lawn dwarf."

"Sweet," I said, appreciatively. "But didn't the fact that you only got two years raise a little suspicion?"

They both snorted. "Like they could add," Larry said.

God forgive me, I was starting to like these guys.

I had an idea.

"You guys know Brett Jarrod?" I asked. "Or Rachael Stark?"

They squirmed again. "We might," Larry said cautiously, "if it doesn't leave this room."

"Mum's the word."

Larry sighed. "Yeah, we know 'em. Did a couple of IDs for both. Credit cards, driver's licenses. Why?"

I ignored the question. "You met them in Texas?"

Sean nodded. "Elvis asked if we knew anybody 'could get fake IDs. Being mass murderers, we said that we, of course, couldn't do it, but we could broker the job."

"Didn't he question why two stone-cold killers like yourselves got out of prison?" I asked.

"Good behavior," Sean said.

"He bought that?"

"Apparently," Sean replied, and scratched his scalp.

My opinion of Elvis was riding a roller coaster. Evil genius, or dumb as a stick?

"Do you remember their real names?"

Larry shifted in his seat. "People who want new IDs aren't all that forthcoming about their real identities. But we just got out of the joint and weren't about to go back. So we followed them." He took another drag off his cigarette. "Got their real names from their plates and home addresses. They weren't cops or connected to cops, so we did the job."

"What're their real names?" I asked.

"Voorhees," Larry said. "Brett and Rachael Voorhees."

I turned my computer screen towards me. Three clicks and Sammy Mayfair's email appeared. John Voorhees was

Sandy Aguayo's second husband, the hunting-accident victim. He had two children, fraternal twins named Brett and Rachael who'd been in Europe when he died and had stayed there during the mess that followed. They'd apparently never met Sandy or Elvis during the chaos, but they both chose to connect with Elvis when he got out of jail, and then they came out here to cozy up to Sandy.

Curious.

"Did Elvis know their real names?" I asked.

"Until a couple of days ago, no," said Sean.

"What's that mean?" I asked.

"When Elvis called us to work you over," Larry said, "he asked us outright for their names." Larry shrugged. "I didn't think much of it, so I told him."

"So he didn't know they were Voorhees when he was in Texas?" I asked.

Larry shook his head. "Nah. I doubt it. Elvis introduced them to us as Brett and Rachael Rogers. That's the name they gave to Elvis...for whatever reason. Plus, they were thick as thieves, stoned most of the time, making plans to move out here." Larry gestured with his hands. "It was a festive atmosphere."

I leaned back and thought about that for a minute. "So, how does Elvis get a hold of you?"

Sean pulled out a cell phone and placed it on my desk. "He's going to call us on this"—he poked at it—"some time this weekend."

I picked it up and another idea emerged. It happens sometimes.

"This weekend, huh?" I mused.

I took out the Dewar's and placed two glasses and a coffee cup on the table, then poured three drinks.

"I have a proposition for you," I said.

CHAPTER TWENTY-SEVEN

We sipped Scotch for a minute or two, like three old friends after a round of golf.

"Proposition?" Larry prodded.

"Yes," I answered. "I propose putting you two on retainer. One hundred dollars a day, each, guaranteed for five days."

They didn't look too impressed. I decided to sweeten the pot.

"I'll also put you up in a motel, again for five days, and absorb the cost."

Still not impressed.

"And," I said, raising a finger, "I'll refrain from putting a .38 slug into your spleen."

They seemed more receptive.

"What do we have to do for this,"—Larry sought for a word—"largesse?"

I leaned forward. "When Elvis calls, you'll set up a meeting." I took out a card and slid it across the desk.

"Then you'll call me." I punctured him with a stare. "And then I'll fuck him up."

They both sighed and leaned away from my card. Sean shook his head. "That wouldn't be ethical."

"Ethical?" I almost choked on it.

"Technically," Larry said, "no crime has been committed." He paused. "True, Elvis did engage us to commit a felony. However, said felony was never executed." He spread his hands.

"Therefore, by assisting you, we'd be abetting a criminal endeavor."

"Abetting?" I howled. "Who are you, Johnnie fuckin' Cochran?"

"No," Sean said, "but we're not going to set some guy up just because you're pissed off at him. That wouldn't be right."

Larry nodded. "Wouldn't be right."

I paused, then poured another shot into each of their glasses.

"Drink that. You're going to need it."

They eyed me suspiciously for a second, then drank their medicine.

I was silent for a minute then sat back, put my elbows on the armrests and steepled my fingers.

"Elvis Boone beat Rachael Voorhees to death yesterday," I said quietly. "I found the body."

They went pale.

"Her face looked like the inside of a raw sausage."

I poured myself some more medicine and drank it. After a moment, I exhaled.

"And that's why,"—I looked them in the eyes, so there wouldn't be any misunderstanding—"I'm going to fuck him up."

They gently put their glasses down.

Larry released a long, mournful breath.

"Jeez."

Sean gestured toward his glass. I poured.

"That poor girl." His eyebrows pressed together. "She was just a kid."

Larry also gestured. I obliged. He took half of it in one gulp.

"Fuckin' Elvis," he growled.

"Yeah," I said. "Fuckin' Elvis."

CHAPTER TWENTY-EIGHT

In like lions, out like lambs. Larry and Sean didn't seem to be bad guys, aside from their critique of my dialogue. I'd made a call to the Sea Captain Motel, out on Lombard Street, and reserved a room with my credit card. Seventy-nine bucks a night, with a continental breakfast.

We shook hands like gentlemen and they left with mumbled apologies and a promise to call me when they were settled in.

It was only nine o'clock, but it already felt like I'd put in a full day's work. I checked my e-mail and discovered that I could increase the length and girth of my penis in 30 days, as well as meet hot single nymphos who liked to be spanked.

My fax, though, yielded something of value. Octavio had sent over the article and photo we found yesterday at Rachael's, and to my surprise, some letters from Jenny Monroe's apartment. The letters were from Sandy Aguayo, and I blushed as I read them. They were filled with passion, oddly poetic and it made me feel cheap because I was violating something so obviously genuine. For the first time in years I was embarrassed, but I'm pure of heart and long of limb, so I got over it.

The big surprise was the letter from Rachael Voorhees to Jenny Monroe—less poetic, but it still left little to the imagination. This put a new dynamic into the equation. Maybe the argument between Jenny and Elvis at the dinner party had been territorial; maybe Elvis was telling Jenny to keep her hands off his girl. Or maybe not.

I called Octavio.

"Hey," I said.

"What's up, Roy?" he chirped. "You get my fax?"

"Yes, and thank you. You got any news?"

"A little. You?"

"A little."

"Spill," he said. I bit my tongue.

I filled him in on my morning, leaving out a lot, and told him we'd identified Brett and Rachael.

"Bueno," he said. "I've got an address on the phone number Ruby gave us yesterday. I'm going out there to see if I can roust Brett." He paused like he was debating something. "You wanna' come?"

"Absolutely."

"Good," he said. "You're driving."

"All right, I'll pick you up in front of the Hall in 20 minutes."

"I'll be the handsome guy," he said, "with the nice suit."

"Got it," I said. "I'll look for a jockey, dressed like a pimp."

"I resent that," he said, laughing.

"What's not to resent?" We hung up.

I locked up and did a fast six-block walk to my car. I got to the Hall of Justice at 850 Bryant Street in exactly 20 minutes. True to his word, Octavio was waiting out front, in a nice suit. I pulled up close to the curb and he hopped in.

Octavio had on a snappy four-button construct, as blue as a Sri Lankan sapphire. A white shirt served as a canvas for a cerulean silk tie with tiny pink stars and octagons and other shapes that I would've recognized had I passed geometry. The suit's buttons matched the tie perfectly, and speculating on how he'd managed that was giving me a headache. His shoes were cobalt.

"Where in God's name did you get those shoes?" I asked, incredulous.

He smirked. "If I told you," he said, "everybody'd be wearin' 'em."

"Not on this planet," I mumbled as I pulled out. He ignored it and handed me a sheet with driving instructions. "We're going to Emeryville," he said. I handed it back. "Navigate for me, will ya'? I can't drive and read at the same time."

"Are you chewing gum?" he asked.

"No."

He blew out a sigh of relief.

We headed out to the Bay Bridge and I swung onto the gray span. Halfway across, he put the knife in.

"Where's Larry and Moe?" he asked.

"Larry and Sean," I corrected.

"Whatever."

"They high-tailed it back to Texas," I lied.

"You should've let me talk to them."

"I know."

I could feel him fuming next to me. I knew that if I'd handed them over, Octavio and Petey would've set up what I was setting up. But they were going to arrest Elvis, put him into the system. My way was more efficient. I was going to kill him.

"Listen," I said. "I made a judgment call, probably wrong. I apologize."

"I'm not stupid, Roy." he said, annoyed. "I know you've got something going with those two. Don't think for a minute that I won't clamp you in irons if you fuck with me."

"Let's hope it doesn't come to that," I said.

"It's up to you, cowboy," he answered.

We were silent going over the bridge, the conflict brooding between us like a third passenger.

"Take the Macarthur turnoff," he said as we neared Emeryville. "Stay on the left and then take West Macarthur."

I did as he instructed. More minutes of silence.

"Left here." He pointed. "Peralta. Then get on San Pablo."

A couple more curt instructions and we passed the Pixar Animation Studios on Park.

"It's right up here." Octavio pointed to a brick warehouse that looked like it had been converted into live/work lofts.

I circled the block, twice, until I spotted a Mercedes pulling out of a space. I slid into the vacuum and turned off the ignition.

"Look, Octavio, I might be holding out on you or I might not. But we've got a bird in the hand here with Brett. Can we put Larry and Sean on the back burner and cross that bridge when we come to it?"

Octavio got out of the car shaking his head, but his mouth hinted of smile. "Three clichés in three seconds." He looked up the street. "That's gotta' be a record." I got out and followed him to the loft/warehouse conversion.

318 Park had a brick façade and was stacked to four stories. Each story was about 20 feet high, with monstrous mullioned windows taking up most of the face. It was a square, standalone building, with corners sharp enough to shave my legs. The result was Industrial Revolution meets Tao, and like all good architecture, gave me a sense of the grandeur of the human condition.

"This building gives me a sense of the grandeur of the human condition," I said.

Octavio scowled at me. "Don't be an idiot. They bought an old warehouse, turned it into lofts, and sold them for a million apiece." He shook his head. "I got your grandeur," he mumbled.

Plebian bastard.

We had to go to the middle of the building, which meant the middle of the block, to get to the front entrance. We faced an enormous stainless steel door with a thousand holes punched into its surface, each about one-inch square, lined up in perfect symmetry. Behind the steel was glass, and the whole thing must've stood 10 feet tall and weighed a thousand pounds. A glass transom sat on top, and clear glass on either side let you see into the long, bare lobby.

Octavio checked the directory for names. "What were the names on Rachael's IDs?"

"Stark, Parker, Simpson and…." I thought for a second. "Rogers."

He pointed to a name. "B. Rogers. Loft 1441."

I stepped back and looked at the door. "How in the hell are we gonna' get into this place?"

"Like this." Octavio had his finger on the *building manager* button.

"I knew that," I said. "I was testing you."

A voice came out of the speaker. "Yes?"

"My name is Octavio Sequoia; I'm with the SFPD. I've got some questions I'd like to ask you."

Thirty seconds went by.

"Be right out."

About a minute later, a very tall, very old gentleman shambled out into the lobby. He must've been at least six-nine, and wore a red and white checkered shirt under faded bib overalls. His face was all loose skin and big jowls, with a nose descended from Romans. Cornflower-blue eyes that smacked of Siberian husky stared at us over gold-rimmed glasses, and his ears looked like they could've gotten him airborne in a high wind. His hair was white as a Klansman's hat.

Something clicked, and the door swung in on silent hinges.

"What can I do for you?" he asked, friendly.

Octavio fished out his badge. "I'm a homicide inspector," he said. "I need to talk with one of your tenants. I believe his name is Brett Rogers."

The old giant stroked his chin. "What was your name again?"

"Octavio Sequoia." He waved a hand toward me. "And this is my trainee, Roy Jobe."

I probably deserved that.

The old guy held out his hand. "Clete Hicks," he said. "Pleased to meet you."

We shook hands.

"Well, no point standing around drawing flies," he said. "C'mon in."

We followed him into the lobby and down the hall about 40 yards. He opened a door on the left and motioned us in. We entered a wonderland.

The place was about 3,000 square feet, with no dividing walls. It was painted white up to 40 feet, then went light blue for three stories to a glass skylight. It must've been an airshaft of some kind, perhaps expanded to fit the floor plan. Large windows were embedded in the walls starting at the second floor, and I assumed they were installed to provide light for the units above. To the left, a staircase led up to a sleeping loft that jutted out to cover a third of the ground floor. A bright blue canvas covered the sleeping area, providing privacy from the windows above.

The most astonishing feature, though, was the babbling brook. It meandered sinuously through the space like a liquid python. The stream was about two feet wide and divided the home into three sections: kitchen, living room and work area. A light maple floor crossed over the baby river here and there in little wooden bridgelets. The stream was black-bottomed, to give the illusion of depth, and the source and endpoint seemed to disappear under the wall at opposite ends of the space.

"Nice," I said.

"Beautiful," Octavio added.

Big Clete smiled. "Thank you," he said. He waved toward the living room peninsula. "Grab a seat. I'll bring some coffee."

Octavio and I crossed the water and settled ourselves into some chairs. I whistled the theme to *Bridge On the River Kwai* at Octavio. He shushed me.

Clete brought over a tray with a coffee service and set it down on the aptly named coffee table. He poured three cups into bone china and we tailored to taste.

"So, is Brett in some kind of trouble?" Clete asked.

"Not that we know of," Octavio said, "but he'd be doing himself a favor by clearing the air." Octavio paused. "You know him?"

Clete sipped some coffee. The cup looked like a toy in his massive hands. "Yep," he said. "Brett rents a unit on the ground floor."

"1441?" Octavio asked.

"Yep. It's one of 10 I own, besides this one. I've got 35 units sold, five vacant," he said deprecatingly.

"You built this place?" I asked.

"Yessir. Bought, planned, built and sold. I'm an architect by trade and a contractor by choice."

"You seem to be good at both," I said, glancing around.

"Thank you."

"What about Brett?" Octavio asked. "Is he at home?"

"Soon's we finish our coffee," Clete said, "we can go find out."

That seemed to make sense, so we sat and admired the environment while we sipped our coffee.

After a few minutes, Clete was ready. "Okay, gentlemen," he said, rising, "let's go knock on his door."

We followed Clete over the river and through the wood and took a left in the lobby. The lobby had a high ceiling and was painted a glossy fire-engine red. The exposed pipes that were 20 feet up were also glossy, but black.

"Why this color scheme?" I asked Clete.

He looked back at me while we walked.

"It gives a visual contrast to the lofts' interiors," he said. "After being jarred by the hallway, the soothing colors inside the lofts are accentuated."

"Very Zen," I said.

He smiled. "The Devil's in the details."

"Amen, brother," Octavio said.

After walking for what felt like a mile we stopped in front of 1441.

Clete rang the door buzzer. A minute went by and then the door opened a crack. Brett's face peeked out at Clete and he started to smile, but it vanished when he saw Octavio and me. He started to close the door, but I jammed a foot between the door and jamb. I saw Brett reach down and set something under the door and knew instantly it was a wedge. He had been expecting an occasion like this. The wedge effectively held the door while he disappeared from view.

"Help me," I said to Octavio and Clete. With the three of us pushing, the door begrudged me enough room to get in. I saw Brett at the far end of the unit, already easing through the plate-glass sliding doors leading out to an open patio. I rushed in, with Octavio hot on my heels, just as Brett raised a revolver toward my chest.

"Gun!" I screamed, and jumped to the side.

Brett fired two rounds through the glass, missing me by inches. I heard a surprised yell behind me and saw Octavio spin down to the floor.

Brett was climbing the wall and was getting away. Chase Brett or help a man down? I barked a curse that would've embarrassed a sailor and turned back to Octavio. He was lying on his stomach, clutching his side.

"Clete!" I pointed toward the living room. "Call 911! Officer down!"

Moving surprisingly fast for a six-foot-nine old guy, Clete spotted the phone and punched in the numbers, while I knelt by Octavio.

"Where you hit?" I asked.

"In the side," he hissed. "I think it went clean through."

I rolled him over and helped hold the wadded lower portion of his suit to the wound. There was plenty of blood, but the pressure was working.

Octavio raised his head and looked toward the patio. "He get away?"

"Gone," I said.

"Goddamn tragedy," he growled.

"Yeah," I said, nodding in agreement. "Just missed him."

"Not *him*," Octavio snarled. "My *suit*."

CHAPTER TWENTY-NINE

After EMS got to us, and before the Emeryville Police arrived, I beat it out of there with Octavio's blessing. We both agreed that it would be better if we had at least one man out on the street, rather than two left behind doing paperwork. And since Octavio had a hole in his suit...

I cruised the area around the warehouse just in case Brett was stupid enough to show his face. He wasn't, so I drove back across the bridge.

Octavio's shoes were on the passenger seat, keeping me company. They made a nice contrast to my beige leather interior. Octavio had insisted I take them, for their own protection. The man had just been shot, so my clever riposte had never made it past my lips, proving once again that I'm a man of compassion.

I slipped a Dandy Warhols CD into the dash and let them wail at me all the way across the Bay Bridge. It wasn't until later that I realized that Elton John would have been more appropriate for a man with cobalt shoes in protective custody.

I parked my car and called Petey while I walked back toward my office. I also lit a cigarette, which was quite a feat considering the tiny keypad on my phone and the blue shoes tucked under my arm.

"Petey?"

"You got my partner shot," he accused.

"Looks that way," I said. "What's the latest?"

"It was a flesh wound, didn't hit any organs or arteries." Petey sighed, relieved. "It nipped a love handle and sailed on through. He'll be okay."

"I'm sorry it turned out this way, Petey," I said. "Octavio's a good man."

"That he is," he agreed. "Fill me in, Jobe."

I gave him the rundown of this morning, leaving out large portions of my conversation and subsequent arrangements with Larry and Sean.

"You should've let me talk to them," he admonished.

"I know. Octavio already threatened me with incarceration."

"He mention the cattle prod?"

"No," I said, "but it was implied."

"Good. What else you got?"

"Nothing," I said, "except for the possibility that my client is a jewel thief."

Petey grunted. "That's not my problem. Fact of the matter is, someone upstairs wants me to keep that little piece of information confidential until it's sorted out diplomatically."

"Diplomatically?"

"Yes." Petey said. "Peter Aguayo knows people."

"The governor?" I asked.

"The president."

"Jesus Biggie Christ," I groaned.

"I'm sure you can appreciate my position," he said. "I let you tag along with Octavio, who, by the way, is a *real* detective. I let a civilian stomp around a crime scene, maybe tamper with evidence."

I started to protest, but Petey silenced me with something approximating a bark. "You know something you shouldn't, Roy," he continued. "So here's the deal: you were never in Rachael's house. You never found those documents about this jewel, both of which are now in the possession of my captain. You never got the fax from Octavio that yielded said information. You will never speak of this under penalty of me kicking the living crap out of you. Do we understand each other?"

"My lips are sealed," I said solemnly.

"I mean it, Jobe. We're talking about getting bounced from the force. I'll get my pension, but Octavio will be screwed."

"I know, Petey. You have my word."

He grunted.

"You find out anything from Sandra?" I asked.

"Ahhh," Petey said disgustedly. "She knows nothing; she sees nothing. She cosigned the gold Lexus for Elvis; he's supposedly making the monthly payments. The only other things I got out of her are that she and Jenny Monroe were lovers, and that Elvis was with her around the time of Jenny's murder."

"She admit that Elvis is her brother?" I asked.

"Of course she did," he said. "No law against that."

"What'd she say about the relationships with the others?"

"Same elusive crap. Just friends she gets together with occasionally. She got hissy with me when I brought her past up, said there was no need to relive it, it was all on record. She also asked me how Chief Penderson was doing, dropping a big, fat hint that she knows people too."

Petey emitted a noise that an annoyed ocelot might make. "She's pretty slick, that one."

"And smart," I said. "Did she use any words you didn't understand? 'Cause I can explain them to you."

"Fuck you in the neck, Jobe. You owe me. I'm up to my ass in political horseshit and you got my partner *shot*." He was almost yelling now. "I'm spending most of my day unfucking a situation when I should be out looking for murderers, which by the way, is my *job*." He paused to spit out some of the nails he'd been chewing. "You need to bring me something I can use, Jobe. Bring me something *now*."

"All right, Petey, I'll come through for you," I said. "You have my word."

"That's two promises I'll hold you to," he said, then calmly asked, "Am I going to see you at the gym tonight?"

"Yes," I answered. "I'll need you to tape my hands."

"A pleasure," he said. "See you tonight."

"See ya', Petey.

That had been a four-block conversation, which put me a half block east of the Haj Delicatessen. I veered left and dumped my cigarette before entering. Inside I was faced by a long glass display counter, with big blocks of roast beef and salami and cheeses and liverwurst and a ton of other stuff that made my mouth water. Haj had big bowls of potato salad and macaroni salad and other unfathomably complex salads behind the glass, and more sausages than Jimmy Dean.

There were about 12 people milling menacingly, like Pacific tuna around a smelt ball. I joined them. When my number came up, I ordered a prosciutto and Swiss on light rye with mustard, mayo, romaine, tomatoes and Bermuda onions cut so thin they were translucent. On the side, a cola in a can and no chips.

I paid and, as was my custom, dropped a dollar into Haj's tip jar. Haj had shown up last year to our regatta, trailing five kids. I figured anyone with five kids could always use an extra buck.

Ten minutes later I was in my office, with the mess that was my lunch opened on my desk. My stomach was rumbling angrily.

I was feeling pretty lousy about Octavio, but a flesh wound was better than the alternative. Maybe a good meal would help assuage my guilt over getting a good man shot. I focused on the smell of onion, cheese and Parma ham, the combination of which threatened to overwhelm me. I somehow remained conscious.

I was about to gnaw off a chunk of the assemblage when Sandy Aguayo walked in. On the verge of tears, I put it down.

"Sandy," I said, rising and wiping my hands on a napkin.

"Don't get up, Roy," she said as she nestled into a chair. "No need to be formal."

I sat.

Sandy, as usual, looked stunning. She wore a black double-breasted suit coat with a matching skirt. Anne Klein, I'd wager. Under the coat was a graphite-colored collarless silk blouse. A simple gold band graced her left ring finger, but the other hand sported a flawless black pearl slightly smaller than a whale heart.

I wondered what the hell she was doing here, but I figured I'd find out soon enough. I was concerned that my suspicion about her possible complicity in Rachael's death, and my vow to burn her down if she was, might be revealed in my manner and language, so I decided to play it casual.

"Hungry?" I asked.

She eyed my victuals. "Starving."

I unfurled a napkin and placed it at her edge of the desk and carefully transferred half of my sandwich onto it. I got a coffee cup and poured some cola into it and placed it next to the sandwich.

We ate in silence—she daintily, me like a malnourished wolf. Somehow, we finished at the same time.

"That was *good*," she said with her mouth half-full. Had I done that, I'd have come off as a slob; she came off as an empress. She waved at the blue shoes on my file cabinet. "Where in God's name did you get those?"

"If I told you," I said, "everybody'd be wearin' 'em."

She laughed, and I felt a twinge for stealing Octavio's line. It passed.

"I had a visit from your friend at the SFPD," she said. "Detective Dempster."

"So I've been told."

"He's a good interviewer," she said. "Asks good questions, doesn't get flustered."

"You should know."

She frowned; she didn't like that.

"You got a cigarette?" she asked.

I pulled out a pack and slid them toward her. She put one in her mouth and waited for me to light it. I slid my lighter across the desk instead. She waited a beat, then picked it up and torched her fag. She exhaled.

"You don't like me very much, do you?" she asked.

"That's irrelevant."

"That's right," she said quickly, "and don't you forget it."

Which annoyed me. Considerably.

"What do you want, Sandy? What are you doing here?"

She flicked an ash. "I'm here to see if you've found Jenny's murderer."

"I'm working on it."

She stubbed out her cigarette. "What can I do to help?"

"You can stop lying."

"Fuck you, Roy," she snapped. "I've never lied to you. You just haven't asked the right questions."

I leaned back in my chair.

"Was Elvis with you at the time of Jenny's death?" I asked.

"Yes," she said. "He was with me all morning."

"Doing what?"

"Telling me things I already knew."

I gave her a disgusted look. "All right, Sandy. I'm tired of dickin' around. What's going on with you and Elvis?"

Her glare was hard as a hangman's smile. She knew that I knew about her past. But she hadn't figured out how much I knew about the present, which, unfortunately, wasn't much.

We stared at each other for a while, then she reached for the Gaulloises again and shook two out. She flipped one toward me and I put it between my lips. She leaned over to light it, before lighting another for herself and inhaled deeply, then vented a geyser of bluish-white smoke.

"Let me tell you a little story," she said.

CHAPTER THIRTY

S andy adjusted her position and re-crossed her legs. Her eyes examined a photo on the wall of myself, my godson Jake, his dad Dan, and a 200-pound halibut Jake had hauled out of the waters off the coast of Alaska. It was a good photo, but it didn't warrant the attention she was giving it.

"When I was little girl," Sandy started, "I lived with monsters."

My skepticism radar was on full alert. It always goes on full alert when the beautiful wife of a multimillionaire with two dead husbands in her slipstream and a murdering psychopath of a brother starts telling me a story. But that's just me.

Sandy sat up a little straighter and somehow tore herself away from the halibut.

"I was pretty and blonde and I played with dolls," she continued. "I went to school and baked brownies and had a crush on my fourth-grade teacher." She took a long breath. "And when I was 10 years old"—her eyes started blinking in Morse—"I watched my father beat my mother to death."

Admittedly, that caught me off guard. I flinched, but she didn't notice. Sandy smoothed a lapel and fussed with her skirt hem.

"My father came home one night, stinking of well liquor and another woman," she said. "He sat down to an overcooked four-dollar roast, which only got that way because he was two hours late."

She moistened her lips. I searched her face for guile, deceit, duplicity or any combination thereof, but came up short.

"That didn't matter, though," she said. "The only thing that mattered was that daddy's meat wasn't cooked the way he wanted. Daddy liked his meat *rare*."

Sandy paused and stared out my window. Her fists were compressed little balls, white around the knuckles.

"The punishment for overcooking a roast was usually a couple of punches to the ribs," she said, "and maybe a bloody lip." She paused.

"But well liquor is cheap, and Daddy had lost another job."

Sandy carefully lifted her cigarette from the ashtray's groove. It was the action of a drunk walking past a squad car, too deliberate and too precise. She took a nervous drag and put it back.

"He started beating my mother with a piece of firewood, hitting her in the legs so the neighbors wouldn't see the bruises."

She flashed a smile bitter as a lover's lie.

"Daddy was *smart*." Sandy played with her pearls for a minute, fingering them like prayer beads.

"My mother started crying." she said. "She tried to protect herself, but couldn't. She *begged* him to stop."

A long pause this time. Sandy's eyes roamed over my desk, settling on nothing.

"But Daddy just got angrier." Sandy took another deep, shuddering breath. "And he started beating her in the face with that big, splintery piece of firewood." She looked at everything but me. "Until she stopped moving."

Thirty more seconds ticked by. They went by on the back of a fat man wading through water. I still couldn't tell if she was selling this story, but I knew plenty of guys who would've broken out their checkbooks. Maybe even me.

She continued.

"Daddy smiled and pointed to my mother's face." She was almost whispering now. "He said: 'Now *that's* rare. *That's* the way I like it.'"

Sandy became quiet and stared at her shoe. I lit a new cigarette from the first, something I never do.

"Daddy ran away for a few years," she said, detached, "and left me alone with my big brother. We moved in with an aunt and shared a small trailer outside of town."

Sandy took another long drag from her cigarette. Her hand trembled. She placed the cigarette neatly back in the ashtray.

"Unfortunately, my brother is his father's son." Sandy's little smile was as cynical and as vicious as I'd ever seen. "He started coming into my bed, asking me to do things." Her voice was flat, like she was reading off a grocery list.

"I complied," she said, "because I was afraid of my brother, but I was more afraid of being alone."

Sandy had become flushed, her breathing shallow. Her face had shame and anger fighting each other for shotgun.

"This went on for a couple of years, until my father came back. He moved us into a shack. He saw that his little girl had grown up, so on his first night back, he took turns with my brother, using me."

I felt my sandwich lurch for an exit. I didn't want to hear this.

"At that point I did pretty much whatever I was told." She smiled, ruefully. "Even servicing some of my father's friends when they came over."

I was getting nauseous, and I felt a red blossom of anger raging directly behind my sternum.

"Then I was told to marry a rich man in town." She flicked her hand. "Which I did without question. I was married for almost a year." Sandy frowned. "He made me perform like a circus act. I was 15." Sandy shook out another cigarette, even though she already had one burning. This time, I lit it for her. "Thank you, Roy," she said, quietly.

She was quiet for a while. I thought to prompt her, but I wasn't sure I wanted to hear anymore.

"My first husband died," she continued, "and I got some money, which the men of my family were happy to grab. A while later I was told to marry another man." Sandy's lip twisted into a half-snarl. "*He* used me as a toilet."

I rubbed behind my ear. My lump was starting to throb again.

"Somehow or other, my second husband died too, and I got some more money." Her eyes came up to mine. "But I wasn't a little girl anymore." Sandy smiled again, this time like a cat with feathers on its chin.

"I kept most of the money," she said, "and ran away." Sandy reached over and took a sip from her coffee cup.

"Daddy and big brother weren't too happy about that." Another feral grin. "Like I gave a fuck."

Sandy noticed she had two cigarettes going and crushed them out.

"I eventually met a nice man," she said. "A man who treated me with kindness and respect, who gave me a wonderful child, who gave me the closest thing I've ever had to love."

She leaned forward and showed me some canines.

"I would do *anything*," she said tightly, "to protect them." Sandy stared at me for a moment, then sat back and waved at the air.

"And that's the end of story time."

I fiddled with a pen and pushed some things around on my desk. I let some time burn off. I was flattered, angry and suspicious at the same time.

Flattered because she'd confided in me and wanted badly for me to be on her side, angry because if any of this were true, then there were men out there who needed killing...and suspicious because that is my nature. But if she was playing me, she was doing a masterful job.

"So," I finally said, "Elvis is back and wants his pimp's cut." I paused. "And you're paying him off with the credit card scam." She twitched at the mention of the scam. "He threatens to take Peter out, but you hold him off with promises of riches. Then the Star drops into your hand." I pulled on my cigarette and watched for any reaction. "And it looks like you might be able to get Elvis out of your life."

Sandy glanced at me coolly. "I thought about it, yes," she said, "but I never took the Star." She grimaced. "Someone beat me to it."

I nodded like I believed her.

"Where's your father? What happened to him?" I asked.

Sandy gathered her purse and stood up. "That's what keeps me up at night."

"You don't know where he is?"

"All I know is the man's still alive," she said. "I can feel it in my bones." She turned to go.

"Sandy?"

"Yes?"

"Elvis was with you when Jenny was murdered, right?"

She nodded, almost reluctantly. "Yes."

"So someone else murdered Jenny."

"Yes," she said. "Without question." No lie was apparent in her voice, or if there was, I couldn't hear it.

"You still want me to find her murderer?"
She slumped a little.
"Yes," she said. "Yes, I do."

CHAPTER THIRTY ONE

Sandy's story had been like a blow to the face. It felt like it had sucked the life out of the room, leaving a vacuum. Now that she and her horror story were gone, there was a hole in my office, one that needed to be filled with ideas. I sighed and propped my Doc Martens up on the desk. I had my best ideas when I could see my feet.

Sandy's little tale seemed to bolster Eddie's theory. She might be trying to protect her family, by any means necessary. Hence the credit card scam. Elvis had shown up about six months ago, unknowingly leading Brett and Rachael to Sandy's world. The Voorhees twins had befriended Elvis—Brett with drugs, Rachael with sex—and had attached themselves like barnacles to the reunited Boone clan. Jenny Monroe was already in place, an established part of Sandy's life.

If Eddie's theory was correct, Sandy was paying off Elvis regularly, and Brett and Rachael were waiting around for— what? Revenge? Justice? Then Elvis discovers from Larry or Sean that the Brett-Rachael duo were the children of the man he'd killed, and that he'd been played for a chump. He subsequently flips out and murders Rachael.

Brett might have thought that since I was working for the Aguayos, I might also be working for Elvis, and that could be the reason he got skittish when I showed up in Emeryville, especially after the death of his sister. Still, it was no excuse for ruining Octavio's suit.

Jenny had been Sandy *and* Rachael's lover, which would explain Sandy's less than flattering description of Rachael. But if Elvis' alibi was real, he had been with Sandy when Jenny had been killed, which left another killer out there.

Or maybe Sandy was the killer. Could she have been in a jealous rage and driven over to Jenny's, with or without Elvis, and put a bullet in her head? That didn't feel right. Jealousy over Rachael's relationship with Jenny didn't seem like a strong enough motive for murder, but I could be wrong. The bottom line was that Sandy didn't strike me as an impulsive person, and impulsive rage didn't suit her, or else Elvis would have been dead a long time ago–if her story were true. That meant someone else, with another motive, killed Jenny.

And why had Rachael been planning to move in with Joey Kimble, that skinny maitre d' at the Millennium Restaurant? Was it for convenience? Rachael had already gotten a taste of Elvis' knuckles, so maybe Joey was just a safe place to land. She probably sensed that Elvis could escalate the violence at any time, so maybe she was looking for a hideout. Maybe she sensed her subterfuge couldn't last forever and decided to cut the cord. She couldn't stay at Brett's—Elvis knew where that was.

But then again, why did Brett have another place in Emeryville? Was it just a bolthole, or something else? And what about the $50,000 in the bag? And while I'm asking questions, where was Sandy's father? And where in the hell was the Star?

This case was laying the foundation for a world-class ulcer.

I tilted the iMac toward me and checked my e-mail. Sammy Mayfair had sent over a background on the Aguayos' butler, Samuel Becker. He'd pulled a blank on the Star of Siddhartha, but I couldn't fault him as the Star of Siddhartha was nonexistent.

Samuel was exactly the person he claimed to be, which in this case was quite refreshing. Becker had been a Marine, became a master gunnery sergeant, then retired. He started working for Peter Aguayo five years ago, right after Peter and Sandy's marriage, and if there were any skeletons in his closet, I wasn't seeing them. No joy there. I had been harboring a fantasy that Samuel might be the mysterious long-lost psycho degenerate father of Sandy Aguayo, but no soap—it was a soap-free zone. "All Ye Who Enter Here, Abandon All Soap," I said aloud, to amuse myself.

But maybe it was just as well. I kinda' liked Samuel, and I wouldn't be able to face my friends at the SFPD if I had a case where the butler actually did the crime. That's one cliché I'd never live down.

I stared at my feet in disappointment.

"You're failing miserably as a source for ideas," I said to them. "I'm seriously thinking of firing you."

Just then a knock came at my door. Maybe Sandy had forgotten something.

I gave my feet a stern look. "I'll deal with you later," I said curtly. I looked up. "Come in," I said. "It's open."

My door opened and a woman's head peeked in. The rest of her followed shortly thereafter. It wasn't Sandy. She was older than Sandy, considerably, and had gigantic glasses that magnified her eyes to the size of my forming ulcer. She was about 70, with her hair done up in one of those perfect coifs that only 70-year-old ladies can carry off. The hair was champagne-colored, as was her skin. She had on a powder-blue Adidas running suit made of some kind of microfiber. Her shoes were white with pink accents and candy-striped laces that matched the running suit. Her headband, to my dismay, matched her shoes.

"Mr. Jobe?" she said.

"I am he."

"It says on your door that you're a private investigator."

"It does?"

She got flustered. I felt bad.

"I was just kidding," I said guiltily. "It does indeed say 'Private Investigator.'"

She looked relieved.

I gestured.

"Please, have a seat."

She sat, and looked disapprovingly at my ashtray. I whisked it off the desk and dumped the whole thing into my wastebasket.

"What can I do for you, Ms.—?"

"Eunice," she said. "Mrs. Eunice Hudson."

"Very well, Eunice, how may I assist you?"

She looked around my office. "I've never met a detective before."

"Then consider yourself lucky," I said. "We're a bad lot."

She laughed politely. So did I. She fidgeted a bit before speaking.

"I have a problem," she said. "A rather unique one."

"They usually are, Eunice. That's what I'm here for."

She held a fanny pack in front of her, on her lap. "It involves a smell," she said, embarrassed.

"A smell?" I asked.

"Yes. A bad one."

"Hmmm...." I scratched my chin. "Those are the worst kind."

She gave me a schoolmarm look, a stern one, and I knew I'd better start behaving. "This smell, Eunice," I said, "where does it originate?"

"That's why I'm here, Mr. Jobe. I can't seem to find where it comes from."

I tapped my fingers on my desk. "And you would like to employ my services to find this odor?"

She brightened. "Yes, I would."

I thought about it. The Aguayo case wasn't going anywhere any time soon. I needed a distraction, and I needed to do something positive. I had to get the specter of Sandy's story out of my head, and put some perspective on the woes of the too-rich, the too-good-looking and the too-dramatic. I itched to "give something back to the community," as every professional athlete who got caught beating his wife has said. On top of that, Eunice seemed like a really nice old lady, and nice old ladies shouldn't have to spend their golden years fretting about unpleasant odors. It's simply not cricket.

Eunice started babbling. "It's from somewhere outside my window, at my apartment. On some days it's there and on others there's not a trace. It's got me so upset that I can't think straight." She took a breath. "I want it to stop. I bake peach cobbler once a week, and then this horrid odor wafts in from God knows where and fills my kitchen with its stench."

She looked like she was going to cry. I wasn't equipped for that. I'm never equipped for that.

"Needless to say," she said, somehow holding it together, "my cobbler tastes like that smell." She paused. "And I have to throw the whole batch out."

I felt a cold hand grip my heart. "You throw freshly-baked peach cobbler into the garbage can?" I asked, aghast.

"Yes." She was getting teary. "Four full baking pans."

I stood abruptly. "Not on my watch, lady. Homemade peach cobbler is my all-time, hands-down favorite." I put some passion into my voice. "This will not stand!"

She looked a little frightened. I pointed at her.

"Where do you live?" I demanded.

"On Commercial," she squeaked, "two blocks up from here."

I squinted. "Let's go, Eunice," I said grimly. "There's not a moment to lose."

CHAPTER THIRTY-TWO

E unice stared at me like I was a multi-tentacled squid creature from Mars. "Right now?" she asked, uncertainly.

"Yes," I said. "We need to nip this thing in the bud."

She thought about it, then bolted to her feet, eyes afire. "Right," she said, "time to lock and load."

Huh?

I followed Mrs. Eunice Hudson out of my building and we power-walked the two blocks to Commercial Street. She kept a good steady pace and had a look of grim determination about her. Halfway there we overtook a group of teenagers, chittering away like songbirds. As we passed, I felt their energy and optimism pulsing off them in waves. It was a welcome tonic to Sandy's story.

We took a quick right and entered a four-story apartment building, probably one of Eddie's, and went up to the second floor. Eunice got her keys out of her fanny pack and unlocked the doorknob and the three deadbolts. I thought the three deadbolts were overkill, but I'm not 70. I followed her in.

Her apartment's floor plan was remarkably like mine, with a small hallway leading into a large living room and a bright, open kitchen. The decor was contemporary, which surprised me. I guess I was expecting spindly Victorian pieces and fussy woven rugs and a lot of doilies and knickknacks. Instead, Eunice's tastes ran toward the European, with sleek furniture and a bunch of colors with names like latte and sea foam. Her living room had a large, light-colored sofa with two matching chairs. The coffee table and matching side-tables were made of spalted poplar and smelled of Lemon Pledge. No doilies.

I trailed her into the kitchen. It was immaculate, with new-looking appliances and white tile everywhere. She pointed to the window over the sink.

"That's how the smell gets in," she said. "I have to leave it open when I bake. Otherwise it gets too hot in here."

I leaned over the sink and stuck my head halfway out the window. It looked out on the building next to it. About 25 feet of air separated the two. I looked straight down at an alley with a number of blue dumpsters lined neatly against the walls. To the left was a slice of Commercial Street, with the occasional flash of pedestrian. To the right, about four feet from my face, was a brand-new, galvanized vent shaft that ran down Eunice's building and disappeared into the wall at street level. It was rectangular, about one foot-by-two. I looked up and saw that it continued all the way up to the top of the building. Having spied the shaft, I deduced the source of the odor to be a small break in one of the shaft's sections, slightly below Eunice's window. Someone was probably brewing something foul in the subbasement and venting it up the side of the building and letting it spew over the rooftops. Whatever it was, it wasn't city-approved. This area was zoned residential.

I pulled my head back into the apartment.

"I'm pleased to report that I've broken this case wide open," I said confidently. She looked at me like I was an idiot, but I forged ahead. I described to her what I'd seen and asked her if she knew what was happening in the basement.

"It's the laundry area, Mr. Jobe," she said, face scrunched up, "but there are rooms I've never been in."

"Is there a superintendent I can speak to?" I asked.

"Yes, but I've called him several times," she said. "*He* says I'm imagining things." She looked indignant, and rightfully so.

"How long has this been going on, Eunice?"

"On and off for about three months."

I nodded. "Okay, give me his number. I'll talk to him."

Eunice went to the Rolodex on the kitchen counter and rummaged around for a minute. She found the number and wrote it down on a piece of paper. I tucked it into my wallet and handed her one of my cards.

"I'll give him a call and see what I can do," I said. "In the meantime, if the smell returns, call me right away."

She nodded. "We haven't discussed your fee."

I thought for a moment, rolling over in my mind the cost benefit ratio, vendor fees, supply chain management issues and, of course, shipping and handling.

"I'll take it in trade," I said. "One pan of peach cobbler, once a month, for three months."

She beamed. "Deal."

CHAPTER THIRTY-THREE

I descended to the basement and found a long, low room filled with washers and dryers. The floor was cement and the walls were unpainted cinderblock. It was clean and warm and smelled of fresh laundry. I headed to where I thought the vent should enter the building, but ran out of space. The vent was behind a wall at the far end of the room, and the only access seemed to be a stout steel door with a keypad instead of a lock. No chance of picking *that*. The complexity of the locking mechanism made me suspicious; it was expensive and entirely too sophisticated for a storage or boiler room.

Outside in the alley, I checked where the vent punched into Eunice's building. It was two feet above my head and went flush into the wall, with clear plastic caulking sealing it cleanly. A dead end.

I returned to my office and checked phone messages and e-mail. Nothing. I called the number Eunice had given me and left a message for the building super to call me back. Calling Eddie, I left a message asking him if he knew who owned Eunice's building. Next I contacted Jumbo Choi and Rupert Park and spoke briefly to both. I e-mailed Sammy Mayfair and asked him to look into Joey Kimble, the maitre d' at the Millennium Restaurant and Rachael's boyfriend. Phoning the Sea Captain Motel, I dropped a message for Sean and Larry, then called the hospital to check in with Octavio. He was sleeping.

I locked up and went to my apartment, where I stripped, did stretches for half an hour, then took a long, hot shower. I crawled into bed and took a nap. I had a busy night ahead me.

CHAPTER THIRTY-FOUR

I woke up at five, feeling like a basket of fresh strawberries. Someone somewhere in Chinatown was cooking something in red chili oil and garlic, with a suggestion of oyster sauce. The fragrance oozed into my apartment via a process akin to osmosis and made me react like Pavlov's dog.

I went into the kitchen and put two cups of water into the blender, then added a banana, two scoops of vanilla-flavored whey protein and tossed in some blueberries. I gulped it down and made a flagon of French roast. Sitting in my favorite chair, I sipped my coffee and read John Burdett's *Bangkok 8* for about an hour.

At 6:30 I changed into gray cotton sweat pants and a white long-sleeved t-shirt. I put on my black, calf-high Adidas boxing shoes and laced them up tight. I went to my gym bag and pulled out a groin protector, thought about it, and tossed it aside, and did the same with my headgear. Checking to make sure I had gloves, tape, mouthpiece and scissors, I then threw in a change of clothes, shaving kit, a white towel, my wallet, cell phone and handgun, then zipped it up.

I shadowboxed for about 15 minutes, working up a thin sweat, then stretched some more. Keys in hand, I jogged to my car, keeping the sweat going.

I made my way out to 2576 Third Street. The Third Street Gym was a newish boxing gym with two full-sized rings and no parking. It had spectator seating and heavy bags, speed bags, double-end bags, uppercut bags and a full complement of weights. The clientele was upper income and not too pretentious, mostly guys and gals trying to get into shape. The guys who ran the place had been Golden Glove champs at one time or another, so the joint had credibility.

I'd been here a number of times and liked it, but I remained faithful to my home gym. My gym, McCoy's, was old school, a seedy place under a freeway overpass that smelled of mildew and Pine-Sol, with patches in the mat and ring ropes that sagged. The showers begrudged only tepid water, and the heavy bags were more duct tape than canvas.

What's not to like?

I circled Third Street a couple of times until I spotted a semi-legal parking spot and snagged it before a busload of crippled orphans or blind nuns beat me to it. Parking in the City takes a heart of stone.

I grasped my bag and jogged to the gym, ducking through the door.

The place was packed. I immediately deduced this wasn't the regular crowd, as most were cops. Some were still in uniform, and I had a work-based acquaintance with most. I walked through the crowd, nodding hellos, then approached Petey.

"What the fuck?" I asked, eloquently.

Petey shrugged.

"I might have mentioned you'd be here," he said, "in passing."

I looked over the throng. There were close to 30 cops here, talking shop and passing money. Some were from Oakland, a couple from Berkeley. About five of the cops were youngsters, clustered around the far ring, watching Sean Stewby warm up.

I shook my head.

"Fuck me, why didn't you just sell tickets?"

"What makes you think I didn't?"

I laughed and followed Petey to the ring where Stewby was sparring.

I took off my shirt and, as usual, heard the murmurs. I'd gotten used to them, just like I'd gotten used to the scars that caused them. I had a beaut that started at my right collarbone, blazed its way across my chest and ended just under my left nipple. That was a gift from a South American guerilla who didn't like American Marines, out of uniform, traipsing around his country. I had a nice star-shaped bullet scar on my left side, very much like Octavio would now have, from a psychopath I was trying to arrest for the murders of three nurses. I'd shot him in the eye shortly after he shot me. My back displayed a large half-moon burn scar where my father had pressed an iron skillet to my bare skin, with his boot, when I was 13. Nine small puncture scars dotted the left side of my back from shrapnel, to round everything off. And that was just above my waist.

Am I macho or what?

Petey asked me, again, where I got the scars, and again, I informed him they were the result of under-tipping a French waiter. It's a running gag. You had to be there.

As he taped my hands, I watched Stewby prance around a kid a little shorter than me and a little wider than a Nile ferry, poking him with a decent jab. Stewby had good footwork and good fundamentals, as he'd been brought up in a boxing family. His dad, Sean Sr., was now Deputy Chief Stewby and had been a pretty fair light heavyweight in his day and his grandfather had boxed professionally as a welterweight, before electricity.

But none of that was going to help him. Not tonight.

Petey laced my gloves and rummaged in my bag for my mouthpiece. He held it up; I shook it off. I went through the ropes into the ring, followed by Petey and waited in my corner.

The big kid sparring with Stewby gave me an ugly grin and exited. I made a note to have a chat with him later.

Petey went to the center of the ring and motioned Stewby toward him.

"Sean," he said, "Roy here,"—he waved me over—"would like to know if you'd be willing to spar with him, you know, friendly like."

"Ain't nothing friendly about it, fatman," Stewby said, pointing a glove at me. "We both know what we're here for. Let's quit fuckin' around."

"I'll take that as a yes," Petey said.

Stewby glared at me. My terror knew no bounds.

Prompted by Petey, we retreated to our respective corners. I looked over the crowd and felt guilty. Most of these guys had come here on their time off and were expecting a show. I was just here to administer a lesson.

Petey pointed to us, raised his hands and backed out of the way.

Stewby circled me warily, like a hooker eyeing an unmarked. I kept my hands down by my waist. He juked like he saw it done on television and threw some head fakes. My hands stayed down. This made him mad, as it exhibited a complete lack of respect for his pugilistic skills.

His first punch was a haymaker, which he telegraphed from Machu Picchu. I slipped it easily and looped a vicious overhand right into his throat. He staggered back and clawed at his neck, which is hard to do with boxing gloves on. I ripped two left hooks into his ribs and thought I felt one snap. He was defenseless at this point and he wanted to fall, so I stood him up with a crisp uppercut. The combinations that came next made him a walking testimonial not to fuck with me.

The first punch broke his nose; the other four or five made it mush. It took three guys to pull me off him, and even then it was a close thing.

I came out of my haze and let myself be pushed to a neutral corner by Petey.

I held my gloves out to him.

"Cut 'em off."

Petey had a goofy grin on his face.

"Sure, champ."

"What's so funny?" I asked.

Petey kept cutting and smiling.

"See those guys over there?" He poked the scissors at the group of young cops. "The ones with the long faces?"

I hummed a yes.

He chortled.

"I just made 'em lighter by 500 bucks."

I gave them all a long, unpleasant look.

"You ought to be ashamed of yourself, Petey, shearing the yearlings."

He shook his head.

"Uh-uh, they came to me. I just accepted their wagers."

I tsked.

"You're a pirate, Petey, a regular Morgan."

Petey's smile faltered a little as he looked over at Stewby. My opponent was prone on the mat, with a couple of guys kneeling next to him. A ruby towel that used to be white was clutched to his face.

"You really fucked him up," Petey said quietly. "Sometimes you scare me."

I didn't feel bad about it. Not one bit.

I stared a couple more holes into Stewby's friends.

"Fucker had it coming," I said.

CHAPTER THIRTY-FIVE

I stepped out of the ring and meandered toward the showers. A lot of cops smiled and nodded, but most were too smart to congratulate me outright. Stewby's father was still the deputy chief, and there was nothing to be gained by glad-handing the guy who had just beaten the living shit out of his son. The out-of-town cops had no such restraints and slapped my back with some "well dones" and "about times." Apparently, Stewby's assholism had reached the point of legend.

I showered, basking in the joy of a continuous stream of hot water. I dried off and changed into some loose-fitting Nautica jeans and a gray long-sleeved t-shirt. I then slipped on some dark blue Nike basketball shoes, and doffed a Raiders cap, bill in front, because that's how God wants it.

When I came out of the locker room, Stewby and most of the cops were gone. Petey was there, and much to my surprise, so was Liz Ishida.

Petey gave me a look, smiled at Liz and left.

Liz was out of uniform. She wore blue jeans and a white blouse. Her hair was loose and hung to the middle of her back.

"Been here long?" I asked.

"Long enough."

I paused. This was where women started looking for an excuse to be anyplace else.

"Sorry you had to see that," I said.

She eyed me like an archeologist over a fresh dig.

"You're a very violent man."

"Yes," I said quietly. "I am."

"How come?"

I sighed. "A thousand reasons," I said, "none of which I understand. It's just part of my nature."

She raised a brow.

"I never saw this side of you," she said, puzzled. "Not that I've seen that much. I mean, I didn't pick it up on my mandar." She looked disappointed in herself. "I'm usually pretty good about things like that."

"Don't be so hard on yourself," I said lightly. "You're not the first to miss it." I paused again. "And you're not the first to bolt because of it."

She frowned. "What makes you think I'm going to bolt?"

"Your face," I said. "And experience."

She crossed her arms and looked at me askance. "Uh-uh." She shook her head. "You're not off the hook." Her hands went to her hips. She looked combative. "I'll admit, it's a little unnerving, but I don't scare easily."

We stared at each other. Activity surrounded us. The treadmills kept up a mechanical hum as a backbeat for slapping feet. People were in the rings sparring. Men and women were hitting the bags and clanking weights. Gym chat buzzed.

Somewhere, my mind registered the sounds and smells, but I was only seeing myself reflected in her eyes.

Liz smiled.

"You hungry?" she asked.

"Starving."

She hooked her arm in mine and led me to the door.

"Take me to my place," she said, "and I'll whip up some food."

"That's an offer impossible to refuse."

The corner of her mouth tugged up.

"I know."

Outside, it had darkened, and the breeze had some teeth in it. I barely felt it. I put my arm around Liz and held her close. Her arm encircled my waist as we walked to my car.

"How'd you get here?" I asked.

"I hitched a ride with Petey," she said. "I figured you wouldn't mind giving me a ride back."

"Presumptuous of you."

"Yep."

Liz lived on Polk, near Washington. I loved this neighborhood. It was filled with small shops and cozy bars and corner markets with old Italian men who remembered your name. There were sidewalk cafes, trendy clothing stores and florists with wares spilling out into the street. People were everywhere. On a summer's night like this, the streets buzzed with energy. Movement, colors, smells and sounds swirled like a million baitfish up from the depths. I felt alive and electric, due in no small part to the woman sitting next to me.

We made a game attempt at finding a parking spot, but settled for a garage about five blocks from her apartment. We took our time walking back, grazing the scene like indolent cattle. I hadn't felt this relaxed since I got medicated for my last surgery.

Liz led me through a doorway set between a jewelry shop that sold hand-carved bead necklaces and a used bookstore. Liz lived on the top floor of the three-story building. She gave me the tour. It was a one-bedroom place with a living room that had shiny wooden floors and walls painted a muted cream. A fat sofa and matching chair were in the middle of the room, with an Amish-built coffee table atop a throw rug. Her kitchen was at the back, with high ceilings and stand-alone sinks that you could take a bath in.

Liz sat me down on the couch and disappeared for a minute. She came back with two icy Sierra Nevada ales and sat next to me.

"What's for dinner?" I asked.

She took a long, unladylike pull from her beer. I respected that.

"Pan-seared petrole sole in a butter cream sauce, homemade chicken-and-prosciutto raviolis with pesto, sautéed baby carrots, snow peas, shallots and pine nuts"—she took a another healthy swig—"paired with white wine in a jug."

"Righteous." I salivated. "Need some help?"

"After our beers," she said.

We sipped our beers in comfortable silence. I could feel the day slough off me in sheets. I timed my last gulp with hers and followed her to the kitchen.

Liz poured two glasses of wine and set me up prepping the vegetables. She started water boiling and heated the sauces, then seared the fish to a crispy brown. I had the vegetables ready by then and she tossed them into a pan with a little olive oil and garlic. Our hands were busy and our mouths were shut, and it felt as natural as rain. Liz arranged the feast on plates and instructed me to set the table with cutlery, placemats and linen napkins.

We sat down and I toasted her.

"Hail to the chef."

"Mud in your eye," she said.

We dug in. It was perfect.

Just like at our lunch, Liz ate neatly. She cut pieces of fish that were proportionate with the vegetables, and each ravioli was halved before disappearing into her mouth. We made small talk, and I was surprised to find that I held my own. There seemed to be an unspoken agreement not to talk shop, and I had no trouble upholding my end of the bargain.

We finished and stacked the dishes into the sink. I started to soap them, but Liz stopped me.

"I'll do those tomorrow," she said. "Let's finish our wine."

I topped off our glasses and we sat at the table.

"That was delicious, Liz. Thank you."

"You're welcome."

I sipped my wine and enjoyed the glow she brought to the room.

"Not to sound ungrateful," I said, "but what's for dessert?'

Liz put her glass down and came over to my side of the table. She sat on my lap and put her arms around my neck. The kiss that followed was long, deep and soft.

"Me," she said.

CHAPTER THIRTY-SIX

Liz's alarm went off at half-past midnight, and as is my habit, I awoke instantly. Without shifting position, I reached over and slapped it off. Liz was nestled deep in the crook of my arm, and her warmth was that of bread five minutes out of the oven. Her skin was soft and velvety, and she smelled of soap and light rain and good dreams. I kissed her neck and she stirred; her eyes fluttered open. She reached up and pulled my head down to hers and gave me a long, wet kiss. Her mouth was liquid fire. We made love again, this time slowly, with the patience of familiarity. It was different than last night, when we had consumed each other like hungry lions. Even our noises were softer, more sigh than scream, more moan than roar.

Once again, we finished in concert, sated and content.

The buzz of Polk Street had settled into a gentle hum, softened by the blanket of night. It murmured quietly, like a receding tide over pebbles.

On our backs, we stared at the dark ceiling, taking in each other's scent.

"I have to go," I said.

"I know," she said, from somewhere deep in her throat. "But I don't have to like it."

I got up and pulled on my clothes.

"When we gonna' do this again?" she asked, wickedly.

I smiled.

"As soon as humanly possible."

I kissed her goodbye and left.

Outside on Polk, most of the shops were closed, but the bars still had some life to them. I stopped by an all-night market and bought a pack of Gauloises and lit up. When I was with Liz, I hadn't even thought of cigarettes, but now that I was back on the hunt, my addiction screamed for attention.

I got to my car without mishap and paid the bored attendant enough money to finance a coup. I drove to Chinatown and located a spot a block up from the Red Pagoda.

Inside, Jumbo Choi was bussing the tables, and I noted he'd recruited Rupert Park to stash the well liquor into the back cabinets. Aside from them, the place was empty. They looked up when I came in.

"'Bout ready?" I asked.

"Five minutes," Jumbo said. "Help yourself to a drink."

"Thanks."

I went behind the bar and put two fingers of Dewar's into a highball glass. I sipped it while I toweled down the bar.

Jumbo and Rupert pulled up a couple of bar stools and I opened two beers for them. I stayed behind the bar.

"The Joy Boys should be over on Hang Au by now," I said, "starting their day. Let's give 'em another 10 minutes before heading over."

Jumbo grunted; Rupert nodded.

We finished our drinks and Rupert and I walked outside. Jumbo shut down the jukebox and the lights and met us on the curb. We hiked up Clay a block and a half and turned onto Hang Au Street. Toward the end of Hang Au, we ducked into an unpleasant-smelling alley with standing puddles of water. It curved to the left and dumped us at the back door of a noodle factory. The back of the factory was mostly window, with wired panes painted dull black. Three stairs led up to a wide cement loading dock, and a battered light arched out of the building's wall above the door, illuminating a 50-foot circle. The heavy door was ajar and a number of barrels and crates were stacked on the platform. On the platform were six young Asian men. Five were Joy Boys; the other guy was Randall Tang.

The Joy Boys were dressed in young men's attire: hyper-baggy jeans with "beater" t-shirts under short-sleeved checked shirts, untucked. Enough gold chains hung around their necks to tow a garbage scow, and each had a one- or two-carat diamond stud in the left ear. All the Joy Boys sported a trademark 18-carat gold Rolex Cosmograph Daytona with a diamond face, hanging like a bracelet from each skinny wrist. Everyone knew a Joy Boy by his watch.

Randal Tang was dressed like Roy Orbison.

They smoked cigarettes and yakked, and stopped doing both when we came into view.

I approached them with arms spread wide. Jumbo and Rupert hung back.

"Gentlemen," I said. "I simply can't describe what a pleasure it is to see you."

They all stared at me with eyes that would make a pinball machine look tranquil. The Joy Boys made their money from crystal meth, and they were users. I wish I could say they were simply unfortunate youths, products of broken homes, but most of them had made the dean's list in college and had carried a grade-point average higher than my cholesterol. They were businessmen, hard as rocks. They saw meth for what it was, a homegrown product you didn't have to smuggle past the Coast Guard and the DEA. You could pretty much make it anywhere; and since at least three of the Joy Boys had degrees in chemistry, it was easy as baking a cake.

"What do you want, cracker?" Randall asked.

I pointed at him.

"You."

He laughed and looked over at his new cohorts. They stared back at him with eyes suddenly gone flat.

Realization dawned on Tang's face. He looked like he'd just bitten into a jelly doughnut filled with maggots.

"So that's how it is," he stated.

The Joy Boys continued staring.

"Fine," he said.

Randall Tang hopped down from the platform and moved toward me. When he was 10 feet away, a buck knife appeared in his hand. It was about four inches long, with a satin finish and a bone handle. He was moving at me pretty fast, so in a blink, I bent my knee and transferred my .38 to my hand. If the quick draw was an art, I was Picasso.

I shot him in the shin.

Tang went down, screaming. The Joy Boys, looking shocked, pulled out their nine-millimeters and held them at their sides. I wasn't worried. Jumbo had a sawed-off double-barreled 10-gauge and could take out all five if it came to that. Rupert had his hand inside his jacket, the threat implicit.

I walked over to Randall Tang and kicked his knife away. I motioned to Jumbo and he tossed a Louisville Slugger to me. He kept this bat behind the bar, and it had cracked its share of heads.

I went to work on Tang's leg and noted that one of the Joy Boys vomited over the edge of the platform.

I tossed the bat back to Jumbo. Tang had passed out. I put on my latex gloves and picked up his knife. Pinning his leg with my foot, I cut his pant leg lengthwise, then quickly dug out my .38 slug. No ballistics trail meant I wouldn't have to get rid of my gun. I liked my gun. I put the bloody slug into a handkerchief and slipped it into my pocket.

"Get him to an emergency room," I said to the Joy Boys. "Then put him in a car back to Seattle."

I pointed at them.

"If I see him around town again," I growled, "you're next."

I turned and walked to Jumbo and Rupert. They backed away from the Joy Boys, keeping their eyes open for any sudden, stupid moves.

On the way back to the Pagoda, Rupert gave me a look.

"What?" I asked.

He shook his head.

"Nothin'," he said.

"Fucker had it coming," I said, for the second time in a day.

"That's a fact," Jumbo said. "How about we get a couple of drinks?"

I smiled. "A sterling idea."

We went back to the Pagoda and did just that.

CHAPTER THIRTY-SEVEN
Friday

I woke up a couple of hours later with a mechanic's rag in my mouth. My head hurt from drinking with Jumbo and Rupert, and my hands, torso, knee and the lump behind my ear were thundering down the home stretch to see who could be the most unpleasant. My knee was winning by a nose, but my hands were going to place in the money.

I got up, creakily, and made some coffee. After the first cup I felt like a lower-rung marsupial, which was a vast improvement. After the second, I'd evolved to a creature just below human. I believed that was as good as it was going to get.

I showered, shaved and dressed in a cream suit over a pink shirt. I got my one and only Rolex out of my document safe and slipped it on. The Rolex was an extravagant gift to myself after a big case with an equally big paycheck, and it had a blue face with a stainless-steel and 18-carat gold band. It was a Submariner, which meant I could solve mysteries while under 200 feet of water.

I checked myself in the mirror and decided I looked like a Miami pimp, but the colors and the flash of the Rolex made me feel better, so today, a pimp I'd be.

I scooped the paper off my doorstep and limped down to the café. I sat down and watched as Wei Lee, with a forearm cast and wired jaw, walked to my table. He pointed to his face.

"Not you fault," he said. "You try to help." He put out his good hand. "Thank you."

I shook his hand and my knee suddenly felt a lot better, although I was thinking; with friends like me, who needs enemas?

Wei left and was replaced by Eddie. He had a cup of coffee in one hand and a Bloody Mary in the other. He put them both down in front of me and sat.

"Jumbo left a message, said you might be needing this." He nudged the drink closer. "How're you feeling?"

I gulped down half the Bloody Mary. "Better, now."

He looked at my suit. "Been watching reruns of *Miami Vice*?"

"Ha ha."

"Everything taken care of?" he asked.

"Si."

He nodded. "Bueno."

Wei brought Eddie a coffee and followed that shortly with my breakfast. It was fresh cantaloupe with cottage cheese, scrambled eggs with diced ham, and whole wheat toast with lots of butter.

I poked a fork towards the kitchen. "Looks like Wei's doing all right, considering."

"Yeah," Eddie said. "He insisted on working, said he wanted to keep busy."

I grunted. "You got any information on Eunice's building?" I asked.

"Yep," Eddie said. "It's owned by a holding company out of Arizona." He sipped some coffee. "Carlisle Property Management in Foster City handles the details."

"What about the superintendent?" I asked.

"Sonny Itakura's in charge. Takes care of three other buildings in Chinatown."

"You know him?" I asked.

Eddie smirked. "Of course. I know everybody in real estate. Sonny worked for me a few years back. I gave him the boot."

"Oh?" I said.

"Uh-huh," Eddie said. "Caught him fencing hot PCs out of one of my offices."

"You don't say?"

"I do say."

This was getting interesting.

"What's happening with the Aguayo case?" Eddie asked.

"Plenty," I said, then brought him up to date with all the lurid details.

Eddie grimaced. "So you got a detective shot?"

"Well, technically, yes," I said, "but the way you say it, it sounds like a bad thing."

He laughed. "Silly of me," he said. "Call me tonight."

"All right."

Eddie went back to work, and I finished breakfast then went to my office.

I fired up my iMac and perused my e-mail. I cross-referenced what Sammy Mayfair had given me with the notes I'd made in my composition book. I wrote out a summary of events and stared at it for a while.

Nothing magical happened. No flashes of inspiration, no dots connecting, no breathtaking moment of clarity. Except...

I carefully reread a fact Sammy had dug up for me and felt a muscle twitch in my head. I could only hope it wasn't an aneurism. I felt it flicker and sputter, like a moist fuse, and I fought hard to keep it lit. I almost lost it, but then it caught.

I went online and Googled a little and was surprised to get three hits. I felt another twitch, this time with a little more power, and tucked it away. I couldn't tell if it changed the bottom line, but hope springs eternal.

Ultimately, solving this case boiled down to finding Elvis and Brett, and if Sandy's story was to be believed, maybe finding her long-lost father. I emailed Sammy and asked him to research Sandy's father, then picked up my ringing phone.

"Roy Jobe." I said.

"Roy? Petey."

"What's up?"

"Plenty," he said. "We've got a body in Pacifica, on Sharp Park Golf Course. You know the bulrushes along the beach hiking trail?"

"Yes," I said. "I believe I deposited a number of name-brand golf balls in its environs."

"I'm not surprised," he said. "Anyway, a body fitting the description of Brett Voorhees was found by some hackers."

"Any ID on him?"

"Yeah. Driver's license says he's Brett Rodgers. You're the only guy I know, besides my shot-up partner, who's seen him; I need you to come down here and ID him."

"Give me 30 minutes." I hung up.

I jogged to my car and headed out to Highway 101, then got on Interstate 280 to the Coast Highway. I aimed south, past Colma and Daly City, and took Sharp Park Road to the golf course. Traffic was normal so I was only 15 minutes late.

Sharp Park Golf Course, while in the city of Pacifica, was a San Francisco City public golf course and was run by the San Francisco Parks and Recreation Department. Don't ask me why. It was built in 1931 and designed by Alister MacKenzie, one of the top golf-course architects ever to grace the planet. He had designed Pebble Beach's Cypress Point, also in 1931, and Georgia's Augusta National in 1933.

Sharp Park was an unpretentious, blue-collar golf course, rough around the edges, which made it one of my favorites.

It had a small nylon cage where you could hit practice balls into the mesh, and cast-iron ball washers that worked only when they felt like it. The parking lot was half gravel and half asphalt, and there were as many Mercedes there as pickups.

I slid into a parking spot between a Lexus and an '84 Buick and went into the clubhouse.

The clubhouse was a one-story white stucco building that had seen better days. It boasted a tiny pro shop on the right and a restaurant and bar on the left. The carpet was threadbare and shredded by golf spikes, and the walls hadn't been painted since Nixon. But you could get a great breakfast here with a wonderful view of the first tee, and the bar was the kind you'd be comfortable bellying up to.

I told the starter I was with the police, and he gave me an ancient golf cart to drive out to where Petey and the CSU crew were processing the scene. Weaving my way out to the fifteenth hole, I inhaled the perfume of moist grass and the Pacific Ocean. The sun was out in force and had burned off most of the fog, leaving only a few weak tendrils to fend for themselves.

I cut across a couple of fairways to the derisive hooting of outraged golfers and pulled up next to the CSU van. The morgue van was between it and two Pacifica PD patrol cars and Petey's unmarked. The vehicles made a half circle around where I presumed the body to be.

Petey waved me over. "Hey!" he yelled. "Ice cream man!"

Jeez. Dress in some festive colors and everyone turns into a smartass.

"Thanks for coming, Roy," he said, eyeing my suit.

"No problem, Petey." We shook hands.

Petey had his jacket off and the sleeves of his white shirt rolled up, exposing beefy forearms. His tie was loosened and his straw porkpie was tipped high on his forehead. About 15 feet from where we were standing, a body lay on its back. It was at the edge of the rough, where the grass ended and the tule marsh began. Drag marks and broken bulrushes told me that someone from CSU had waded into the marsh to pull him out. There was no doubt that he was Brett Voorhees.

"Well?" Petey asked.

"That's him, all right," I said. "What happened?"

Petey gestured over at four very pale golfers clustered around a Pacifica PD patrol car. They all looked to be retirement age, with sun faded golf bags strapped to the ass end of their carts.

"Guy sliced his drive over this way," Petey said, "poked around in the marsh with his ball retriever and saw a hand." Petey grinned. "Surprised the hell out of him."

I studied the golfers as they pulled nervously on their cigarettes.

"How about we tell him his golf ball killed Brett," I said. "Really freak him out."

Petey laughed. "That would be mean. Funny as hell, but mean."

"Yeah." I said. "What's the cause of death?"

"I'll let Lisa fill you in."

Lisa Yuen was a coroner with whom I'd worked when I was still with the SFPD. She was a petite, pretty woman who dreamed of being five-foot. She wore jeans and a blue oxford shirt that she must've bought at the boy's department at Macy's. Her feet were tiny and encased in blue Reebok high-tops. I walked over to her.

"Hey, Lisa," I said.

She gave me a bright smile. "Roy! How the hell have you been?"

"Good, how about you?"

"Couldn't be better," she said. "I've got a one-year-old now, and I'm down to part-time at the morgue."

"I heard," I said. "Congratulations."

"Thanks, Roy. Wanna' see a picture?"

"It would complete my life."

Lisa pulled out a photo of very possibly the most beautiful baby I've ever seen. "This is very possibly the most beautiful baby I've ever seen," I said.

She snorted. "I know you, Roy—you say that to all the girls."

"I'm serious."

"So am I."

I smiled. "All right, what you got?"

Lisa squatted next to Brett's body. She maneuvered the head to the side and pointed to a gash.

"Blunt-force trauma," she said dispassionately. "Dollars to donuts it's the business end of a claw hammer. One hit and dead." She looked up at me. "He a friend of yours?"

I shook my head. "No. Petey asked me to ID him. I met him briefly during the course of an investigation."

Lisa gave me a look. "The scuttlebutt," she said, "says you've got two other bodies in your wake." She lifted a brow. "This one makes three."

I shrugged.

"It's a gift."

She smiled. "Let's not make this a habit, okay?"

"Sure, Lisa. Good seeing you again."

"Ditto." She winked. "Nice work on Stewby."

I grinned and went back to Petey. "What do you think?" I asked.

"The killer parked somewhere along the course," he said. "Plenty of access points." He paused. "He walked Brett out here and bashed him one. No witnesses. There's not a more deserted place on earth than a golf course at night. He rolled the body into the bog and went home. The grounds crew mowed the fairways and rough this morning, so no footprints or cigarette butts or nothin'."

"You think Elvis?" I asked.

"For lack of a better suspect," he said, "yes, I think Elvis."

We let it stew while we watched Lisa and her crew stuff the late Brett Voorhees into a body bag. Within minutes Brett was in the back of the van and we were waving goodbye to Lisa.

"Elvis can't be working alone," I said. "This town's not that big and we've got Oakland, Berkeley and the Peninsula looking for him."

Petey made a face. "Yeah," he grumped. "He's got help. Somewhere to stay, a clean car. Maybe he's using Rachael's BMW with stolen plates?"

"Could be," I said. "Around here, black BMWs are like freckles on a Mick."

"Watch it," Petey warned. "I'm half Irish."

"Who isn't?" I replied.

We watched a foursome tee off. One guy knocked it 230 yards down the middle of the fairway. The next guy hit it as far, but it went over the embankment between the golf course and the ocean. On the beach, literally.

"You got anything for me on Jenny Monroe?" Petey asked.

"As a matter of fact, I do."

"What?"

"It's just a hunch, but I'm going to follow up on it this afternoon," I said.

"How good a hunch?"

"Are you familiar with the odds on winning the state lottery?"

Petey shook his head. "Christ. I'm a dead man."

I patted him on the back. "Hang in there, Petey. I said I'd come through for you."

"Yeah," he said glumly."

"Trust me," I said, and left.

CHAPTER THIRTY-EIGHT

I hustled back to my office to find Eunice Hudson waiting for me in the hall. She had on a mauve running suit with wide alternating vertical pink and blue stripes that matched the laces on her black running shoes. On her head, she sported a pink tam-o'-shanter set at a rakish angle. She looked upset.

"Mr. Jobe," she said haltingly, "the smell is back."

I gawked at her outfit, then looked at my watch. Ten o'clock.

"All right, Eunice, let's get over there."

We did the power-walk thing again back to her apartment. The minute she opened the door I knew what we were dealing with.

I told Eunice to stay in the hallway. She covered her nose and nodded. I went in.

Her apartment reeked of a combination of ether, ammonia and acetone. It was a sickly-sweet stench that grew stronger the closer I got to her kitchen window. I took a deep breath and poked my head out to make sure the break in the vent was still there. It was.

I returned to Eunice.

"Take this," I said, handing her the key to my apartment. "Go to the American Café and ask Eddie Lee to let you into my place. You know where the café is?"

"Yes," she said, confused. "But why?"

I scowled and chewed on my lip a little. "I'm pretty sure

you have a meth lab in your basement, Eunice. Do you know what that is?"

Her eyes went big. "Yes, I do," she said. "I saw a documentary about them on KQED." Her mouth tightened. "You gonna' bust them?"

"I'm going to go down there and roust them, yes," I said.

Eunice thought for a moment.

"Then you're gonna' need backup," she said grimly.

Before I could stop her she slipped past me and disappeared into one of the bedrooms. Thirty seconds later, Mrs. Eunice Hudson came back to the front door with the biggest handgun I'd ever seen. She was loading slugs as thick as my thumb into the chambers as she walked towards me, then snapped the cylinder shut and gave it an expert spin. She held the gun up.

"Eighteen forty-eight second-model Dragoon," she said. "Forty-four caliber black-powder rounds, takes six. Case-hardened frame, walnut handles, blued barrel."

My mouth was agape.

"Anybody makes a move on you," she growled, "I'll pop a cap in his ass."

I took the gun away from her.

"Jesus, Eunice. Be careful with that."

She looked disappointed. "You're going to need help," she said. "I'll watch your six."

"Absolutely not. You're going to go to my apartment and wait."

She started to protest, but I held up my hand. "Don't worry, Eunice; I'm going to call a cop friend of mine to back me up." I paused. "I promise."

She frowned. "You sure?"

"Yes, Eunice," I said. "Let me handle this. It's what I get paid for."

She squinted at me, then sighed. "All right," she said grudgingly. "I'll go to your apartment. You got cable?"

"Yes, I do. And help yourself to coffee or anything else there. Okay?"

"Okay," she said. "You gonna' call me?"

"Yes. I'll call you in two hours, regardless of what happens. Let me have your house keys."

She handed me her keys, looked at her bazooka wistfully, and left.

I went to Eunice's kitchen and put her hand cannon on top of the refrigerator. *Jesus Christ.*

I went back out in the hall and locked her door behind me. Downstairs, on the sidewalk, I dialed Liz Ishida's cell phone. She answered on the first ring.

"Liz here."

"Liz, it's Roy."

"Hello, handsome."

My knees felt weak. "Hello, gorgeous."

"What's up?"

"It depends. Are you paired with Stewby?"

"No," she said. "Stewby's taking a few vacation days. They paired me with Floyd Meriwether."

That was good. "I know Floyd," I said. "He's a good man."

"He's a breath of fresh air, is what he is." She laughed, then paused.

"You calling me for a date?"

"Absolutely, but I've got some business you might be interested in first."

"Let's hear it."

I filled her in on what was happening and what I suspected. She put Floyd on the line and I explained it to him also. I liked

Floyd. He was a 15-year veteran and a stand-up guy. He agreed to meet me at Eunice's place in 20 minutes.

I hung out front and smoked a cigarette. Twelve minutes later a patrol car pulled up onto the sidewalk and Liz and Floyd popped out. I shook hands with Floyd and Liz, even though I wanted to throw a lip lock on Liz. Propriety and all.

"So," Floyd said, "what you got?"

"Let's go into the alley and I'll show you what's happening." I took them into the alley and pointed out the vent. "There's a break just outside Eunice's window," I said in a near-whisper. "I'm 99 percent sure it's a meth lab."

Floyd and Liz walked up to the vent and eyeballed it. They looked impressed.

"Let's go upstairs and you can smell for yourselves," I suggested.

We trudged up to Eunice's apartment and entered. Immediately, Floyd and Liz covered their noses.

"You're right, Roy," Floyd said. "Reeks to high heaven." Floyd and Liz went to the window and took turns checking out the vent.

We backed out of the apartment. "Definitely a meth lab," Floyd said. He looked over at Liz. "Remember this smell, Liz. File it away for future reference."

Liz nodded. Floyd was a good training cop, because he imparted knowledge without condescension. I could tell Liz appreciated it.

"How do we get to the basement?" she asked.

"Follow me," I said.

We went downstairs and I led them to the laundry room. I put my fingers to my lips and motioned to the steel door at the end. Floyd put his ear to the door and listened for a minute.

He gestured us out to the hall. "I heard movement in there," he said quietly. "Roy, let us take it from here. I'm calling for backup." He looked back at the door. "This the only way in?"

"Yes," I said. "I checked around the building and couldn't ascertain an alternate egress."

Liz and Floyd gave me a funny look.

"All right," Floyd said. "Liz, go out to the car and call Sergeant Garza on your cell. Don't radio; they might have scanners. Tell him I want three squad cars and a battering ram. After you call, get back here with the riot gun to back me up."

Liz nodded and left.

"Roy, stick with me until Liz gets back." He looked at my ankle. "You packin'?"

"Always," I said.

"Good."

We watched the steel door for a few minutes until Liz got back.

"Ten minutes," she said.

Floyd smiled, then pointed at me. "I appreciate the heads-up on this, Roy, but you gotta' go now."

"And miss all the fun?" I asked.

"'Fraid so."

I pouted. "All right."

"By the way," he said, "nice work on Stewby."

Word gets around fast.

I turned to Liz. "Can you call me on my cell after it goes down? I've got Eunice holed up at my place."

She arched an eyebrow. "You have a woman in your apartment?"

"Only in a professional capacity."

"Uh-huh. Okay, I'll call you."

"Be careful," I said, a little intensely. She grinned and Floyd looked at us with curiosity, but he didn't comment.

I left and returned to my apartment. Eunice let me in after the first knock. "How'd things go?" she asked.

"The police are there now," I said. "They're preparing to storm the ramparts."

"Awesome," she said. "We should go down there. I've never been in on a drug raid before."

I shook my head in dismay. "No, Eunice, please stay put. I have to go to my office for a minute, and then I'll bring some sandwiches over." I gave her a stern look, which she chose to ignore. "I don't want to have to worry about you," I said, "getting caught in a crossfire or something."

"But I've never seen a perp walk," she argued. Eunice looked defiant. This was not the meek woman I'd met yesterday.

"Please promise me you'll stay here," I pleaded.

She scrunched her face. "All right. I promise." She sighed. *"Days of Our Lives* will be on soon. I'll catch up on what's happening."

"Thank you, Eunice," I said, relieved. "I'll be back in about an hour. What kind of sandwich would you like?"

"I'll leave it up to you," she said. "I'm feeling adventurous."

"I noticed," I said. "Stay put."

"Roger that." She smiled. "And thanks for helping me out, Roy."

I smiled back. I liked Mrs. Eunice Hudson. "No problem, Eunice. My pleasure."

I left Eunice to her soaps and revisited my office. I called Octavio's hospital room number on my landline.

"Hey, Octavio, how're you feeling?"

"I have a hole in my side," he grumped. "Other than that, not bad."

"Yeah," I said, "sorry it went down that way."

"Que sera," he said. "How're my shoes?"

I'd completely forgotten about Octavio's cobalt shoes. I pulled open the file drawer I'd dumped them in. They looked none the worse for wear.

"I only left them alone for a minute, Octavio. I swear. As soon as my back was turned, they made a break for it."

He laughed. "What's happening with my case?"

I brought him up to speed on Brett Voorhees' fate and told him about the meth lab operation.

"Any news on Elvis?" he asked.

"Nothing. But I'm following up a hunch on Jenny Monroe this afternoon." I told him what I'd gotten from Sammy Mayfair, and the results of my online research. He agreed that my gut might be right and told me to keep him posted.

"When they gonna' spring you?" I asked.

"Tomorrow some time. I'm supposed to stay off my feet for a couple of weeks...as if."

"I hear you," I said. "You've got a date with Ruby next Saturday night. Maybe you can leverage your bullet wound into some sympathy sex."

"It's worth a try." He laughed. "Holla' back."

"Count on it," I said, and hung up.

My phone rang the instant it touched the cradle.

"Roy Jobe."

"Hey Roy, it's Sean."

"What's up, Sean? How's the Sea Captain?"

"A palace," he said. "A continental breakfast second to none. Bearclaws the size of your head." He paused. "Elvis called. I set up a meeting with him."

Finally, a break.

"That's good news," I said. "How'd he sound?"

"Pretty pissed off. Wanted to know why we hadn't put you in the hospital."

"What'd you tell him?"

"I told him you and two of your friends got the jump on us. Told him you guys put a bad beatin' on Larry and me."

"How'd he react?" I asked.

Sean laughed. "'Tough shit' were his exact words. He was going to cut us loose until I convinced him to meet with us."

"How'd you do that?"

"I told him we needed a couple of cheap handguns, said we were going to take you out," he said.

"That's quick thinking, Sean," I said, impressed. "Where and when?"

Sean gave me the details and I wrote them down on a slip of paper. I wasn't going to put this in my notebook in case I got hit over the head again. This was personal, anyway.

"Okay, Sean, thanks. I'll pick you guys up an hour before the meet," I said.

"See you tomorrow, Roy," Sean answered.

I locked up my office and walked down to Haj's Deli. While I walked, I rolled over in my head how I was going to handle Elvis. Gang tackle was what I was most comfortable with, but Elvis would be armed and I'd have to finesse it. I was concerned because finesse is not one of my strong points.

Inside Haj's, I waited my turn then ordered a turkey, swiss and avocado on wheat for Eunice, and a ham and provolone on light rye for me. I got some soft drinks and strolled to my apartment.

Eunice let me in and we sat down and watched Erica destroy a life or two while we ate. The food helped a little, but I was nervous and jittery about Liz. It was hard to sit here knowing that she was in the process of taking down a meth lab, but she was with Floyd and a bunch of veteran cops and they'd take care of her. I hoped.

I was thoroughly engrossed in *Days of Our Lives* and was actually annoyed when the phone rang halfway through someone getting caught in bed with another man's wife or mother or proctologist.

"Jobe."

"Roy? It's Liz."

The relief I felt surprised me.

"Are you okay?" I asked, a little too loudly. "How'd it go?"

"It went great, and everyone's fine."

I could hear the adrenaline in her voice, her breathing coming in short, excited bursts. She was ecstatic.

"I'm so pumped," she said. "This was a great bust." She took a gulp of air. "I love being a cop!"

I laughed.

"I can't talk now, Roy," she said. I could hear loud voices in the background. "Except to say that they're evacuating the building and bringing in a HAZMAT team. It's a major lab. There are 55-gallon drums of toxic material. The cleanup is going to take a while." I thought I heard her giggle. "Looks like your guest will be staying with you for a day or two."

I looked over at Eunice.

"They'll let her in for about five minutes later today to get some clothes and whatnot," she said. "Maybe her Victoria's Secret collection."

"You'll apologize to me for that crack later," I said. "Count on it."

"We'll see," she said. "I gotta' go. I'll fill you in later."

"All right. And Liz…I'm glad you're safe."

I could hear the smile in her voice. "That's music to my ears, Roy. Call you later."

"You bet," I said, and rang off.

I put the phone back in my pocket and found Eunice staring at me.

"Well?" she asked.

"All's well that ends well," I said. "They couldn't give me the details, but it looks like it was a clean bust."

"That's all you got?" she asked, disappointed. "Did anybody get shot? Did they have to Taser some punk bitch?"

"Eunice! The language!"

Her lip curled. "I'd'a Tasered him," she sniffed. "Fifty thousand volts of rehabilitation."

I stared at her. "Eunice, do you watch a lot of cop shows?"

"Why?"

I shook my head. "Never mind," I mumbled. I took a sip of my soda. "There is a slight hitch, though. They've evacuated the building so the Hazardous Materials Team can go in and clean up."

Eunice frowned.

"I can take you there later this afternoon or this evening to get some things, and you can stay here for the duration."

She looked worried. "That would be an imposition on you, Roy. I don't want to be a burden."

"It's no burden, Eunice. I like having you around. Consider it part of my service."

She smiled. "That's very kind of you, Roy Jobe. I appreciate it."

"You're very welcome, Eunice Hudson."

"How long do you think they'll be?" she asked.

"I'm not sure. A couple of days at the most." I got up and brushed some crumbs off my slacks. "I have to go into the office and do some work, though, and then I'm going to make a quick trip. Will you be all right alone for a while?"

She waved a hand in the air. "I've been taking care of myself for over 20 years now. I think I can handle it."

I smiled.

"Yes, I believe you can."

CHAPTER THIRTY-NINE

I left Eunice and somehow maneuvered my car out of the lot. I took a slip of paper with an address on it out of my shirt pocket and double-checked it. It was an East Bay address, on Prince Street off College Avenue.

Prince Street was in the Rockridge district of Oakland, on the border of Berkeley. The neighborhood was a concoction of '60s hippy kitsch and well-kept homes and apartments. The main drag, College Avenue, was jammed with small restaurants, independently owned espresso joints, head shops, an honest-to-God Birkenstock store, very trendy clothing stores, antique shops, the wonderful Elmwood movie theater and three or four small bookstores not named Barnes & Noble.

It took me 40 minutes to get to Prince Street and I slowed to a crawl to eyeball the addresses. I found what I wanted and parked about three blocks up.

Prince Street was a mellow tree-lined lane with old apartment buildings interspersed with neat little bungalows and beautifully maintained Victorians, with a couple of English Tudors thrown in for flavor. The address I was looking for, 2820 Prince, was a stately three-story apartment building with an elegant arabesque facade and a crenellated roof. The front entrance was inset about 10 feet into the building and had beveled glass doors with varnished wood borders.

It wasn't a security building, so I let myself into the wide lobby and looked around. The floors and walls were white marble with gray veins and there was a bank of brass mailboxes taking up the right wall. I found the name I was looking for and the corresponding apartment number and ascended the stairs to the second floor. I knocked lightly on number 236.

Joey Kimble opened the door. His face designed itself into a mixture of surprise, sadness and dread. He was wearing blue running shorts and a white tank top with blue and gold ASIC running shoes. Cal Berkeley colors. His legs were all muscle and sinew, built to eat up miles. My first take on the kid had been right. He was made to run.

I stuck out my hand. "You probably forgot my name," I said. "Roy Jobe."

He took my hand. "What can I do for you, Officer Jobe?"

I didn't bother to correct him. Shameless and duplicitous and self-serving. I almost felt bad about it.

"May I come in?" I asked.

Joey stepped away from the door and I went past him into the living room. The apartment's interior motif was frat house, with a big green couch that was 60 percent duct tape. The obligatory wire-spool coffee table had more scars on it than a Maasai elder, and there were just enough plastic patio chairs to host a Klan rally. The place was clean, though, and the carpet, while cheap, was relatively new.

I sat in one of the plastic chairs while Joey took the couch.

"I'm doing some follow-up on Rachael's murder," I started, "tying up some loose ends."

Joey sat forward and dry-washed his hands.

"So you haven't found Elvis?" He asked.

"Not yet, but it's only a matter of time," I said.

He looked disappointed.

I pulled out a small notepad with nothing on it and carefully read the blank page. "There's a connection here that's been bothering me though, Joey. It seems that Jenny Monroe and Rachael were lovers. You know anything about that?"

He didn't flinch. "No, nothing."

"Did you know that Jenny Monroe had been murdered?" I asked.

He acted surprised, but badly. "No, I didn't. When did it happen?"

I put the pad away. "On your day off."

He frowned. I saw a spark in his eye. It was either fear or anger, but I couldn't tell which.

He licked his lips nervously. "What's that supposed to mean?"

I sighed. "It means that you were a member of the NRA Collegiate Shooting Program; that according to the Civilian Marksmanship Program, you're an expert marksman." I took out my pad and read some more from the empty page. "You were a junior champion in the .22 caliber pistol category."

Joey's face flushed a little. "So?"

"So, Jenny Monroe was shot with a .22 caliber gun," I said, quietly. "Jenny was killed by someone she knew. There was no break-in, no signs of struggle. She opened the door and let her murderer in."

Joey's face went crimson. "And you think it was me?"

"I *know* it was you," I said, sharply. "You found out that Rachael and Jenny had a thing going, after Rachael swore up and down that you were her main man. You couldn't accept that. So you took out your target pistol and loaded it. You wrapped it in a towel or put it into a gym bag and went over to Jenny's house. You knocked on the door and she let you in. You asked her point-blank if she was Rachael's lover. She laughed at you and said, 'What of it?' You pulled out the gun and made her kneel in front of her coffee table; you put the barrel to the back of her head, *and then you pulled the trigger!*"

Joey's face was bright red, his breathing short and hot.

"After the deed you felt bad about it, Joey, because you're not a hard case at heart. This was a crime of passion, which, by the way, doesn't count for beans in the state of California. The thought of Jenny lying there for days, her body crawling with maggots, got to you. So you called the murder in from a pay phone and slept a little easier that night."

"You can't prove that," he said, a little too fast.

"The fuck I can't." I waved at the apartment. "You're buried in college loans—I checked. You make a mediocre living at the restaurant—I checked. Your degree in journalism hasn't paid off yet-that's obvious. You're barely scraping by."

Joey's eyes got sharp and crafty. "So what?"

"So what?" I scooted my chair forward so our knees were almost touching.

"I'll tell you 'so what.' A competition Ruger .22 caliber will set you back 500 bucks. That's the low end, stripped down. An expert like you would need something substantially more expensive: custom sights, molded grips, balancing…it adds up fast. You've been shooting for years, since you were a kid. Your father has been in and out of jail your entire life, which translates into very little discretionary income around for you and your two sisters. So it's not much of an assumption that owning an expert-level competition pistol equates to a significant financial sacrifice."

He wasn't looking so crafty now.

"I'm a marksman. So what?" he snapped, "That doesn't prove dick. Why would I kill Jenny? Why would I risk life in prison for a dyke?"

He spit the word 'dyke' out of his mouth like it was a bluebottle fly.

I looked at my notepad and flipped a couple of pages.

"According to my notes, you've had two restraining orders issued against you, both from women you dated for less than a year. One when you were 19, the other just last year."

I glanced up from the pad.

"And a judge sentenced you to an anger management course on the last offense," I said.

I put the pad away again.

"You've got issues, pal."

His eyes narrowed to coin slots.

"Where's this going?"

"This is going to your bedroom closet," I said, "or the top shelf of your pantry. This is going directly to a murder weapon that is still in this house, a murder weapon that you cherished and couldn't bring yourself to part with. This is going to a .22 caliber shooting piece that you coddled and saved up for and that won a young geek like you a lot of recognition and respect." I pointed at his face. "I'll *tell* you where this is going, *motherfucker*—this is going to land your ass in jail for the murder of Jenny Monroe!"

I never saw the mule that exploded the kick into my chest. I landed on my back with my ass in the air and my dignity somewhere off the coast of New Brunswick. Out of the corner of my eye I saw Joey bolt for the hallway.

I bounced up and sprinted after him, down the stairs and out to the street, with him 50 feet in front of me. I kept up with him the two blocks to College Avenue, and then he kicked it into another gear and pulled away from me like I was Barry White in sand. His arms were pumping in an almost hypnotic rhythm, and I watched helplessly as he showed me the bottom of his shoes in staccato flashes. I kept running for another block, but my knee started behaving like the 40-year-old, stitched-together, one-operation-too-many joint from hell that it was. It was hopeless. I stopped and bent over to catch my breath, just as two blonde 20-somethings with nice tans and bared midriffs came out of a salon.

"Are you okay, mister?" the one with the pierced naval asked. "Do you need a doctor?"

Waving them off, I felt a little part of me die. Insult to injury.

I limped back to his apartment and closed the door behind me.

I went through the place carefully, with my latex gloves on. It only took 15 minutes. Taped to the back of his bed board was a long, slim metal case. I carefully removed it and placed it on the bed. Inside, a custom-made Walther target pistol, surrounded by protective foam, confirmed my theory. A Zeiss pistol scope nestled in its own indent. I closed the case and taped it back where I found it.

I went back to the living room and sat down. I called Petey.

"Dempster."

"Petey, Roy."

"What's up?"

"Remember our conversation about the odds of winning the lottery?" I asked.

"Everything you say is etched forever in my mind."

"Well," I said. "Our numbers just hit."

I filled him in on my experience with Joey and led him through my deductive construal. I told him I figured Joey was the one who called in Jenny's murder, because he got a case of conscience and didn't like the thought of Jenny's body bloating from rot. Pure speculation, but that's my business.

"That's good detective work, Roy."

"I learned from the best."

"Goddamn right," he said. "Wait for me there. I know a judge who'll give me a down-and-dirty search warrant. Did you touch anything?"

"Not without gloves."

"Good boy. I'll be there within an hour."

CHAPTER FORTY

Tue to his word, Petey showed up about an hour later. He had with him two patrolmen, a search warrant and a big smile. I was outside Joey's apartment, in the hall, and had conveniently left the door unlocked.

Petey motioned to the patrolmen. "Go inside. Take the kitchen, living room and bathroom. I'll do the bedroom."

After the uniforms entered the apartment, he turned to me.

"Where is it?"

"Taped behind the headboard," I said. "Can't miss it."

He hummed something happy.

"I owe you one, Roy."

"I'll say."

He smiled.

"How long before you get ballistics back?" I asked.

"Already got 'em. Everyone upstairs wants this one put to bed."

"Fast track," I stated.

"Yep. But anything that keeps a friend of the governor happy is okay with me."

He waved at the stairs.

"You better take off. No need to complicate matters."

"Yeah. Contact me later."

"Right," he said.

I went out to my car, still limping, and started it up. I pulled out and circled the block a couple of times and cruised

College Avenue for a while. No Joey. I drove back across the bridge and parked in my little piece of San Francisco.

I found Eunice mopping the kitchen floor of my apartment. The place smelled of Pine-Sol and Comet, and everything chrome had a deep sheen to it.

"What's this?"

Eunice had a dishtowel wrapped around her head and her sleeves rolled up. Her face was flushed and she was breathing hard. She looked elated. "I got bored," she said, "and your place needed a little sprucing up."

"You didn't have to do that, Eunice."

"I know. I just like to keep busy."

I looked around the apartment. My bathroom was sparkling; my bedroom, the spare bedroom and living room were freshly vacuumed. Every window had been scoured, inside and out. Dust was nonexistent.

Eunice was giving the kitchen floor a couple of last licks.

"Thanks for cleaning up. That was very considerate of you."

She blushed.

"It's nothing, just returning a kindness."

I matched her blush and quickly changed the subject.

"Let's go over to your place and get your things," I said. "Then we'll get you settled in."

She nodded. "Okay. Give me a minute."

Eunice returned the cleaning gear to the closet while I wiped down the kitchen counter. She got her purse, took off her do-rag, and put her tam-o'-shanter back on.

We walked to her apartment building and stopped to gawp at the HAZMAT crew in their white jumpsuits, air masks and yellow gloves. They looked like spacemen excavating alien artifacts.

I approached the patrolman at the entrance and explained that Eunice lived there and needed her stuff. He asked her for some ID and waved us in.

"Ten minutes," he said.

Eunice sniggered.

He gave her a look; she gave one back. He looked away.

Forty-five minutes and two very large, very heavy suitcases later, we emerged from her building. The cop mumbled something, but not loud enough for Eunice to hear. Smart man.

I lugged Eunice's stuff up to my place and put the suitcases in the spare bedroom. I got some ice out of the freezer and wrapped it in a towel, and rolled my pants leg up and set the ice pack on my knee while Eunice put away her things.

Fifteen minutes later she came out and pointed. "Bad knee?"

"Old too," I sniveled.

She harrumphed and went back into the bedroom. She came out with a jar festooned with Chinese characters and unscrewed the top. "Dragon Balm," she said. She took the ice off my knee and slapped on a big glob of something that smelled sharply of eucalyptus, mint and old people. "Rub that in," she said. "It'll change you life."

I did as instructed and was surprised to find that she was close to right.

"This stuff is great. What is it?"

She looked at me balefully. "If I told you, I'd have to kill you."

I chuckled. "I've got to go into the office. Make yourself at home."

"Thanks, Roy."

She went into the kitchen and rooted around in the refrigerator.

"I'm going out to do some grocery shopping," she said. "This place is too bachelor."

I dug out my wallet. "Let me give you some money."

She shook her head. "No, I got this."

"But Eunice—"

"Shush. What do you want for dinner?"

I shrugged.

"Okay," she said, "three-bean salad it is."

I blanched and she laughed. "Relax. I was kidding," she said. "Be back by 7:30"—she paused—"sharp."

"Yes, ma'am."

I walked to my office, sans limp, and opened my outer door. My hand was on the doorknob of my inner office entrance when my internal alarm started keening. I turned quickly, with my hands protecting my face…to find Samuel leaning against the doorjamb.

"Jesus, Samuel, wear a bell or something."

He didn't smile. No smile existed in him today. Bad news rode across his features like a stock ticker.

"We have a situation, Mr. Jobe."

His face was pale and drawn, with frown lines deep enough to wedge a quarter. He was dressed in a light brown suit with a khaki shirt, strung by a deep brown tie with tiny, red dots.

I opened the door and waved him into my office. As he passed, a bulb went off in my head.

"Take a seat." I said.

I moved behind my desk, sat down and appraised him. "You're the guy," I accused, "that hit me over the head the other day."

He grimaced. "Yes," he said. "I apologize."

He didn't look all that apologetic.

I waited. He kept staring.

"And you hit me over the head because…"

He looked annoyed, like I'd asked him to explain the obvious.

"It was imperative for me to know what you were on to—due diligence."

"So you hit me over the head and went through my files."

"I believe I just confessed to that."

I thought about giving him a steely look, but I knew it'd be wasted on him.

"Had it occurred to you that there might have been another, less unpleasant way to get your information?" I asked, reasonably.

"It never crossed my mind."

I grunted. At least he was honest.

"You know, another man might be tempted to retaliate." I rubbed my lump absently. "That really hurt."

"I'm aware of that," he said, "but it's a risk I was willing to take."

So much for contrition. I decided to drop it.

"All right, never mind. What are you doing here, Samuel?"

He cleared his throat and adjusted his tie.

"As you've probably already guessed," he said, "this case has more factors in it than were presented to you."

"No kidding," I groused. "Fill me in."

Samuel shook his head. "No. I can't do that. I can't control what you find out on your own, but much of this has to remain confidential."

"Like the fact that Peter Aguayo is a jewel thief?" I asked.

Samuel shrugged. "Among other things."

I stewed for a minute.

"Are you babysitting me?" I asked. "Making sure I don't dig too deep?"

"Too late for that," he said. "I'm here on another matter."

I waited.

Samuel shifted in his seat and rolled his neck.

"Little PJ has been kidnapped."

CHAPTER FORTY-ONE

A screech of tires and a sharp horn bark outside my window distracted me for a moment. But only for a moment.

"Christ," I groaned. I rubbed my eyes and pinched hard at the bridge of my nose.

"When did it happen?"

"This morning," he said. "It seems that PJ was plucked from the park while playing with some friends. I believe it's called a play date, when parents with children of the same age bracket..."

"I know what a play date is, Samuel."

Samuel stared blankly.

"Yes, of course you do."

I watched him fidget for a while. He was rattled and jumpy, like a pensioner after a bad day at the track.

"It was Elvis, wasn't it?" I asked.

He nodded.

"Yes," he said. "A man fitting the description of Sandra's brother was seen running from the park with PJ in his arms... and I have a note."

I tapped my finger on the desk.

"Let's see it," I said.

Samuel removed a folded sheet of paper and handed it to me. I motioned for him to place it on my desk. I took out a pair of latex gloves from my jacket and a plastic bag from a drawer.

With the gloves on, I carefully unfolded the note and read. When I finished, I placed the letter in the plastic bag and set it to the side.

Samuel looked embarrassed.

"I should've known better," he said, pointing. "My prints are all over it."

"Don't worry about it." I said. "Due diligence."

He eked out a smile.

"So," I said, "Elvis wants the Star and one million in cash, or, if you choose the option plan, five million straight."

I picked up the note again and glanced at it.

"That was nice of him."

Samuel nodded again.

"Sandra is hysterical. She's more than willing to comply, but she has no idea where the Star is," Samuel said.

"Where's Peter?"

"In Boston, making arrangements."

"What kind of arrangements?"

Samuel adjusted his tie.

"Gathering five million dollars in small, unmarked bills is a lot harder than it sounds. Even for a man of Peter's wealth."

"I wouldn't know."

He shrugged.

"Not many do," Samuel said.

I looked at the note again.

"So Elvis is going to call on Monday with instructions."

"Yes."

"What about the police?"

Samuel shook his head.

"No police," he said. "Sandra and Peter don't want to take any chances." He made a sour face. "They'll pay."

"You don't agree?"

"Not in the slightest."

"And that's why you're here."

"Yes."

I rubbed my knee a little and looked out the window. I scratched my face and gingerly felt the knot he'd given me. I tapped my foot and pulled at my earlobe. I did a bunch of useless things I do when I need time to think.

"You think Elvis will kill PJ?" I asked.

"I have no doubt in my mind."

"Why?"

"Because keeping PJ alive after the money is in his hands would be *inconvenient*."

A harsh assessment, but one with which I might be inclined to agree. PJ might be Elvis' nephew, but tigers have been known to eat their young.

"I have a meeting set up with Elvis," I said, "for tomorrow."

Samuel's mouth jerked itself into a bestial smile.

"I was hoping for something like that," he said. "You don't disappoint."

I scanned his face. His lips were two thin slashes. His eyes had havoc in them.

"Who are you, Samuel?"

"A man much like yourself."

"That doesn't tell me much," I snapped.

He squirmed, at least as much as a man who seldom does it can.

"There's a line between law and justice," he said quietly. "Sometimes it's a thin fissure, and sometimes it's a chasm. I'm a man who is unafraid to bridge that gap." He paused and waved towards me. "Much like yourself."

"How would you know?"

"Mr. Aguayo still has many friends in the British Intelligence community, and I have my own resources. I know a lot about you, Mr. Jobe."

He peered around the office.

"May I have a drink?"

I stared at him for a couple of heartbeats.

"Of course, Samuel. My apologies." I pulled out my Dewar's bottle and held it up. "Scotch all right?"

"As long as it comes in a bucket."

I laughed and poured two drinks.

He held his glass up in a toast.

"Semper Fi," he said, then downed it

"Semper Fi," I replied, and did the same.

I poured two more.

He sipped the second drink before continuing.

"You're a Marine, Mr. Jobe," he said, "as am I. It may have been a long time ago for you, and even longer for me, but we're still Marines. We've both looked into the black abyss that is death, and have, for whatever reason"–his smile was light as new snow—"maybe by the grace of God, come out on the winning end."

He swirled his Scotch around and stared at it.

"You worked for a government organization known by an acronym." He looked at me. "As did I. You've done some things that will take a lifetime to forget, and, based only on my gut instinct, I believe you'll be spending the rest of your life trying to put those things right." He took another sip. "Like me."

My response was to take another gulp of Scotch. It was a good description and a better assessment, and I'd be a liar if I didn't admit that I was a slightly unnerved by its accuracy. I was also slightly unnerved, and deeply impressed, by the fact that he had that information. The confidentiality of that part of my life was supposed to be ironclad. Obviously, it wasn't. I tried to be annoyed, but couldn't muster the enthusiasm. It was like losing a sneeze.

"And why should I trust you?" I asked.

"Because we have a common goal."

"So you say."

He put his drink down.

"What can I do to gain your trust?" he asked.

"Information," I said.

"Such as?"

I leaned forward.

"Tell me about Sandy's father."

Samuel hooded his eyes and swirled his Scotch some more.

"A monster," he hissed.

He looked out the window behind me and searched for the Chinese coastline.

"They exist, you know. Monsters. You might've met a few as a homicide inspector."

I nodded.

"Sandra's father is the most insidious of monsters, Mr. Jobe. Intelligent, charming, seemingly trustworthy."

He sipped.

"He certainly had me fooled."

"How so?"

Samuel finished his drink.

"He married my sister, with my blessing."

My stomach went tight.

"She was my only sibling. Our parents passed when I was 19, and she was the only family I had left. In those days I was in the field a lot: Cambodia, Laos, Thailand, Vietnam. Sara was a year older than me and worked as a nurses' aid in Houston."

He fidgeted a little and kept his eyes away from mine.

"I got a letter from her saying she was getting married, so I hopped on a transport to meet her beau. His name was Travis Boone. Real tall, real lanky Texan with a winning smile. Said he was in oil and promised to take care of my sister through thick and thin."

Samuel's jaw muscles flexed.

"I stayed with them for a week and left thinking she would live a full, happy life."

He put his glass on my desk and pointed at it. I filled it halfway.

"I was scrambling all over Asia back then, going from disaster to disaster, performing nasty little tasks for Uncle Sam. Sara and I exchanged fewer and fewer letters, until eventually we only communicated once yearly through Christmas cards. I remember getting letters announcing the births of Elvis and Sandra, but I never responded."

A skein of sadness, guilt and regret suddenly draped his shoulders.

"I learned of Sara's murder a year after the fact, while I was in Walter Reed, undergoing treatment for severe depression."

He stared at his drink. A bag full of minutes limped by.

"At the time, I was in no shape to do anything about it."

Shaking his head, he muttered, "I'm ashamed to say that I didn't even bother to check to see if the kids were all right."

"How long were you in Reed?"

He shot me a level look.

"Five years."

I took another sip of Scotch and let it roll around in my mouth for a while.

"You all right now?"

He smiled.

"I'll never be all right."

We were quiet for a while. I listened to the sounds of the street while he listened to the echoes of what might have been.

"Sandy gave me a brief family history," I said. "Sounded like a nightmare."

"It was."

"Does she know you're her uncle?"

"Yes."

"So you're just playing at being a butler."

"Yes, but I do it well."

"How's she feel about you being a bodyguard?"

"Grateful."

We let that simmer for a minute.

I felt the need to either get some fresh air or move the conversation away from this horror show. I moved the conversation.

"Tell me about the bag with 50 grand in it I found in Rachael's locker."

More simmering. Samuel cleared his throat and scratched his ear. But he looked obliged for the change of subject.

"Rachael and Brett Voorhees approached Mr. Aguayo with a business proposition the day after the dinner party," he started. "The twins showed Mr. Aguayo a number of documents they'd stumbled upon in their ongoing research of the Aguayo family." He paused and took a deep breath. "The Voorhees were two very intelligent, very thorough siblings, and were able to link Mr. Aguayo to the disappearance of the Star of Bombay."

"You knew who they really were for a long time, didn't you?"

"From the start," he said.

"And you're using the past tense to describe both the Voorhees twins, so you know that Brett was found dead this morning," I said.

"It's been conveyed to me."

He took a long swallow of Dewar's. Me too. I believe we were both getting a little drunk.

"Mr. Aguayo agreed to pay the twins $50,000 to go away." He continued. "I was the bag man. We both knew, however, that they'd be back. As I said, Mr. Jobe, the Voorhees were two very intelligent people. They knew they could milk Mr. Aguayo for a lot more than the initial payment." He stared at his drink again. "We knew that too."

Something clicked. Another couple of pieces fell into place.

"So you tipped Elvis off about who they really were," I said, "hoping he'd take care of your problem."

He looked surprised.

"I might have made an anonymous phone call," he said, "to that effect."

Rachael Voorhees' broken face swam into view. I felt a spike of anger. I wasn't liking this case, and I wasn't liking any of the players.

"And you knew Elvis would ask around to confirm your claim, and having done so, would take action," I growled, "probably deadly action."

Samuel glared.

"Don't be naïve, Mr. Jobe. Rachel and Brett Voorhees were not innocent little children. They had every intention of bringing ruin to the Aguayo family. They weren't a couple of low-level grifters who overplayed their hand." He leaned forward a little and gestured at nothing. "They were both independently wealthy; the money was irrelevant. Their motivation was, simply put, revenge. They blame Sandra for the death of their father and were bent on destroying her and anyone close to her." He paused. "Unfortunately, they toyed with fire and got burned."

I sipped my drink while I thought it over. Scotch was good for that.

"Why didn't you just take them out yourself?" I asked.

Samuel gave me a look cold as an editor's pen.

"Their actions hadn't yet warranted it."

That offended me. "Who the fuck are you to sit in judgment?" I barked.

His face slackened a little.

"The Aguayos are the only family I have." He brushed at his sleeve.

"The Voorhees were threats to my family, Mr. Jobe, and as such, deserve no quarter."

I pointed at him.

"You're only one step removed from beating Rachael Voorhees to death," I said. "You didn't see her face. I did. When you called Elvis, you signed both their death warrants."

Samuel nodded.

"Perhaps," he said, calmly. "Ultimately, I left that decision in Elvis' hands."

He then gave me a look that would've scared a man with something to lose.

"But if anyone else were to threaten my family, I'd do the same."

Another piece fell.

"You ransacked Elvis and Rachael's place," I said, "looking for Rachael's evidence."

"I was there, yes," he said. "But Elvis was the one who ransacked it. I simply sifted through the rubble. I waited for Elvis, but he never came back to the apartment. Then you showed up with your friend and it was time for me to be scarce."

"And if Elvis had come back to the apartment," I said, "what would you have done?"

"Given recent events, in retrospect, I would've done the same thing you intend to," he replied.

He had me there. Holding the high moral ground was difficult for a man like me. But Rachael's death had affected me deeply, so maybe there was still hope. Regardless, I was angry, but that's nothing new. I slowed my breathing down like my ex-therapist taught me. It helped a little. I looked at Samuel and wondered if I'd be in his shoes, 20 or 30 years from now, trying to forget, spending every day working to make things right. I wondered, too, if the faces of the men I'd killed, all of whom marched past my mind's eye each night before sleep, each of whom nodded acknowledgement of my sin, would stop visiting me when I reached Samuel's age. I hoped so. Maybe I'd ask him about it some time.

I sighed. Nothing about this case was making me happy, but last time I checked, I didn't get paid to be happy. I got paid for results. A young boy was still in the hands of a murderer, and spending time untangling the ethical nuances of Samuel's actions, or mine, wasn't getting us any closer to PJ.

Samuel must've been thinking along the same lines.

"Can we get back to PJ?" he asked.

"For now," I conceded.

He nodded, relieved.

Something had passed between us. It was an intangible awareness of being in the presence of a like-minded man, of sharing a commonality that couldn't be verbalized. I wasn't sure if I liked it, because I wasn't sure if I liked myself. The jury was still out on that.

"How did you set up this meeting with Elvis?" he asked.

I rubbed my face and sighed again.

I described my encounter with Sean and Larry, and the reason why we had an encounter in the first place, then illustrated the subsequent arrangements.

"Before you walked in here I was confident Elvis would show up for it," I said. "But now I'm having second thoughts."

I worried a molar with my tongue.

"You think daddy's back in town?" I asked.

"Yes." No hesitation. "Travis Boone is the one behind PJ's kidnapping. I have no doubt."

"Then Travis won't let Elvis make this meeting," I said. "It wouldn't make sense. They've got their hands full with arranging a swap. They've got to keep a little kid stashed for the weekend, if not longer. I'm not worth the time."

Samuel was shaking his head.

"He'll be there," he said.

"How do you know?"

His lip went into a half curl.

"I know a little about my nephew," he said. "I've been monitoring him for a long time." He paused. "He's a classic sociopath. He's manipulative, has no conscience or empathy. He also suffers from narcissistic personality disorder, in that he's filled with self-importance and has an almost desperate need for admiration. Throw in the fact that he's got an unhealthy dose of persecutory delusions and you've got a guy who will hunt down anyone who's slighted him."

Samuel pointed at me. "I take it you've slighted him?"

"A little."

"And you're an obvious threat."

"Probably."

"Then he'll show up."

I cocked a brow.

"You know a lot about him," I said.

"Huntsville gave him a psych evaluation. Makes for interesting reading."

"I'll bet."

I slid the dregs of my Scotch onto my tongue and sloshed it before swallowing.

"You make him sound completely one-dimensional, Samuel," I said.

"He is."

"But his father isn't," I stated.

Samuel stroked a nonexistent moustache.

"No," he said, abruptly sullen. "The father isn't."

I thought about refilling my empty glass, but for some reason, good sense stayed my hand.

"Why have you and Peter tolerated Elvis? Why didn't you, or at least Peter, put him away?" I asked.

"Same reason as the Voorhees," he said. "His actions hadn't yet warranted it." He blew a breath out in frustration. "And Elvis is still my nephew, and I was hoping, erroneously, that he might've changed."

"That's bullshit," I said.

Samuel flinched and went a little red.

I leaned forward and let my right hand drop to my side, near my gun.

"You and Peter were overjoyed to see Elvis." I pointed at him with my left hand. "Because you knew his father wasn't far behind. You let Elvis play out his little charade for six long months, waiting for Travis to show his hand. But he never did. That wasn't cutting it. You got impatient and decided to prime the pump with the Star. That's the only reason in the world, besides the wedding, which frankly was stupid, that Peter would risk exposing himself as a jewel thief."

Samuel became redder.

"You called me in to stir things up," I said, "hoping I'd flush Travis out. Peter was never concerned about Sandy killing him. This isn't about Sandy or the Voorhees or even Elvis, this is about Travis. The three of you want him dead."

Samuel tapped his fingers on his chair's arm. He calmed a little and his face went back to being Caucasian.

"Yes."

"This whole thing is a set-up," I grumbled, "designed to bring Travis out of the shadows and into the killing ground."

He nodded, reluctantly.

"Sandy hasn't had a full night's sleep since she was a child," he said. "She's been looking over her shoulder, waiting for that monster to drag her back into hell."

He leaned forward and peeled back his upper lip.

Wrath of God came to mind.

"That's not going to happen," he whispered.

I decided that good sense was an overrated concept and poured another shot into my glass. Samuel held his up and I refueled it. The bottle was almost empty, but I always had a backup in the drawer, just in case.

"Where's the Star?" I asked.

Samuel paused with his drink halfway to his lips.

"We don't know."

I was incredulous.

"Someone really took it?"

"Yes." He sipped. "A completely unexpected and extremely unfortunate turn of events...a real hairball."

I chuckled, then giggled, then laughed. After a few seconds, so did he.

"Never saw that one comin'," I wheezed.

He wheezed back.

"Neither did we."

I shook my head appreciatively and wiped some tears away.

"Fuckin' hairball."

"Classic."

We laughed again, like drunken frat brothers, then eventually got it under control.

"Alright, Samuel, be here tomorrow at eight. We've got some work to do."

He finished his drink and placed the glass on my desk.

"Thank you, Mr. Jobe."

He got up, smoothed his suit and walked to the door.

"Samuel."

He turned.

"I think it's about time you started calling me Roy."

He smiled and left.

CHAPTER FORTY-TWO

I was slightly less than a little drunk. I finished my drink and lost the slightly less designation. I called Liz and got her voicemail. I assumed she was buried in paperwork, probably about three hours' worth. I left a message. I made another phone call, rinsed out the glasses, then closed up shop and drifted toward the Red Pagoda.

I worked on my plan, such as it was, on the walk over, and it almost coalesced by the time I reached the door.

Elvis wasn't working alone, which meant my original plan of hammering him into the ground was no longer viable. It was looking like I'd be forced to employ some restraint, which is simply not part of my makeup. Ultimately, I only had one option, and I needed some warm bodies and some halfway intelligent logistics to make it happen. This called for finesse, and finesse usually came to me on a barstool.

I stood inside the Pagoda for a minute, blinking away the late afternoon sun. Eventually my eyes adjusted and the bar's darkened interior started to make sense.

Jumbo stood behind the bar talking with Khan and Rupert Park.

I sat next to Khan while Jumbo built a Dewar's rocks for me.

"Thanks for coming," I said.

"No sweat," Khan said. "Rupert tells me you handled Randall Tang nicely." He popped a peanut into his mouth. "I appreciate it."

"Not much to it, really," I said. "The Joy Boys are still children."

"Yeah," Rupert said, a stool down. "I heard they lost a major meth lab." He gestured toward Berkeley. "Around the corner."

I hadn't thought of that, but it made sense. The Joy Boys and a slick meth lab. You gotta' love it. It takes balls to manufacture product in the heart of the city, right under everyone's noses. I guess they figured it was less risky than transporting meth from somewhere up in Humboldt County, where young Asian men with a lot of jewelry would stick out a bit. It did my heart good to see that the Joy Boys' college educations weren't going to waste. They just hadn't factored in Eunice.

Jumbo brought my drink over and chimed in.

"Someone told me they saw you go into that building," he said, "with your mom."

"Ha ha," I said. "Her name's Eunice Hudson." I took a jolt of Dewar's. "She's a nice lady and a client of mine. She hired me to investigate an odor, and that led me to the meth lab."

I sipped my drink in silence. All three looked at me for a while, then Jumbo gestured impatiently.

Smiling, I went over my dealings with Eunice, beginning with her walking into my office. Like all good stories, there was little need for embellishment; it stood on its own. They especially enjoyed Eunice's "punk bitch" reference. I had all three chuckling satisfactorily and decided this was a good time to call in my favor. I explained my situation, mostly to Khan, and laid out what I needed. It wasn't a complex plan, and didn't involve illegality or money, so there weren't any sharp intakes of breath. Not too many anyway.

Jimmy Khan looked over at Rupert before speaking.

"All right, we can do that."

"Of course," I said, "I don't expect you to participate, Jimmy." I grinned. "You being upper management and all."

He shrugged.

"I haven't gotten my hands dirty in a while. A little field work might be fun."

"Good. How about we meet at my office tomorrow morning at eight?"

Everyone nodded.

"We'll go over the details and I'll hand out the walkie-talkies," I said.

"We'll be there," Khan said.

"Thanks."

I finished my drink and wobbled back to my apartment. The minute I walked in I was hit with the aroma of more pleasant things than I could name. I picked out the obvious: garlic, basil, mushrooms and beef, but the rest just melded into a good reason to be there.

Eunice was in the kitchen, whisking something in a bowl. My four-burner stove was at full occupancy, with covered pots wisping steam. Something was happening in the oven too. Chez Jobe.

"You're early," she chirped.

I looked at my watch. Seven o'clock.

"A first," I said.

"I took the liberty of inviting that nice Eddie Lee from downstairs," she said. "He said he'd be here at 7:30."

"Good. I need to talk with him anyway." I lifted a pot lid and Eunice hissed at me.

"Leave it."

I raised both hands.

"Okee dokee," I said.

"Have you been drinking?" she asked, suspiciously.

"Yes."

I noticed an opened bottle of red wine and a glass with lipstick on it next to the blender.

She giggled and poured me a glass.

"Me too."

We toasted.

"Go in the living room and watch a game or something," she said. "You're getting underfoot."

"Right."

I did as instructed and turned on an A's game. They were playing Texas. I called Eddie and asked him if I could borrow six Nextel walkie-talkies from his various employees. He said he'd arrange it. I watched the A's pummel the Rangers for a while, then Eddie showed up.

Eunice put out a traditional beef roast with baby onions, carrots, mushrooms and new potatoes. We had sides of wild rice cooked in chicken broth with fresh peas and shallots, two different macaroni and cheese dishes, string beans with butter and baked potatoes with sour cream and chives. Comfort food squared. All through dinner the doorbell rang with Eddie's employees dropping off their walkie-talkies. Eunice invited each one in and fixed him a plate. By the time dessert was served, a baked Alaska, I had eight people at my table or on the couch, and there was still going to be leftovers.

CHAPTER FORTY-THREE
Saturday

I woke up a half-hour before my alarm did. My head was killing me. I got up, brushed my teeth and shaved. I dressed in a gray sweat suit, put my running shoes on and pulled an elastic knee brace over the offending joint. I made some coffee and knocked down two cups. Eunice was still sleeping, so I did everything quietly. I left her a note and went downstairs.

Outside, the air carried the foretaste of a new ice age. A couple of Halide lamps flickered irritably. The streets were dead as hope.

I drove out to Ocean Beach and parked not far from where I had my little chat with Elvis. I did some stretches and started jogging along the waterline.

At this time of morning the beach was pretty much mine. The sun hadn't yet broken the horizon, but I could see a couple of ghostly runners about a half-mile ahead. I put my hood up and my head down and commenced a four-mile up and back. On my return journey, a quarter-mile from my car, I came upon an old couple walking two equally old dogs. The couple was bundled in layers of wool and their exhalations chuffed out as white vapor. Like mine. Their two dogs romped around my legs a little, tongues flopping like dead eels. The dogs were big, wet and goofy. Happy as the clams they were digging. I waved to the couple as I passed and they waved back.

I got back to my apartment at about 6:30 and found Eunice awake, reading the paper aloud into the telephone. She was decked out in a velour warm-up suit, camel with gold piping. Her head was wrapped in some kind of brown turban with gold spirals and squiggles. She looked up when I came in, but continued reading.

I pantomimed showering and pointed to the bathroom. She nodded.

I cleaned up and dressed in some comfortable jeans and a white t-shirt. I put on a blue oxford shirt over that, tails out. Black engineer boots went on the feet.

Eunice was off the phone when I came out.

"Coffee?" she asked.

"Sure."

She poured a cup and handed it to me.

I gestured with my coffee.

"What's with the paper?"

She looked at me shyly.

"I have a blind friend in the Marina. I read the headlines to her every morning."

"That's damn nice, Eunice."

She shrugged.

"She's a friend."

This gal was a keeper.

"I have a busy day today," I said. "You'll be on your own."

"So do I. A couple of friends and I are doing a 5K circuit. Then lunch. Then shopping," she said.

"Have a good time," I answered.

She pointed at me.

"You be careful, Roy Jobe."

I smiled and lifted my pant leg, giving her a view of my handgun. Then I winked and left.

I drove out to the Sea Captain Motel and somehow found a parking spot. I went up to room 623 and knocked. Larry opened the door.

"Ready?" I asked.

"Yep."

Sean joined us and we drove to a Starbuck's and got some muffins and coffee. We got to my office at 7:30. Samuel waited outside.

We went upstairs and I made the introductions. Everyone shook hands warily. Jimmy Khan, Rupert and Jumbo Choi showed up about 10 minutes later. Two Asian guys I'd never met were a couple of minutes behind them. More introductions, more handshakes, more wariness.

"All right, guys, thanks for coming," I started. "Today we've got a simple foot and car tail." I laid out the walkie-talkies. "These are all on the same frequency. Just push the button and talk."

Everyone except Sean and Larry grabbed one.

"The meeting is going down in front of the ball park, at Willie Mays Plaza. Larry and Sean are going to meet with the guy."

I nodded toward Rupert.

"You and your guys and Jumbo will be on foot. Jimmy, I'll need you in a car. Samuel, you're with me." Nods all around.

I spoke to Jumbo.

"After he does his business with Larry and Sean, tail him to his car. Use the Nextels to keep me posted. If he stays on foot, keep your distance, but keep him in sight. If he gets in a car"—I looked at Jimmy Khan—"we'll take over. Stay a couple of cars behind me, unless I wave you up. Any questions?"

No questions.

"All right, let's go."

We split into groups and took two cars to PacBell Park. I found an illegal stretch of curb that gave a good view of Willie Mays Plaza. Jimmy parked behind me. The foot soldiers disgorged and spread out. Jimmy drove over to the other side of the plaza and idled.

Willie Mays Plaza was a big open space in front of what was very possibly the most beautiful baseball park in the league. A statue of the Say Hey Kid was positioned before a cluster of evenly spaced palm trees. The flagstones were white with some brown stones assembled to look like a baseball.

PacBell Park wasn't called that any more. Not officially. It had been changed to another corporate moniker, but everyone still called it PacBell, just like everyone called the football stadium Candlestick. I hated the concept of "your name here" sports parks, and protested by refusing to acknowledge it. That'll show 'em.

I addressed Larry and Sean over my shoulder.

"Alright, guys. Showtime."

They got out and meandered to the Willie Mays statue.

I looked over at Samuel. Grim would be an understatement.

CHAPTER FORTY-FOUR

A half-hour crawled by, then another. No Elvis. At 10:30, I was considering the very real possibility that he wasn't going to show. Then I saw him.

Elvis was sauntering toward Larry and Sean from the south. He wore a white suit with white shoes and a white shirt. His gold medallion bounced off his chest with every step. He carried a brown paper bag in his left hand. I assumed it held the two handguns he'd promised. He was still wearing Rachael's earring, which made me furious. My hands tightened on the steering wheel.

He reached Larry and Sean and they starting chatting. Elvis looked relaxed and confident, which was a good thing. After a few minutes he handed the bag over to Larry. Larry opened it and nodded. Sean said something and Elvis laughed. The guys who were on foot had spread out on the Plaza, ignoring the meeting. Things were going good.

"Roy!"

I looked around in panic.

"Roy! Roy Jobe!"

Elvis' head swiveled around.

A group of elderly women, with Eunice in their midst, were approaching the Plaza from the west. Eunice was waving at me.

Jesus.

Elvis followed Eunice's eyes to my car. I slumped down.

Too late. His eyes lit up and his face contorted into something close to hate.

Shit.

I popped the door open and ran toward him, with Samuel close behind. Elvis hissed, then spun around and bolted, straight into the arms of Joey Kimble.

They stood there for what seemed like an eternity, clutching each other like lovers. It was a macabre dance that was oddly sexual. Joey moved his hand and Elvis jerked upward, almost on tip-toes. I got to them just as Elvis collapsed. The front of his shirt was bright crimson. He was on his knees and his face was crowded with disbelief. He flicked his eyes at me, then moved them down to the knife handle sticking out of his gut. Elvis' mouth was working like a landed mackerel's, trying to form words that would never come. His eyes jittered here and there and eventually found mine. I saw a familiar look in them, one that I'd seen too many times in too many places. He fell over onto his back and died.

Sean and Larry had Joey by the arms. Jumbo and Rupert were standing behind them. I knelt down and felt for a pulse, knowing there wouldn't be one.

I pointed at Rupert.

"Get your guys into Jimmy's car and disappear."

He gestured to his men and walked away.

I remained on one knee, thinking. Blood flowed over the pavement to the tip of my shoe. I stood up and looked at Larry and Sean.

"I need you guys to sit on this kid." I said, gesturing toward Joey.

Larry and Sean looked skittish.

I pointed to a place near Elvis' shoulder.

"Drop the bag, Larry," I said.

He did.

"When the cops get here, let Jumbo do the talking."

I nodded at Jumbo.

"You guys don't know each other; you were just out for a walk and the shit hit the fan."

"Right," Jumbo said.

I pointed at Larry and Sean. A greenish hue tinted their faces.

"I'll cover you guys. Don't worry. You have my word. Just play dumb."

They grimaced, but bobbed their heads.

I walked over to Eunice and told her to leave, and that I'd explain everything later. She looked a little greenish too, as did her friends.

I got on my cell and called Petey.

"Yeah?" he said grumpily.

"I've got Elvis."

Silence.

"Where?"

"Willie Mays Plaza."

"Is he dead?" he asked.

"Yes."

Dark silence.

"I don't know if I can cover for you on this one, Roy."

"You won't have to. Joey Kimble knifed him."

Shocked silence.

"You got the kid?"

"Yep. Jumbo Choi's here. You know him. And Sean and Larry."

"They witness it?"

"Yes. And they're only doing their civic duty. They had no hand in it."

Petey sighed.

"Alright, I'm there in five. Don't move."

"Sorry, Petey. There's a man I've gotta' see."

I hung up and looked at Joey. He was staring at Elvis.

"Don't give these guys any trouble," I said.

He didn't look up. I doubt if it even registered.

I spoke to Jumbo.

"I'll make this up to you."

He shook his head.

"We're good."

I motioned to Samuel and we walked back to my car.

CHAPTER FORTY-FIVE

I started the car and pulled away from the curb.

"What now?" Samuel asked.

"Now we get PJ."

"You know where he is?"

"I believe so."

I got on the Bay Bridge and headed for the East Bay. On the way, Samuel pulled a Browning .45 automatic out of a shoulder holster and cambered a round. We got to Emeryville and I pulled up in front of the loft conversion warehouse where Brett had shot Octavio. I double-parked and we went to the door. I started pressing numbers at random, careful to stay away from the *building manager* button. The fourth try yielded a buzz that unlocked the door. Samuel and I went into the lobby. He followed me to a door deep in the bowels of the building. I knocked.

After a minute, Clete Hicks opened the door. He stood there blinking, with blue eyes that were an exact match to both Elvis and Sandy's. His six-foot-nine-inch frame filled the doorway. He wore blue jeans and a tight white t-shirt that outlined a well-defined torso, with arms attached that looked like they could tear a phone book in half, even at his age. A thin smile played on his lips, until Samuel stepped into view.

Clete snarled and raised his right hand. I heard a crack shortly before I felt a bullet hit my collarbone. I went down hard.

Out of the corner of my eye, I saw a blur that looked vaguely like Samuel. It threw itself at Clete. The struggle that followed was the most vicious thing I'd ever seen. Elbows, fists, teeth and blood formed a furious ball, whirling insanely. Guttural noises emitted from its center, like the sounds leopards make when they tear the belly out of prey.

I groped for my gun, but my arm was being annoyingly uncooperative. So was the rest of my body. Somewhere I registered the fact that I was going into shock. Whatever.

I wasn't sure how much time passed, but eventually the sounds of struggle stopped, replaced by labored breathing.

Clete came into view. One eye was almost closed and a large flap of skin hung off his cheek. He held a gun.

"How'd you figure it out, gumshoe?"

For some reason, I thought that was hilarious.

I giggled out a reply.

"The Devil's in the details."

Clete cocked a brow.

"Sandy used that phrase when I first met her." I giggled some more. "Then you used it when I asked you about the color scheme. I didn't connect it for a long time; it's not that unique a phrase."

"That's it?" Clete's head seemed to be floating in midair. I thought that was funny too.

"Of course not, *Travis*," I chuckled. "My good friend Samuel the butler described you as real tall and real lanky. That was another piece. A small piece, but a piece nonetheless."

Travis moved closer. He straddled me, with a foot on either side of my shoulders. He kept the gun pointed at my head.

I yammered on.

"And the fact that Brett rented a hideaway here bothered me. So I asked myself, why here? Why not in the City, or in Cleveland?"

I guffawed. That was pretty goddamn funny. Cleveland.

Travis reached down and pushed his gun barrel into my wound. That woke me up a little. I stopped laughing. I yammered some more instead. It seemed really important that he know how I'd ferreted him out. Don't ask me why. "I figured Brett and Rachael probably followed Elvis here, and Brett rented a unit to stay close to the guy who killed their father."

I felt a twitch in my arm. And my leg. Life was returning.

"You don't own this place," I said, suddenly affronted. "You *lied* to me."

Travis smiled. It jiggled his skin flap.

I think I pointed at him with my left hand. Or maybe not.

"You're just the fucking *janitor.*"

His smile disappeared.

"But I didn't put everything together," I said, "until I looked into your son's eyes, *right before he died.*"

He didn't even flinch.

"Very good," he whispered. "But irrelevant."

"Why?"

"Because I'm going to kill you."

That busted me up. My laugh was a high-pitched shriek, edged with madness.

"I don't think so," I giggled.

He looked amused.

"Oh, really?" he asked.

I winked at him.

"Really."

I shot him between the legs.

Travis screamed, and I swear to God, his eyes bulged out of his head at least two inches. He clutched at his groin and fell forward, out of my line of sight. He kept screaming. It was ear-splitting, and sucked the humor out of the room, which, frankly, annoyed me. My right arm was the only thing that was working even remotely well, so I brought it up above my head and emptied my gun at the screams.

"Shut the fuck up," I said.

Then I passed out.

CHAPTER FORTY-SIX
Sunday

I woke up to Petey's face, something his wife Sylvia did every morning. I had no idea how she managed it. I made a note to canonize her.

"Am I in hell?"

"Not yet," he said. "But it's still early."

He poked at me.

"How do you feel?"

"Like a hundred Yen."

I looked around. I was in a hospital room, private by the looks of it. It was painted in soothing colors: gold, ginger and deep brown, and it had a nice couch, a couple of fat chairs and a desk in the corner with a computer on top. There was crown molding and thick curtains and a wall of bookshelves packed with expensive looking leather volumes, probably organized by price. The only difference between this room and the BBC's version of Sherlock Holmes' study was my standard issue hospital bed, the heart monitors, oxygen tank and the IV stand with a tube leading down to a vein in the back of my hand.

And Petey.

"What time is it?"

Petey looked at his watch.

"Six p.m."

"I've been out all day then."

"No. Six p.m. Sunday."

"Oh."

I tried to sit up and immediately realized the idea was pure folly. A sharp pain in the upper left quadrant of my torso sent me crashing back.

"Shit."

Petey grinned.

"You took a slug just above the collar bone. It lodged in your shoulder muscle. I offered to dig it out with my car keys, but they insisted on bringing you here. Mumbled something about 'sterile environment' and 'local anesthesia.'"

"Anesthesia's for pussies," I opined.

"That's what *I* told 'em."

I went somber.

"What about Samuel?" I asked.

Petey sighed.

"He'll live. Took a bad beating. Got a concussion and lost some teeth, but from what I saw, he gave as good as he got."

"Travis?"

"Dead as a doornail."

"He die fast?"

Petey shook his head.

"Died hard. None of your bullets were fatal by themselves. He took six slugs in and around the groin. He died on the operating table."

I harrumphed.

"Fucker had it coming."

Petey looked at me askance.

"That wasn't deliberate, was it?"

"I wish. I was going into shock. All I did was shoot at the noise."

"Alright. Had to ask."

"No problem. What about PJ?" I asked.

"They found him in the bathroom, 'cuffed to a handrail. Assholes hadn't even fed him, but he's okay."

Relief.

"And Joey?"

"Confessed to killing Jenny Monroe and Elvis. Slam dunk. In the system and out of my life."

"Jumbo? Larry and Sean?"

"They're covered," Petey said.

We were quiet for a moment.

I waved at the room.

"Who's paying for this?"

"Peter Aguayo. You're in a private clinic on Parnassas Street. Samuel's next door."

Petey pointed to a large flat panel television on the wall. He seemed a little excited.

"Forty-two-inch high-definition plasma. Sony, no less... and HBO."

"You been here long, bro'?" I asked.

He blushed.

"On and off." The blush went deeper. "I might've spent part of the night here."

"Thanks, Petey."

He waved it off.

"Part of my job."

We left it at that. That's how real men handled it.

"Liz was here too," he said, "and a bunch of other scoundrels. Octavio, Jumbo, Eddie Lee. Also, a woman named Eunice Hudson. She and Liz went out for coffee."

He pointed to a table crowded with about 10 vases filled with flowers.

"Sammy Mayfair left the lilies. In case you died. Wanted me to ask if you were still coming to his show."

"I'll be there."

Petey's face was getting a little hazy. I closed my eyes for a minute, just to rest them, and slept for 12 hours.

CHAPTER FORTY-SEVEN
Friday

My shoulder hurt, and the sling cradling my left arm was pissing me off. I parked my car near the Aguayos' and trundled, like an old man, to the teak door. A Hispanic woman greeted me.

"I'm here to see Mr. Aguayo."

"Bueno."

I followed her into Peter Aguayo's library or den or home office or whatever rich people called 1500 square feet with lots of expensive furniture and walls spray-painted with books.

Peter was sitting behind a large exotic burl desk, doing a good job of being pleased with himself. The desk was covered with a bunch of important-looking papers, a humidor and a leather checkbook.

"Sit down, Roy."

He motioned toward a chair.

"How're you feeling?" he asked, concerned.

"Like a garden spade."

His eyebrows went up.

I gestured with my good hand.

"A tool…?"

His chin tilted.

"Ahh, yes."

Peter opened the tabletop humidor and took out a cigar. He spun the box toward me.

"Cigar?"

"No thanks."

"They're Cuban."

"Okay."

I picked one out of the middle. It was soft and fresh and smooth and smelled like a week off with pay.

Peter cut his cigar and held the trimmer out to me. I waved it off and bit off the end of mine. We lit up.

"I can understand why you might be a little annoyed about being misled," he started. "No one likes the feeling of being used."

I smoked.

"However, everything I did was for my family," he said, "and I won't apologize for that."

I waved again. I was having difficulty remaining indignant. Truth be told, I felt pretty good about myself. I'd saved a child's life, solved four murders and stepped on a bug that should've been stepped on at birth. I couldn't blame Peter for what he did; I probably would've done the same. The hundred-dollar cigar helped a little too.

I reached into my jacket and took out a piece of paper and laid it on his desk.

"My bill," I said.

He picked it up and read for a minute, then opened his checkbook and started scribbling. He tore it out, folded it, then handed it to me.

I looked at it. It was for $50,000.

"This is too much."

He did the wave thing back at me.

"You earned it."

I looked at the check again, folded it and put it in my pocket.

He was right.

I hung around with Peter for about a half-hour, and we talked about everything but the case. Baseball, football, the stock market, why the iPod is just about the coolest thing on the planet and a tiny bit about our pasts. Just a tiny bit.

My cigar was down to about two inches and it was time to go. I stubbed it out and got up.

"I'd like to drop in on Samuel for a while."

"Of course. He's upstairs, third door on the right."

Peter got up to walk me out.

We shook hands. He held on.

"Roy, if you ever need a favor, you call me."

"I'll do that."

I left Peter and went upstairs. I found Samuel's door and knocked.

"It's open."

I went in. Samuel was sitting in a large leather recliner, reading Frank Herbert's *Dune*. His left leg was in a soft cast and he had a cut over his eye with a row of stitches sticking out of it like wild hairs. He smiled and showed off a couple of places where teeth used to be. It was almost comical, but I figured laughing would be inappropriate.

"That's hilarious," I said, laughing.

His tongue felt at the gaps and he scrunched his face.

"And they were real," he said.

"Bummer."

"Yeah. Siddown."

I grabbed part of a couch and looked around. Samuel's place was not so much a room as it was an apartment. We were in the living area and I could see two French doors at the far end with pieces of bedroom furniture peeking at me from the other side. The room we were sitting in could've been an Ethan

Allen showroom, filled with thick, well-built furniture and a small fireplace that would blaze merrily in winter. The walls were covered in a damask paper in beige and gold, and the carpet was dark brown in an oriental pattern. The place looked comfortable and lived in, with personal items scattered around like scent markers. I spotted something mounted on the wall and walked over to get a better look. It was a walnut photo frame with a white background and the Congressional Medal of Honor set in the middle.

I looked at Samuel.

"Vietnam?"

"Yes."

I grunted and went back to the couch.

"How're you feeling?" I asked.

"Better than yesterday," he answered.

I hadn't expected it to be awkward, but it was. We were two grown men who'd shared a life-and-death experience and we didn't know what to say.

After a minute, Samuel looked over at the Medal, then gestured at me. "You were awarded the Navy Cross?"

"Yes."

"You know what Medal of Honor holders call guys with the Navy Cross?"

"No."

"Runner-ups."

I laughed. Not bad. It loosened the atmosphere up a little and we chatted for a while, careful to stay away from Travis and Elvis and other dead people. We had more in common with each other than not, and I knew he was going to be one of those guys who could call me up for any favor and I'd do it without question. I also knew he'd just granted me the same status.

"How're Sandy and PJ?" I asked.

"Good. They're at PJ's therapist today. He still has nightmares, but they seem to be occurring less frequently."

He smiled.

"Sandy's too."

"I'm glad."

I got up and shook Samuel's hand.

"We done good," I said.

"Yes, we did."

Before I got to the door I turned.

"When you get some teeth, I'll buy you dinner."

"I'll hold you to it."

I waved and went into the hallway, careful to close the door behind me.

I looked around the landing, then went to PJ's door. I opened it quietly and went in. His room looked pretty much the same as when I first saw it, a couple of centuries ago. The bed was made and everything was neat as a pin. I rummaged through his drawers for a few minutes, then went into his closet. I searched anywhere a four-year-old kid could reach and found nothing. I went back to the bed and opened his toy chest. I carefully took out some spaceships, racing cars, a number of GI Joes and some electronic learning games that were over my head. At the bottom left corner I pulled out a fire engine with a platinum chain tangled in its ladder. At the end of the chain was a 38-carat alluvial diamond with a ring of platinum disguising five distinct little points.

When I'd first met him, Samuel had told me that PJ went into Sandy's room every night to sleep. "Without fail" was the phrase he used. On the night of the Star of Bombay's disappearance, PJ had gone into this mother's room, as was his habit. He saw the Star, and being a little boy, was mesmerized by its fire. Sandy was probably asleep. He took it back into his room and played with it for a while, then got bored. He tossed it into his toy chest, thinking that he'd goof around with it later, then forgot about it.

At least that's how I saw it.

I admired it for all of 10 seconds, then slipped it into my pocket and left the house.

***

Ashwani Bindal was an Indian man a little older and a lot smarter than me. He sat behind a neat desk in a neat office on the second floor of the Indian chancery on Arguello Boulevard. He was about 5'10" with dark hair and dark skin and eyes of polished onyx. He had a law degree and a Ph.D., had written a number of books on the British colonization of his native country, and had been a member of the national cricket team. He was the number three man in the United States representing Indian diplomatic interests, and he spoke five languages.

I knew this because my very well-connected attorney friend, Gerald Bosworth, told me.

Ashwani held his hand out.

"Mr. Bosworth tells me you might have something of interest for me."

I shook his hand.

"I might."

We settled into our chairs.

"He also tells me that I am not allowed to ask any questions, and that any conclusions, real or imagined, are to remain confidential under penalty of Gerald not inviting me to the Olympic Club for a round of golf."

"You must be shaking in your boots," I said.

"Terrified."

I smiled. He was easy to like.

I took the Star out of my pocket and laid it on his desk. He looked at it like it was a viper.

"What's this?" he asked.

"The Star of Bombay."

His eyes lit up with recognition. He picked it up and examined it, following the five points into the platinum ring.

"Disguised," he said, quietly.

"Ayup."

"Where'd you…?"

"Nope."

He looked at me, looked at the Star, then looked at me again.

"Okay."

We shook hands again and I went my merry way.

EPILOGUE
Sunday

S preckels Lake was as smooth as tumbled glass. A
whisper masquerading as a breeze massaged the four
or five hundred people crowding the banks and the sun
begrudged just enough heat to make wary San Franciscans
show their legs. A small grandstand had been set up on the
south end of the lake, with the mayor and a couple of his toadies
taking in the view and flashing dental work.

I was set up about 20 yards away with the rest of the
Plank Walkers Society. There were 38 of us this year, with one
freshman who'd brought a nice pirate corsair with a square-
rigged foremast and fore-and–aft sails on its main. We were
bivouac on a stretch of lawn that abutted the lake, in front of
several eucalyptus trees and a suspicious looking grassy knoll.

Most of my friends were there, clustered in little groups. Liz
and Eunice shared a spot near the grandstand with Jumbo, his
girlfriend Brittany, Sammy Mayfair, his partner Jules, Octavio
and Ruby Kanzis. Octavio and Ruby had been at Sammy's show
last night, and by the look on their faces, somebody'd gotten
lucky. Liz was in a great mood as she'd parlayed a voice recording
of Sean Stewby making various racial slurs into a transfer and
a new partner. Eunice looked chipper, as did the three or four
members of her posse. Petey and his wife Sylvia sat next to them
in lawn chairs with a cooler of beer between them. Eddie Lee and
his whole clan had just arrived and were unfolding chairs and
spreading blankets and unloading baskets of food.

On the other side of the lake I'd seen Peter, Sandy, PJ and Samuel. They'd been lured here with the promise of a show they'd never forget.

Jimmy Khan's six-year-old son stood next to my director's chair. This was the favor Jimmy had asked for in return for canceling Wei Lee's debt to Randall Tang. Jimmy Jr. was a bright little kid who'd been here last year and had apparently talked of nothing else since. I was going to let him pilot my ship a little in the straight-aways, and I'd take over when we did anything complex.

Our ships were already in the center of the lake, like the Spanish Armada anchored off Calais, except, of course, they were a lot smaller and weren't all Spanish and had little electric motors that were held together with glue. But if you squinted a little, you could imagine them as real, captained by gentlemen of rank with names like Drake, Parma and Nelson, and crewed by hard men who lived on hard-tack and rum.

It was time to start our maneuvers. The flotilla glided out from the center and performed three slow, elegant figure-eights and then reformed into a moving circle. One by one the ships broke from the circle to execute a curlicue. I was behind Stan Keith's abomination, his floating slap in the face, his exact copy of my *Agamemnon*. Since last year, when he'd broken the unwritten code of the Plank Walkers Society by showing up with *my* ship, I'd refused to acknowledge his existence. I did, however, let it be known through other members that there would be a day of reckoning, and today was that day.

I took the controls from Jimmy Jr. and shadowed Stan's ship as it broke from the circle. I could feel the stares from the guys sitting around me, but I was not to be deterred. I moved next to his ship and made contact, nudging it toward the far end of the lake.

"Hey!"

That would be Stan. I ignored him.

Our ships were side by side now, and I pulled Jimmy Jr. closer.

"When I say 'now,' push this button," I told him.

Jimmy nodded.

"What the hell are you doing, Jobe?" Stan barked.

I continued the ignoring.

"Now, Jimmy."

Jimmy Jr. pressed a button on my radio control box.

"Now count to five, kid."

"One, two, three, four…"

A loud BANG echoed from across the lake. Birds bolted from the trees. The mayor's handlers rushed over to him, shielding him with bodies. Every head in the crowd snapped toward the two *Agamemnons*. Jimmy Jr. was laughing hysterically. So was I.

My ship was drifting sideways away from Stan's. His ship was missing its middle third. There was a gaping hole where the center used to be, and splinters and shredded pieces of cloth were fluttering down like snow. It was taking water on by the gallon, and as we watched, it went into a death roll and floated belly-up. The whole sinking had taken about seven seconds.

I'd bolted the firing mechanism of a four-ten gauge shotgun under the deck of my ship, with a radio-controlled servo that pulled the trigger back to fire the shell. Two guys at SFPD ballistics, Mark Gomez and Don Lucas, had rigged it up for me.

"Go to your daddy now, Jimmy."

Jimmy clapped and squealed, then sprinted to his dad. Stan, mouth open, was staring out at the kindling I'd just created. Guys were cracking up all around me. Eddie, Jumbo and Octavio were rolling on the ground. Petey was wiping off the beer he'd spit up on his shirt. Life was good.

Liz walked over. "What the hell?"

I smiled.

"Fucker had it coming."

The End

Made in the USA